Demon Bayou

Tamara A. Lowery

Demon Bayou

Waves of Darkness

Book 2

Tamara A. Lowery

Steele Rose Publishing

Tamara A. Lowery

Demon Bayou

Waves of Darkness Book 2

By

Tamara A. Lowery

1st Edition, Gypsy Shadow Publishing, October 2012 eBook, November 2013 print

2nd Edition, Tamara A. Lowery DBA Steele Rose Publishing, 2022

Cover art, Copyright 2022 Fatima Saddiqa

Interior art, Copyright 2022 Tamara A. Lowery

Published in the United States of America

Print ISBN 978-1-956849-02-8

Ebook ISBN 978-1-956849-03-5

Foreword, Warnings, and Acknowledgement

For those of you new to the Waves of Darkness series, welcome to Demon Bayou, the second book in the series.

Back in 2005, my husband and I thought about how popular pirates were becoming and of the continuing, if slightly waning at the time, popularity of vampires. To our knowledge, no one was combining the two. By 2006, I'd finished initial research on pirates and piracy (you must know the rules in order to properly break them, after all) and begun penning the first book in a hardbound journal someone had gifted my husband.

Of course, I learned later that several iterations of the combination of pirates and vampires were popping up in various formats. I will say that my take on things is sufficiently different enough from other content out there in the same vein (sorry, I had to) to avoid treading on others' toes.

Demon Bayou originally saw publication through Gypsy Shadow Publishing in 2012. I split with them in 2018, mere months after the publication of the seventh book in the series, and all rights reverted to me.

Seeing as how I was unable to secure a new publisher, I decided to revise the books and release the second editions self-published. I plan to release the original seven books in the series, which complete the Sisters of Power story arc, at six-month intervals: namely every May and November.

Blood Curse was released November 2021 in ebook and paperback formats and is currently in production for an audio book edition narrated by Greg D. Barnett.

I have already started drafting a second seven books for the Daughters of the Dragon story arc, which will complete the series. I seriously doubt I can maintain the six-month schedule for their release dates, but I will try to get them out in one-year intervals. I managed to accomplish that with the series' first run, after all.

Now for the warnings.

My pirates are not nice. They murder and occasionally rape. This is not behavior I condone, but it is historically accurate, and I'm NOT writing YA here.

The books are set during the American Revolutionary period, so female characters are subjected to the prevailing male attitudes and treatment of the time. I DO have strong female characters throughout the story, but the ones not magically inclined are written somewhat realistically.

Vampires, by definition, are serial killers.

Viktor Brandewyne can be a massive asshole at times.

Finally, it's time for the acknowledgements. I'll keep them short.

I want to thank my husband, Derik, for helping me conceive this whole hoo-hah. Without him, there would be no Viktor, Grimm, or Belladonna. I also want to thank all my online and convention author friends for their advice and support in getting the tools and knowledge to get these books back on the market. They are too many to name in a short space.

Tamara A. Lowery, April 8, 2022

Tamara A. Lowery

Dedication

To Beth G. for the use of her house ghost

And to Granny Grace, who helped me name
several of the Sisters of Power

Once Upon a Tide....

The lanky boy darted along the wet cobblestones; a heavy-set, red-faced man puffed after him in pursuit. Though remarkably fast for his size, just as the pursuer caught up with the boy and reached out to grab the back of his shirt, the lad leapt onto a barrel and sprang to a drainpipe, nimble as a cat. From there it was a short climb to a rooftop.

"Keep it then, you little shit!" the winded man called after the boy. "If I catch you around my shop again, I'll have you thrown in the stocks and whipped!" He turned and trudged back toward his shop, muttering under his breath.

Grinning over his escape, the boy scrabbled along the rooftops, returning to the waterfront and River Street. He found a way back to the street level and slipped along the shadows of an alleyway. Before long he reached the back door of the Black Flag Tavern. Viktor's sharp ears caught the yowling of a cat coming from the back alley. Looking around to make sure the Captain wasn't paying attention to the kitchen, he slipped over to the stew pot and scooped out a couple of bowls. One more peek into the common room showed him that the old pirate was well into a bottle and busy with his gambling. He eased out the back door, careful to be quiet about it.

"So, you got it, then?" he asked the boy hiding in the shadows.

"It's still warm from the oven. I told you I could, Vik." The boy pulled a loaf of bread out of his shirt. He tore it in half and handed part to Viktor, who passed him a bowl of stew. They both set to eating.

"Mmm! This actually makes it taste good!"

"Aye," Viktor nodded around a mouthful of bread and stew. "Sadie's a fair whore, but not so good of a cook. I've tossed rocks that were softer than her biscuits, Jim."

"You know, you could have told me the fat bastard was so fast," Jim grumbled, good-naturedly. "He damn near caught me before I could make it to a rooftop."

Viktor chuckled at his young friend. "Lucky for you, he can't climb."

Jim made the mistake of taking a bite of the stew without the fresh bread and made a face at the taste. "Gah! Too much salt pork. How can you stand to eat this stuff every day?"

"Better than not eating. Every now and then I can talk Margory into fixing me something."

"Why doesn't the Captain make her the cook, then?"

"She makes more money for him on her back. Face it; men don't come to the Black Flag for the food."

Demon Bayou

They finished their meal in silence. Viktor watched Jim surreptitiously as they ate. He'd met the boy at the start of the month. Vik soon learned he was about four years older than Jim, as best as he could tell.

Formerly a cabin boy aboard a merchantman out of Boston, Jim decided six months under the abusive master of the ship was five too many. The man would whip him raw just for making eye contact. He'd jumped ship the first night in Savannah's harbor.

Viktor and Jim encountered each other when both were trying to burgle the same shop. He'd known right away that the younger boy wasn't a local. He'd also been impressed by Jim's bravado in standing up to his challenge over territory.

The boy was a fair wrestler and would have held his own if the welts on his back hadn't been so fresh. Viktor had been quick to realize that. He'd recognized Jim as being of the same bent of mind as he was. It would be better to have him as an ally than as competition.

He'd snuck the boy back to his corner of the Black Flag's storeroom when old Billy Black had been busy elsewhere. He'd only started working for the old pirate a few months earlier and didn't want to get an ear boxing from him for another mouth to feed. To treat Jim's welts, he'd used some of the salve Mother Celie had given him for the cuts and bruises he always seemed to be acquiring.

The boy had looked up to him ever since. Jim would do anything Viktor asked of him. Viktor discovered that he enjoyed the feeling of power that gave him. He found in Jim not only someone willing to be his tool, but the younger brother he'd never had.

Gathering up the empty bowls, Viktor came to a decision. Young Jim's skills had proven equal to his loyalty.

"Jim, I plan to be a pirate captain one day. It's why I work for the Captain now. He was the best there was in his day, and I mean to learn as much as I can from him. I know I don't have a ship yet, but what would you say to being my first mate?"

"You really mean that, Vik? I'd be proud to call you Captain. Have you got a pirate name? All the famous pirates had pirate names."

"As a matter of fact, Captain Black gave me one when I hired on. Brandee."

"Bloody Vik Brandee. That's a great pirate name!"

"What about you, Jim? You need a pirate name, as well."

Jim shrugged. "Bugger if I know what would be a good one for me. I don't even have a family name. Always been an orphan. I've been called several things, but Jim is the only name I have."

"Well, we can figure one out for you later. Right now, we need to learn all we can about pirating and seamanship, before we take our own ship," Viktor reasoned. "I know the waters along this coast for a few days' travel in either direction. And I've been paying attention in the tavern. I know which trade houses aren't too particular about where a cargo came from or how it found its way to them."

"I picked up how to do the most-used knots and how to splice line, and I learned a bit of how to rig a ship without snarling everything up," Jim offered eagerly. "Good. We can teach each other what we've learned already, as well as anything else we can learn along the way."

He stopped with the door half-open, a slow smile on his face. "I've just the pirate name for you, Jim. Since you know more of it than I do, I'll call you Rigger."

"Mr. Rigger. I like the sound of that." The boy puffed up.

"I better get back to work before the Captain boxes my ear. I get my month's pay tomorrow, as well as a few days off. Come home with me to Mother Celie's, Mr. Rigger. She'll feed you up good and put some meat on your bones. She's always telling me I'm too skinny, and you make me look fat by comparison."

"Aye, aye, Cap'n!"

Tamara A. Lowery

Chapter 1

Hezekiah Grimm found his captain at the railing on the fo'c'sle. Viktor Brandewyne stood looking out at the stars, an involuntary smile on his face. Lazarus was perched on the railing in front of him. The huge black cat emitted a rumbling purr in response to the captain's strokes.

Grimm eyed the cat warily as he joined Viktor. Although he did not know the full story behind the cat, he knew the creature was not natural and was perhaps demonic. It rarely tolerated the touch of anyone other than the Captain. "He really seems to like you, Vik."

Viktor nodded, not speaking.

As uncomfortable as Lazarus made him, Grimm had to admit the cat had a calming effect on Viktor. It was the only thing that convinced him that the creature, which was sometimes a cat, sometimes a bird, sometimes shadow or smoke, was not inherently evil, at least no more evil than the vampire Grimm called Captain.

Never as superstitious as most sailors and pirates, Grimm always believed in making his own luck — and that witches, ghosts, and beasties were mostly stories told to frighten small children or weak-minded fools. He'd not been above using such stories to keep his crew cowed and in line, of course.

These days, however, he'd found himself forced to come to grips with the fact that such beings did exist outside of stories and nightmares.

Since joining his old friend's crew, he'd encountered vampires, witches, shape-shifting familiars, mermaids, and a sea monster. Granted, the sea monster might easily be mistaken for a mermaid by some.

"It's been quiet the past few days," he observed. "How long do you think Belladonna will stay gone?"

"Until I call her back," Viktor answered. "She's busy with some fisherman she caught."

"You keep surprising me, Viktor. Never knew you to share a wench before."

"If it was anyone other than Belle, I wouldn't. I still won't share her with any of my crew."

"But a perfect stranger?"

"Safer that way, Hezekiah. I don't trust her in my bed." He smiled at his first mate. "She's just playing with her food."

Grimm made a face. He'd seen the siren's eating habits firsthand. Anyone foolish enough to go in the water with her was fair game. Even Viktor had felt her teeth, and she was supposed to be there to help him.

Viktor went back to petting the cat. "I was just thinking back to when Jim and I were first starting out. Old Billy Black said Jim was as much trouble as I was."

"Aye and the two of you were damn near inseparable, as I remember. You never have said what happened to Jim."

"No. I haven't." His tone made it clear the subject was not to be broached again. "Was there something in particular that you wanted, Mr. Grimm?"

"There was talk in the last port of a convoy. Spices mostly, but there was rumor that some emeralds were being smuggled."

"I heard the talk, as well."

"I checked over the charts, Captain. The timing is right, and we're in a prime position to intercept."

Viktor thought about it for a while. The right spices could bring a tidy sum, although the emeralds, if there really were any, would be tricky to convert into cash. More importantly, fresh provisions would be welcome: both foodstuffs and prisoners to feed the bloodlust of his small cadre of vampires and himself.

"Very well, Mr. Grimm. Have the lads ready by first light. When the convoy comes into sight, pick us out a fat one."

"Aye, Captain."

"What's the word, Mr. Grimm?"

"Sniff reports five ships in the convoy. They're just to the south of us on the horizon," he answered as he entered the captain's cabin. "Their current heading is north. Three look to be merchantmen. He said the lead and chase vessels appear to be smaller gun boats."

Viktor moved to the window, opening one of the panes to smell and feel the wind. Five specks of white, the topsails of their prey, were just visible where sky met sea.

"Have the riggers furl a third of the sails," he ordered. "Give them a better chance of catching us up. They won't suspect our purpose until it's too late, if they come up behind us, rather than if we turned toward them."

"What colors should we fly?" Even though Sniff, using the glass, couldn't see what flag the convoy ran under, Grimm knew Viktor's eyesight was much sharper than his.

"British, Mr. Grimm."

Even with less sails up, it soon became apparent that it would take the merchant ships most of the day to get remotely close to the *Incubus*. Less experienced or less patient pirates might have turned their ship toward their prey.

Viktor didn't want to spook them into scattering or to provoke their escorts. If he sailed as if they were of no interest, their guard would be down when he did order an attack. Experience taught him that it was an effective ploy when encountering convoys.

At midday, Sniff called down from the crow's nest, "They look to be changing course!"

Grimm took the glass and peered at the slowly approaching ships. Viktor stood beside him, not needing a spyglass. They watched as the ships made an eastward course change.

"Damn. Wasn't expecting that," Grimm muttered. "Most spice traders usually don't head eastward until they're far enough to the north to catch the Trades. Something must have spooked them."

"It is odd," Viktor agreed, "but not as odd as how the middle ship is sailing."

The first mate focused on the vessel indicated. "Interesting. Looks like she's pulling away from the pack and returning to the original heading. Wonder why she'd leave the protection?"

The vampire sniffed the air. Viktor's heightened perceptions greatly augmented his already well-honed weather eye. "The wind is going to hold steady for at least another day. Our stray little lamb should be pulling even with us by dusk. That should be perfect."

"Thinking of trying the harpoon and counterweight system?"

"Aye. It's set up to pull them right to us. I want to see if it works."

"I'll have the lads get the buffers ready to take the brunt of the impact. What's the plan if the contraption doesn't work?"

"It would do my little cadre good to indulge in a fresh feed," he said, referring to the five crewmen he'd turned. "The rum-and-blood blend is sustaining them, but blood is much better in its pure form straight from the source."

Grimm suppressed a slight shudder. He'd seen the vampires in a feeding frenzy back when Viktor had set them on the pirate hunter that had managed to capture the first mate. He'd never wanted to be the target of their Hunger.

"If you say so."

It was moonless that night, a fact that normally would preclude any kind of pirate attack. The merchantman only had one man on watch.

Nighttime, however, was no barrier to Viktor Brandewyne. For that matter, neither was daylight, since his vampirism was the result of a curse placed on him by an irate witch. He had never actually died, unlike his cadre of five. They were now permanent members of his crew, pirates he had killed personally when his blood Hunger had threatened to overwhelm him.

Since the five were true vampires, they had the same weaknesses described in most of the legends: sunlight and holy objects. One discovered another, previously unknown weakness the hard way. Viktor originally made six vampires, but one made the mistake of trying to feed on Belladonna. The siren's blood proved instantly fatal to the vampire.

Brandee ordered the cadre assembled on deck. He'd already ordered all the topside lamps shuttered, so as not to give away their position to the other ship. This rendered the *Incubus* to a dark shadow against the star-studded sky and all but invisible.

Silently, the pirate ship maneuvered alongside the merchant vessel. Large cork buffers hung over the side facing their prey. Using the swivel guns mounted on the rails, the pirates launched several harpoons. As soon as he heard them *thud* home into the wood of the other ship, Viktor gave the signal to release the counterweights.

Line attached to the harpoons passed through small ports in the deck via pulleys and attached to heavy iron weights. Shoving these out the lower gun ports resulted in rapidly pulling the other ship to the pirate. The cork buffers prevented the hulls from damaging each other.

The sleeping crew of the merchantman was taken completely by surprise, jarred awake by the collision. Within seconds, the vampires were on board. Two quickly silenced the lone watchman; he was drained and dead in a matter of minutes. The other three swarmed the rigging, in case any sailors were in the crow's nest.

Quickly and quietly, Viktor sent a large part of his crew over, led by the Grimm Reaper, to secure the ship. Most of the merchantman's crew were still half-asleep, making for a swift victory.

The ship's captain was a heavy sleeper. Not only did the colliding of the ships not waken him, but Grimm also had to shake him a few times to get him on his feet. The man was only half-dressed and disheveled, when Viktor entered his cabin.

"I apologize for this untimely interruption of your voyage, sir, but I believe you and I have some urgent business to attend to." Brandee gave a mock bow. Before he could continue, however, Lazarus darted past him. In a black blur, the demon cat launched himself at the prisoner, clawing and biting any part of the man he could reach. This did not fit in with Brandee's plan.

"Lazarus! Return."

The cat abandoned his attack and leapt to Viktor's shoulder in one fluid movement. He glared and growled at the merchant captain from his perch.

Brandee narrowed his eyes at the man. "My friend does not like you, sir. Have we perhaps met before? What is your name?"

"I've never set eyes on you before in my life!" He spat. "I am Captain Thomas Brumble. Who the hell are you?"

"Brumble? Brumble. Hmm, that would explain it, then. Your father wouldn't happen to be Tobias Brumble?"

"I am his younger son. Who are you, and how do you know my father?"

"Captain Vik Brandee, sir, at your service. You've already met my first mate, Hezekiah Grimm."

The young captain blanched, recognizing the names of the two most feared pirates to sail these waters.

"I don't know your sire personally, Mr. Brumble, but an old friend of mine once spent six miserable months as cabin boy to that cowardly piece of shit. I promised him that I'd pay the bastard back, with interest, for every lash of the whip he'd given my friend unjustly."

"Then I am a dead man. I know the reputations of Bloody Vik Brandee and the Grimm Reaper. All I ask, sir, is that you allow me to dress, so that I may face my fate with some dignity," Brumble requested.

"What say you, Lazarus?" Brandee asked, stroking the agitated cat's head.

Lazarus stopped growling, yawned and stretched out one paw, toes and claws spread. "Meh," he mewed. Then he proceeded to groom the paw and ignore the prisoner.

"Very well, Mr. Brumble. Mr. Grimm, if you will escort our guest topside once he's properly attired? I shall be inspecting our prisoners and new recruits."

"Aye, Captain."

The crew and mates of the merchant vessel gathered on deck, where they had been herded by the pirates. Brandee stood to the side with his second mate, Jon-Jon, watching while their ship's surgeon checked the prisoners over.

Before long, Grimm brought Thomas on deck. The surgeon approached Brandee to report, as they joined the pirate captain. The man gave a curious and mildly astonished look at the prisoner.

"Your report, Mr. Coffin?" Brandee prompted, returning the surgeon's attention to the business at hand.

"Oh, yes, Captain Brandewyne. They are a remarkably healthy lot, given the circumstances." Coffin shot a sideways look at Brumble. It was not lost on Brandee.

"Something about the captain seems to have drawn your attention," he commented.

"Aye, sir. If he wasn't so young, I would swear he was Tobias Brumble."

"Mr. Coffin, may I introduce Thomas Brumble, son of the aforementioned Tobias and former captain of this vessel. Mr. Brumble, this is our ship surgeon, Dr. Matthew Coffin. Now then, why do you say that his crew's condition surprises you?"

"Well, Captain, I remember a voyage I undertook a few years back as a passenger aboard his father's ship. I was appalled at the poor condition he forced his crew to labor under. The man was positively brutal, sometimes having sailors beaten for no apparent reason. These men, however, look to be well-fed and show no signs of recent beatings. The only injuries I see are what would occur as a result of normal sailing hazards: splinters, minor cuts, some rope burns and one missing finger due to a line snapping unexpectedly."

Viktor raised one eyebrow. "Interesting. It would seem that you resemble your sire in appearance only, young Thomas."

The man stood stiffly. "Unlike my father, I've found that a healthy, happy crew is less prone to mutiny."

"Aye, true enough," Viktor nodded. "Of course, I imagine the promise of full shares of the profit on the emeralds you are carrying doesn't hurt."

"I do not know what you mean, sir. We carry only spices."

"Do not insult my intelligence, Thomas."

"Captain Brandee, I know you intend to kill me. I ask that you be swift about it. I know nothing of any emeralds."

"What, no pleas for mercy or begging to be ransomed?"

Without blinking, Brumble told him, "My father will be more distressed over the loss of this ship and its cargo than he will be over the loss of one of his sons. My brother and I were not spared the strap or whip any more than any of Father's crewmen were."

Grimm spoke up, "How do we propose to loosen his tongue, Captain? He obviously fears neither death nor flogging."

"A problem indeed, Mr. Grimm," Vik stroked his goatee thoughtfully. "I believe I do have a solution, however. There are some things more fearful than death."

"Lads," he addressed his cadre, "pick out your meals. I already have mine."

In a heartbeat, he was behind Brumble, one arm holding the man immobile without effort. "Watch and behold your fate," he whispered in his ear; his will forced Brumble to watch. The five vampires seized victims from among the prisoners and proceeded to gorge themselves on the men's blood.

Once satisfied that his prey realized what he faced, Viktor drew him away from the disturbing scene. His blood Hunger ran high, but he refused to let it usurp his control. He did let Thomas see it in his eyes, however.

"Now, I could just tear this ship apart plank by plank and find those emeralds myself, but that would take too much time. Tell me where they are, and I will make your death swift and relatively painless. Keep lying to me," his eyes glowed emerald, and he revealed his fangs, "and I will make your nights pure hell for the rest of eternity."

Brumble crossed himself in terror. "I—I'll show you where they're hidden."

"Very good, Mr. Brumble. Mr. Jon, select some new crew members and give them a round of the good rum, before you put them to work. Put the rest in the larder hold. I want this ship stripped before the next sunset."

"Aye, Cap'n."

Thomas led Viktor past the cabins and gun deck, through one of the holds, and on to the aft powder magazine. He then moved several kegs of powder. It was sweaty work, and the air was close, so he removed his shirt to continue the work. Whip scars covered his torso, front and back, old scars. Brandee had seen similar scars on other men, although rarely so profuse. He was struck by a vivid memory of slathering salve on the fresh welts and cuts that had covered a young Jim Rigger, when they first become partners in piracy.

Lazarus had been watching as well – and listening. He hopped down from Viktor's shoulder and padded over to Thomas. Cocking his head to one side, he gazed at the young man. Then, he rubbed his cheek against the man's ankle, scent marking him, placed a paw on his leg and looked at his master.

"Mrrur?"

Thomas stopped and looked down at the large black cat warily. "I thought he didn't like me."

"It would seem he has changed his mind." The vampire smiled slightly at the cat. *"I think I know what you're telling me, Jim,"* he thought at the creature that had once been his first mate and friend. *"He's not to blame for what his father did to you. Tobias Brumble must be a true bastard to do such a thing to his own son."*

Lazarus returned to Viktor, but remained seated on the floor, watching the younger Brumble.

Finally, Thomas found the powder keg he was looking for. It was only about a foot and a half tall, a foot wide, and bore a slightly different mark from the other kegs. "They're in this."

"Open it."

He took a pry bar down from the wall. Brandee could see him briefly entertain the notion of using it as a weapon. The moment passed, and Thomas did as ordered, prying the top off the keg. Inside appeared to be nothing but black powder. He shook the keg to settle its contents a bit. Glints of green shone through as the emeralds were revealed. Some of the stones rivaled the vampire's eyes in the intensity of their color.

"Lid it and bring it."

Tamara A. Lowery

Chapter 2

Viktor had Thomas locked in one of the unused cabins. He hadn't decided what he wanted to do with the man just yet, but he felt it best to keep him separate from the other prisoners.

Jon-Jon had the salvaging process under control and going quite smoothly. So, Vik and Grimm went back to his cabin with the powder keg, after a brief side trip to the galley for a colander and a tray. Once in the cabin, Vik cleared the table, spread a cloth on it and placed the colander on the center. With a practiced rap, he hit one edge of the loosened lid and popped the small keg open. He then began pouring the contents into the colander. Periodically, he lifted the colander and moved it to sift the powder away from the emeralds and onto the cloth. He emptied the stones from the colander four times, placing most of the loose stones in the tray. The rest ended up on the bed. He and Grimm lifted the corners of the cloth and poured the powder back into the keg.

Grimm whistled at both the quantity and quality of the stones. The majority of them were still rough, but a couple handfuls had been cut and polished. There were also a few pieces of jewelry with what looked to be some of the best stones set into them.

"That's a king's ransom three times over, Vik. May take a while to convert it."

"Aye, the set pieces will be the hardest to get rid of. Too easy to recognize," he agreed. Sorting through them, he lifted out an ornate cross. For some reason, he felt compelled to keep the piece. When he hung its golden chain about his neck, it just felt right.

"It suits you, Vik," Grimm commented.

"Believe I'll keep this one intact," Viktor murmured. "Can't say why, but something tells me it'll be useful. Odd thing to think about a piece of jewelry, isn't it?"

"Aye, but I've a feeling you're right. There's an almost quieting feel about it. Maybe Belle can explain it."

"Maybe. If you see anything you like, go ahead and pick it out."

Grimm sifted through the jewels, drawing out a heavy necklace. Five large emeralds were set into the gold. "I like this."

Vik couldn't resist teasing a little. "I know you don't wear such stuff, Hezekiah. Who's the lucky wench?"

"Now why would I waste this on a whore? Hell, Vik, they pay me, not the other way around. No, I figure I can sell off the stones and melt the gold down to a small ingot. Easier to sell that way," he grinned.

"True; nice sized stones, too," he admired the piece. "Two of them would bring enough to buy a small island. Of course, why buy when you can convince them to give it to you for free?"

"Exactly."

Belladonna growled in irritation when she sensed the vampire's call. Not for the last time, she cursed her predatory nature, which had irrevocably bound her to his will. She wasn't through playing with her latest catch.

The fisherman she had lured to a small, deserted cay was young and virile. Belle's prolonged periods of abstinence aboard the pirate vessel made her rapacious. The young man had been a relief and delight. She'd found his sexual prowess almost equal to her appetite. After four days of multiple rounds of sex he was only just beginning to show signs of exhaustion.

She decided to ignore the summons.

Viktor became more insistent.

Belle hissed in pain. It felt as if someone had driven a marlin spike into her skull.

"Did I hurt you?" the fisherman asked.

She smiled up at him, fighting off the pain in her head. "No, it wasn't you, lover. But I need to cool off. Let's go for a swim."

"I don't know how," he apologized.

She wasn't surprised. It was rare to find a seafarer that could swim. Most felt it useless to fight the fate of drowning.

"I'll teach you," she smiled coquettishly.

He let her lead him into the surf. He was so enamored and trusting that he never noticed when her legs fused and shifted to a black shark tail. She pulled him into a searing kiss.

When she finally pulled back, he smiled, drunk with lust. "I've never met anyone like you, Belladonna."

"I know, and you never will again."

His expression was more one of surprise than pain when she stabbed her talons up through his gut and deep into his chest. The last thing he saw, before his vision went dark, was the siren tossing his heart into her impossibly wide mouth lined with razor-sharp teeth.

It galled Viktor somewhat that the siren tried to ignore him. His desire to have everything under his control and his admiration of her ability to resist his will tore at his psyche. When he opened the bond between them to get a feel for what was distracting her so much, he found himself consumed with an overwhelming surge of jealousy.

Each had avoided bedding the other, despite a strong desire to do so on both their parts. Viktor resisted temptation out of a sense of self-preservation. Belladonna refused to give in because of her fear of binding herself even closer to his will.

But none of that reasoning lessened the sting of knowing she was enjoying herself with another man. Viktor had always been very possessive of women he considered to be his. Grimm had spoken truth; he did not like to share his wenches.

As a result, his second summons carried more force. He felt no regret for causing Belle some minor pain. He could sense it got the point across. She would finish her meal and return promptly.

"Now, what to do with young Brumble?" he thought. Aloud, he said, "Lazarus, come forth."

Obediently, the cat materialized. "Mrrrurr."

Viktor smiled as he caressed the cat's head. Lazarus leaned into his hand, then put his paws onto his friend's chest to rub his cheek against Vik's face.

"What do you think, old friend, should I ransom the lad, feed him to the sharks, or make him part of the crew?"

"Meh!"

"Keep him?"

"Meh!" Lazarus purred. Viktor took that as a yes. He wished the cat could talk. Although he would never admit it to anyone, he missed his friend.

The irate siren barged into the captain's cabin without knocking. The sight of the vampire lowering a drained body to the floor took some of the edge off her anger.

"Well, at least you have a peace offering for me," she nodded at the body. "Now, what was so bloody important that you felt it necessary to give me a splitting headache?"

Lazarus leapt onto the corpse, crouching and growling, when she moved toward it. Viktor stopped her before she could get close enough to try to physically dislodge the cat. "I've given him to Lazarus. I do not owe you a 'peace offering,' Belle."

"You're going to waste that on him? It will start to rot before he can eat all of it. And yes, you do! What makes you think that it is perfectly all right for you to cause me that kind of pain on a whim?"

"He's not going to eat it. Brumble is to be the replacement for Griffin among my cadre. And no, I do not. If you had not tried to block me out, I would not have had to be so forceful. Nor did I summon you on a whim. I have need of your expertise and knowledge."

Belladonna blinked at him. She had thought he had merely been trying to interrupt her prolonged encounter with her prey. She'd sensed his jealousy just before the psychic blow. But he was claiming to have a legitimate reason for the summons. This Her curiosity was aroused.

"What do you need to know?"

He drew out the emerald-encrusted cross. As it twisted slowly on its chain, it seemed to not only sparkle but to glow softly in the lamplight. Both he and Lazarus seemed to be mesmerized by the piece of jewelry.

She moved closer to examine it but did not try to touch it. Instead, she sniffed the air around it. "Interesting and pretty. What exactly do you want to know about it?"

Viktor's voice was peaceful, when he answered, a fact that caught her attention more sharply than the jewelry. Viktor Brandewyne could be many things, but peaceful was not on that list.

"This was among a cache of smuggled emeralds I recently liberated from young Brumble there. I want to know why I felt compelled to keep this particular piece and why it seems to have such a calming effect."

The siren tilted her head, thinking the situation over. She was relieved that he was at least aware of the cross' effect on him. That told her its effect was not an adverse one.

"What I know is this has been blessed. I've seen various 'holy' items over the centuries, but this is one of the few that really are holy. I can only guess that either it is something you will need later and were meant to find, or it simply is damping to the power of the curse on you. That is what it is doing and would explain your calm right now. But it is not a cure."

"Hmm, I have been less – Hungry since acquiring this."

She nodded. "That does not surprise me. Should be useful during long stretches when no prey is available, but I wouldn't change your feeding habits for the present, unless absolutely necessary. It's been my experience with similar objects that, although they replenish their power, heavy use will drain them quickly and make the power buildup take longer."

He took the cross off and locked it in a small chest he kept for such trinkets. "So, you are saying if I use it too much, it may not work when I really need it."

"Exactly."

Viktor went to the door of the cabin and summoned the cabin boy. The lad always stayed near but was more often attending his first mate than him – especially when he wished to feed.

"Danny, fetch Anvil. Tell him I need this body taken down to the ballast hold to join the cadre. Be quick about it. Sundown is approaching."

"Aye, sir." The boy darted off to carry out the order.

He shut the door and returned his attention to the siren. Something in the change in his posture put her on the alert.

"You know I do not summon lightly or on a whim. Why did you ignore me?" His voice remained neutral, making it difficult to judge his mood.

"I wasn't through playing with my food." She couldn't keep the sullenness out of her tone.

"Yes, I noticed that. I do not care much for your manner of playing."

She crossed her arms and glared at him. "Oh yes you do. It's the same way you play with your food. You just don't like that I am playing with someone else."

His eyes flashed green fire. Belle had hit right on the mark. "No, I do not, when I see you doing so."

"Well, you wouldn't have seen, if you hadn't 'looked!'"

"I wouldn't have looked, if you had responded rather than ignored me," he snarled, throwing it back at her.

She returned his snarl, getting up in his face. "I have needs other than my hunger, and you are not meeting them."

He needed no further goading. He knew of one sure way to ensure she understood he was not to be ignored. Lightning fast, he had her wrist behind her back, forcing her arms up. Shoving her forward, he bent her face down over the table, leaving her no leverage to free herself.

"Is this what you want?" he growled in her ear. "It is, isn't it? You want it." His laugh was both lustful and cruel. She felt his hardness against her butt through the fabric of their clothes. Writhing, she tried to throw him off, but she was pinned.

"Come now, Belle, you can do better than that," he laughed. "I'm not even trying."

"Get off me!"

"Make me." He managed to get both of her wrists into one of his hands, then used the other to rip her breeches apart at the seam. The remnants effectively tangled her legs, so she couldn't kick him.

Bared to him with no leverage, Belladonna became acutely aware of her lack of control of the situation; an unfamiliar predicament for her. She already knew he was physically stronger than her, but she found it unnerving to not have control. It frightened her and excited her, which frightened her even more.

Her fear translated into her scent and voice, making the latter shrill. "Viktor, get off me!" Her struggles became frenzied.

"But you don't want me to, pet," he purred in her ear. Her behavior fired every predator reaction in him.

She realized she was acting like prey but didn't seem able to stop herself. "Please Viktor, let me go."

Her plea got through to the part of him still able to reason. He still didn't let her up, but he became gentler.

"Is that really what you want, Belle?"

"Get off, get off, get off!" Her voice came out panicked.

Just like that, he released her and stood on the other side of the cabin. "There are some spare breeches in the chest at the foot of the bed."

She stripped off the ruined ones and fished a fresh pair out. The entire time she kept a wary eye on the vampire. She didn't understand why he had released her, but she wasn't going to question it at the moment. As soon as she was dressed once again, she began easing toward the door.

Viktor moved there, blocking her escape route before she could reach it. "Don't even think about trying to get out the window, Belle," he warned, when he saw her glancing in that direction.

Her fear quickly dissolved into anger. "What do you want, Viktor?" she snarled.

"Obedience."

"No, you want absolute control!"

"That, too."

She rushed him in an attempt to get out the door. "Get out of my way!" If he hadn't sensed the move a split second before she tried it, she might have gotten past him. But his speed equaled hers, and even though she knew he was physically stronger, she still wasn't used to it. Human men were no match for her.

Once again, she found her arms pinned behind her by the vampire. But this time she was facing him and held against him.

Viktor took a great risk and kissed her on impulse. He was gambling that she was not going to bite a chunk out of him, literally. The gamble paid off.

The kiss caught Belle completely off guard. She'd expected him to try to stop her, even to be rough with her. But the kiss was skillful and gentle. She surrendered to it before she realized what she was doing.

Once he felt her relax and become pliant against him, he released his grip. "That is better, pet," he smiled. "Now, you won't ignore me again, will you?"

"How could I?" she asked, her voice was deepened by lust, but shaky with uncertainty. The pirate confused the hell out of her.

"Exactly."

A knock came at the cabin door. Both growled in irritation at the interruption.

"Mrrow!" Lazarus' yowl reminded Viktor that he'd sent for Anvil to come remove Brumble's body from the cabin.

"Enter."

Anvil came in, but he was joined by Grimm. As the giant smithy bent to pick up the dead man, the first mate met his captain's expectant gaze.

"Sorry to interrupt, Captain, but I think Zeke wants a word with you," he said. "Hell's Breath appeared off the bow a few minutes ago."

"Hmph, well at least he didn't ground the ship this time," Vik grunted. "Let's go see what the old man wants."

Chapter 3

The three of them took a small boat over to the island. Viktor and Belle both felt Uncle Zeke had business with them. Hezekiah went because he just didn't trust the siren. He took his charge to protect Viktor quite seriously.

It didn't take them long to locate Zeke. As usual, the old man perched on a rock, contemplating a small driftwood fire in a barren hollow, obscured from the shore.

"Hope you young'uns didn't forget to bring some smoke for old Zeke."

Of course, Viktor had forgotten, in his irritation. Grimm, however, anticipated and expected the request. The first mate pulled an extra pouch of tobacco out of his vest and tossed it to the old man.

"Thank ye, Hezekiah Grimm, you're a good man to have around," he nodded, catching the pouch one-handed. He filled his pipe and lit it with an ember from the fire. After a few satisfied puffs, he fixed each of them with a stare. "Pull up a rock and sit a spell."

They did as they were bid. Uncle Zeke might have looked like an ordinary old man, but they knew he was much more than he appeared to be. He possessed powers that surpassed anything any of them had ever encountered.

However, Viktor was never one to be intimidated by anyone, regardless of how powerful they were. "I hope you had something more important to summon us for than just to bring you some tobacco."

"You get to be my age, boy, and some days there ain't nothing more important than a good smoke," he teased. "But today there is." Then he went back to smoking in silence.

Belladonna lost patience first among the companions, an unusual reaction for the siren. The recent encounter in the captain's cabin still placed her senses and emotions in a state of turmoil. The wildness of her nature made her want to swim far and fast. Viktor sat across the fire from her, but her instincts recognized him as the greater predator.

She had to put some more distance between them.

With a small, irritated growl, she stood and started stalking off.

"You sit yourself back down, girl," Zeke ordered, as if the siren were a pouting child.

She stopped and glared at him. He just pointed with his pipe at the rock she'd been sitting on. She fought the urge to scream but sat back down.

The old man nodded. "That's better. You want to stay around and hear what has to be said. There might be a meal in it for you."

"What is it you want to talk about, Elder?" Viktor asked with arms crossed.

The formal address drew a sharp stare from Zeke. "Where did you hear that from, boy?"

The vampire just smiled at him.

"You found that hussy Dorada, didn't you?"

"I did."

"Mm-hmm. You got lucky, boy. She is the weakest of the Sisters. She's also not near as clever as she thinks she is and too arrogant for her own good." He puffed some more on his pipe, a perturbed expression on his face.

"You speak as if you know her well, Uncle," Grimm observed.

"Let's just say I've had to put her in her place a time or two."

What the old wizard didn't say was that he had been compelled to summon the earth-witch's successive incarnations to Hell's Breath over the centuries. She was unique among the Sisters in that she had to transfer her power and essence from one host body to another. Her power was fertility-based and required a fertile host. She would never be able to exist in a body whose womb had not awakened yet or had ceased to be viable for childbearing. The problem was that the new hosts would sometimes get drunk on their own power and think they were more important in the order of things than they were.

Zeke tamped out the pipe and tucked it away, then stirred the fire. "But I didn't invite you to talk about that biddy."

"And I ask again, what did you bring us here to discuss?" Viktor reminded.

"You," he fixed the vampire with a mild glare, "seem to need reminding what you need to be about doing. It's been two months since you finished up with the first Sister. There're still six of them out there to find and deal with, boy, and you don't have time to be lollygagging."

"Lollygagging?" Viktor raised an eyebrow. "I would hardly call what I've been doing lollygagging."

"Have you tried to find the next Sister?"

"Not yet. I've been about my business."

"And what business is that, pray tell?"

He was starting to find the old man's needling irritating. "The business that keeps me and mine fed and funded, old man; piracy," he snapped.

Zeke pulled the pipe back out for another smoke. Once he had it going again, he returned his attention to his guests.

"That's all well and good, Viktor Brandewyne," he spoke around the pipe stem. "I know you need to keep your crew healthy and happy."

"But…?"

"But your hunt for the Sisters of Power needs to take first priority, boy." He jabbed the pipe at him to make his point. "You've got to remember your time is limited. Even I don't know how long you've got, so you can't afford to be putting things off."

Vik knew he was right. Old Mother Celie had warned him that the curse *Mamaan* Juma put on him for killing one of her favorites would eventually kill him. But first, it would reduce him to a mindless creature at the mercy of his Hunger. That, more than anything, tarnished his enjoyment of his vampiric powers and abilities. Viktor could not stand the thought of anyone or anything having control over him.

It galled him to be reminded of it. It went against everything in his nature to be chided like a child. He'd tolerated it from Celie, because she had raised him. The only reason he tolerated it from Zeke was that the old wizard had demonstrated that his powers far outstripped those of the vampire.

It didn't stop his voice from going deadly cold, however. "What would you counsel me to do, Elder?"

"You already know what you should be doing, boy. The Sisters are going to eat up enough of your time making themselves hard to find and sending you on all sorts of errands after you do find them. You can't afford to waste time between. Soon as you finish dealing with one, you need to start tracking down the next."

"And what about my crew?"

Zeke cackled, "Trust me, boy, you stay your course, and you'll have plenty opportunities to pirate to your heart's content. I dare say they'll sail right into your path."

Grimm spoke his doubts, "Uncle, how can you be sure of that? We've both been doing this for years. Months can pass without finding a prize."

"If I say it's going to be so, it's going to be so, Hezekiah Grimm. Your captain's done proved he's the One. He was destined for this course. As long as he doesn't stray, the powers that be will see to it he gets what he needs," he stated emphatically.

He then returned his attention to the siren. "You know what you're supposed to be doing, too, girl. You weren't sent along just for the ride."

"He won't let me touch his precious crew," she argued. "I can't have my visions without sacrifice."

"I'll give you one of the new recruits," Viktor told her.

"I get to pick which one?"

"Agreed."

Satisfied that he'd gotten his point across, Zeke tamped out the pipe again. "Well, what are you young'uns still doing here? Go on now, git!" he shooed them.

They wasted no time getting back to the boat. Fog already began to gather as they left the clearing. Seconds after they pushed off, Hell's Breath melted into the fog as if it had never been there.

"That's just unnerving how he does that," Grimm said.

"It's not always Zeke doing it," Belle told them. "Sometimes the island has a mind of its own and will move while you're on it. I've seen

Hell's Breath drop one poor fool that made the mistake of going ashore unbidden in a completely different sea from the one he'd been in."

"If you were there, I'm sure he didn't suffer long," Viktor grunted.

"Long enough," she smiled sweetly. "Seasoned the meat wonderfully."

He should have known better than to agree to let the siren pick her victim. She did abide by his statement that it would be from among the men taken from Brumble's ship. But rather than choose from those destined for the vampire's "larder," she opted for the healthiest, most promising sailor selected to join his crew.

He suspected she did it for spite. Past victims he had supplied her with had generally been among the least valuable of his men.

"Why this one?" Grimm asked the question he knew the captain would not.

Belle looked the sailor up and down, a wicked half-smile on her face. "He looks healthy enough to keep up with me for a while. Besides," she shot a glance at Viktor, "someone needs to learn the definition of sacrifice."

"I agree, pet," the vampire responded to her taunt. "Which is why I forbid you to play with him."

She growled in irritation at him, too angry to speak. He answered her with an arctic smile. "That can be your sacrifice. Right now, we need to know where to start looking for the next Sister."

"Fine," she snarled. "Come on." She grabbed the victim by the arm and started dragging him toward the side.

Up to that point, Viktor had kept the man's mind in thrall to keep him oblivious to the conversation. He released his hold entirely, so his powers would not interfere with the siren's magic.

The victim was surprised but not unhappy to find himself in her hands. In her human form, Belladonna was a striking beauty. She was well-formed with flawless fair skin and hair so red it reminded one of rubies – or blood. He didn't notice that her eyes flashed from sea gray to their true golden amber color.

"You're a strong one, lass," he smiled. "Where are we going?"

Bound by the vampire's order not to play with her victim, she answered truthfully, "We're going to dive into the sea, and I am going to eat you. Strip." She then started removing her own clothes.

The sailor misunderstood her meaning, thinking she was making an *entendré*. He obediently disrobed, revealing that he was well-endowed. She gave a wistful look before jumping over the railing. Eagerly, he jumped in after her.

He didn't even have time to scream when she ripped his throat out with her needle teeth. She made quick work of the body, staying close to the surface rather than diving with her kill.

"Enter, Mr. Grimm," Viktor responded to the knock at his cabin door.

"We have a heading."

The pirate captain just looked at his first mate for a few heartbeats. "Why are you bringing me this news rather than Belladonna, Hezekiah?"

"Apparently, she is avoiding direct contact with you again," he shrugged. "I don't even attempt to understand that female's reasoning for anything she does."

"Very well, if that is how she wants to play it for now. What is the heading?"

Grimm gave him an anticipatory grin, obviously liking the answer. "She said we should start looking in the swamps and bayous close to New Orleans."

Viktor's smile grew to match his, exposing fangs. "Angelique."

The small sloop eased alongside the larger ship. It was plain to her crew that the merchant ship was adrift. They proceeded with caution.

On board, they found the ship stripped and empty: no cargo, no provisions, no crew – and no emeralds.

Tamara A. Lowery

Chapter 4

Swamp water swirled in the wake of a monstrous beast. Moonlight silvered the ripples on the black water, where the faint light could break through the cypress canopy and drapes of Spanish moss. Milky-white skin seemed to glow with its own light in the near-perpetual gloom of the deep swamp. Then it submerged, vanishing back into the cold murk.

The creature wasn't the only one restless that night. In a stilt shack in another part of the bayou, a toothless old hag sniffed the air. Pursing her lips, she dropped a small clay pot on a rough twine cord through a hole in the floor and dipped up some of the tannin-stained water. Peering into it, she nodded.

"Time's almost up. Change is coming. This 'n's the One for sure."

It took the *Incubus* longer to reach New Orleans than her captain would have liked. The sea-witch remained stubborn and uncooperative. For an entire week, Belladonna refused to come out of her cabin or let him in. She even put up a magical barrier to keep Lazarus out. In response, the cat sprayed her door. Viktor toyed with the idea of refusing her entry to his cabin, when she finally emerged and knocked at his door. He decided it would be petty and require too much effort. He would either have to physically hold the door or gamble that his hold on her will was strong enough to keep her out. Either would have been satisfying in a small way but would have only angered the siren further. Much as he hated to admit it, he needed her help.

"Enter."

Belle was in a temper. "That damned cat pissed all over my door!"

"You should have let him in."

"So, you could use him to spy on me? I don't think so."

He shrugged. "What prompted you to grace me with your presence, pet?"

"I couldn't stand the reek anymore." She glared at him.

"I'll have Mr. Jon set someone to scrub your door, if it will make you happy."

"Thank you." Belladonna cocked her head, puzzled by the vampire's even mood. "You seem unusually calm, Viktor. Are you wearing that cross?"

"Not at the moment, but I probably will while we're in port." He waited to see if she would ask. She did.

"Why? It's a busy port. There should be plenty of prey."

He nodded. "Oh, it's a busy port, pet. But I do not wish to waste time hunting for food, when I would rather be hunting for the Sister."

"So just feed well before going ashore," she suggested.

He leaned forward and tented his fingers, elbows on the table, and peered at her. "And therein lies the problem, pet," he smiled. "My larder is running low. My cadre will have to remain on board, and they will need provisions to tide them over. It would not do for them to be loosed on the port or start feeding on the crew."

She narrowed her eyes at him, crossing her arms. "Sarcasm does not become you, Viktor. You know you can order your little vampires dormant for the duration."

"I do not know how long this is going to take or how far from the ship I will have to go. I would rather not risk my hold growing too thin or faint. Besides, I need to be free to concentrate on what obstacles, tests or hostile magic this Sister decides to throw at me."

He got up and retrieved one of his bottles of blood mixed with brandy then returned to his seat. "Of course, this wouldn't have been as much of an issue, if we could have made better time," he stated matter of fact. "If the weather and winds hold, and given the currents, it will still be another week before we make port."

She went on the defensive, recognizing his reproach for what it was. "I sensed no fear or urgency in my vision. This one is not going to run from you."

"Oh, I forgot. You were not present when Uncle Zeke told me I cannot afford to lollygag." In a split second he was behind her, hands on her shoulders and whispering in her ear, "Just because this Sister is not going to run from me does not mean I can take my time getting to her, pet. Have you ever been in the swamps and bayous along the Louisiana coast or upriver there?"

"No," Belle's voice was soft, her body reacting to his touch and proximity against her will. "I am a saltwater creature."

Viktor enjoyed that the siren was so soft and amazingly compliant under his fingertips, but he did not allow it to distract him. "The Sister will not have to run from me. She has only to hide. Those swamps are a deadly maze of bogs, quicksand, and waterways that frequently alter courses. Most of the creatures that inhabit them are deadly, as well."

She turned to face him but did not try to move away. The fact that he was not using his power on her seduced her more surely than if the vampire had forced his will through the blood and flesh bond they shared. "What do you want of me, Viktor?"

His smile was both gentle and, at the same time, self-satisfied. He could sense that, for the moment, she would do anything he asked of her. Leaning down, he kissed her. She returned the kiss with a passion.

He laughed lasciviously, as he pulled away from the kiss. "I appreciate your fervor, pet. But for now, I only need you to sing up a wind to speed me on my way."

Belladonna pouted, wrapping arms around his shoulders and wriggling against him. "Are you sure? I could do oh so much more for you."

"Of that I have no doubt, but it will have to wait. I need that wind now, however, or I will have to hunt before looking for the Sister."

She stepped back from him, her eyes trailing down. What she observed brought a wicked smile to her lips. She left the cabin chuckling, knowing his eyes were following her.

A courier waited patiently outside the office door at Brumble & Sons Shipping in Boston. He'd been given instructions to return the proprietor's reply, and he hoped for a tip for his trouble. He was soon disappointed.

Tobias Brumble opened the door and thrust a scrap of paper that had been folded over several times into the boy's hand. "Can you read, boy?" his voice was gruff with barely contained rage.

"No sir. Never had no one to teach me."

"Good. Letters would be wasted on a little gutter rat like you," he sneered. "Take this back to the man who sent you." When the lad didn't leave right away, he barked, "What are you waiting for?"

The boy held out his hand. "Can you spare any coin, sir?"

In response, the elder Brumble backhanded him, knocking him to the stair landing. "Let the bastard who sent you here pay you, whelp. If you don't hie yourself back right now, I'll take my quirt to you!"

He got up, rubbing his bruised jaw, then scrambled down the stairs and out through the shipping house. Brumble slammed the office door and stormed back to his desk.

Later that night, Samantha Brumble realized something troubled her father. She knew he was prone to be ill-tempered with almost everyone except her and her departed mother, but his mood was exceptionally foul this evening. He barely touched his food except to shove it around on his plate.

She waited on him, because he'd already broken the nose of one of the household servants that evening. The remainder of them had hidden out in the kitchen, terrified to go near the man. Samantha hoped to defuse the situation, before her father decided to randomly single out one of them for an arbitrary beating.

"Papa, you've barely touched your roast," she chided. "What's troubling you?"

He snorted in response. Downing his wine, he refilled his glass and then half-drained that. It was not a good sign. She knew he did not drink to excess, unless he was very angry or very worried.

Thinking it might lighten his mood, she said, "We should get good news from Thomas soon. Isn't it close to time for him to return?"

Brumble threw the glass across the room to shatter against the far wall. Wine dripped down from the wainscoting.

"Papa?!"

"He won't be coming back, Sam," he growled. "Got a message today. His ship fell to pirates, apparently."

She blanched. "No. Has there been any demand for ransom?"

"Ransom be damned! I should have known better than to trust that useless whelp with a ship!"

"You don't mean that, Papa. Thomas is your son and my brother, and he is a fine sea captain. You trained him yourself."

He rounded on her, but she didn't flinch from him. "The hell I don't, girl," he sputtered. "He must not have learned much from me. The boy just handed everything over to them without a fight. He is weak! He is not worthy to call himself my son!"

Samantha gave her father a stony stare. She knew the reason he thought Thomas weak was because her brother treated his crew like men, instead of animals to be beaten into submission. She agreed with Thomas but knew she could never say so to her father. He would just dismiss it as female foolishness.

Tobias often underestimated his only daughter's strength and intelligence. He had no idea she knew about not only how his trade business was run, but about the smuggling operation, as well. She knew not to let him know that she was aware of exactly what was going on. He had always been indulgent and gentle toward her, but she saw how he treated everyone else, even her brothers. She did not trust him to not turn that violence and rage against her eventually.

Silently, she turned and set about cleaning up the broken glass, gathering the shards in a napkin.

Brumble stood and grabbed the decanter. "I'm going to my study, Samantha. I am not to be disturbed for any reason."

"Very well, Papa." She did not look back at him.

Once safely ensconced in his favorite chair, Brumble poured a fresh glass of the wine and brooded. His contact was losing confidence. The report he got was that other than some slight damage to the ship's side, there was no sign of any kind of a struggle, not even a bloodstain to show where any of the crew had been killed. It was enough to make the contact think Thomas and his crew had deliberately stripped their ship and transferred to another vessel.

If Tobias' heart had truly been hardened against his youngest son, he too would have suspected him of making arrangements with another buyer for the emeralds and faking his disappearance. He preferred to believe Thomas had fallen to pirates. He only hoped that the next shipment, being carried aboard Zachary, his elder son's, vessel would be transferred successfully.

The transaction would restore his buyer's faith and cement their relationship.

Demon Bayou

The favorable winds the siren conjured shaved almost three days off their estimated travel time. Viktor's choice to anchor the *Incubus* well away from the main harbor aroused her curiosity, however.

"I don't trust other pirates, pet," he explained. "New Orleans has a fair share of them, as well as those who fancy themselves pirates. This ship is too tempting a prize, especially since I intend to allow most of the crew shore time. Why leave her where she's easy to board?"

"What's to stop someone who's truly determined from trying to steal it?"

"My cadre would not let them get far." His smile was smug and sinister.

Her laugh matched it. "No, now that you mention it, I imagine they would not."

Tamara A. Lowery

Chapter 5

Once all the crew went ashore, they scattered throughout the city. Viktor made sure they knew to keep a rotating watch back on the ship, both to protect it and to keep an eye on his vampires. He harbored no worry of any of them conveniently forgetting their turn. He'd made sure all the crew received a good double helping of rum before going ashore. What they didn't know was that he'd tainted the rum with a few drops of his blood to keep them bound to his will.

Unlike many pirates, Vik Brandee preferred absolute control rather than the traditional shipboard democracy, where the crew chose their captain from among themselves depending on the prize they were after. It kept things simple, made sure things got done, and cut down on the risk of a mutiny.

Only Hezekiah was exempted from the special rum. In Viktor's opinion, his loyalty was beyond question.

He split off from Viktor's core group, when they went ashore, to hunt down one of his personal contacts. He planned to put out feelers for a potential buyer for the emeralds. It would be much easier to divvy up shares once the gemstones were converted to gold coins.

Jon-Jon and Belladonna stayed with the captain. The second mate fully expected to be entertained watching the siren's reaction to where they were going. Viktor felt glad she had accidentally bound herself to him. It would make it easier to keep her from causing trouble with his information source.

Before long, they found themselves at the gates of a well-appointed manse in the Garden District. A foppish gate attendant in a powdered wig came out of the gate house. He looked them over with a sneer at their attire. Amazingly, Vik ignored the implied insult.

"May I help you?" the man's tone made it plain that he doubted it.

"I've business to discuss with Angelique," the vampire got right to the point.

The attendant raked his eyes over Belladonna, before he smirked. "She's pretty enough and might even clean up well, but I'm sorry, *Madame* is not in the market for new talent at the present."

Jon-Jon put a hand over his mouth to hide his grin. The siren very quickly caught on to what had just happened. "Why you scrawny little puffer fish! I am not for sale!" she sputtered furiously.

Viktor caught her hand as it transformed into a talon, forcing it behind her back before the unwitting flunky could see it. "Easy, pet," he soothed. "Given the nature of this establishment, it was an honest mistake." He turned his attention to the now indignant attendant. "I am not here to sell. I am here as a customer. Take this to your mistress."

He handed a small parchment scroll and a few coins to the man. He took them, holding the scroll as if it were unclean, but pocketing the coins. "Very well, *m'sieur*, but I doubt *Madame* will receive you. She is very select about her clientele."

Viktor's eyes flashed emerald briefly. "You will give Angelique the message, and you will return my coin, you worthless little eunuch."

Looking befuddled and nervous, the man retrieved the money and returned it, then gave a half bow and scurried off to the main house.

Jon-Jon couldn't contain his laughter any longer. Viktor soon joined him. Belle scowled at both of them, not understanding the joke. This, of course, made them laugh even harder, which led her to believe she was the object of their amusement.

"I don't have to take this," she growled at them. "I'll just go back to the sea and you can find the bitch on your own."

"Be still."

The power behind those two words proved enough to stop the siren where she stood. Even Jon-Jon's laughter died as if it had never been. Viktor glanced at his second mate, "Not you, Mr. Jon."

He gave his captain a shaky smile and rubbed the back of his neck.

"We were not laughing at you, pet," Vik smiled wryly. "The butt of this joke is that mincing little idiot I just sent in there." Seeing the irritation leave her eyes, he released his mental grip on her.

"What exactly is this joke? Does it involve causing the little wretch lots of pain?" She looked hopeful.

He smiled wide enough to show fangs. "It just might, my little fish."

She grinned, her true teeth showing.

"Now, now, pet," he chuckled, "our new toy is on his way back. We don't want to frighten the unsuspecting humans."

Shortly after, the attendant returned, with another servant dressed identically. The newcomer went into the gatehouse. The original gate tender bowed and opened the gate. "Please follow me, *ma'm'selle et m'sieurs. Madame* will receive you now."

They were shown into a beautifully decorated parlor. It managed to look both tasteful and decadent at the same time. A stunningly beautiful woman lounged on a velvet-covered chaise. She wore her golden hair coiffed in the current fashion. Her dress, of some sheer fabric draped about her body and held in place by a golden cord and some jeweled pins, looked to favor more of a Greco-Roman style.

She smiled and held a be-ringed hand out to Viktor. "*Mon cher*, it has been far too long."

He took the hand and placed a kiss on her knuckles. "Indeed, Angelique."

"I see you brought the strapping Mr. Jon with you, cher. Who is this lovely creature you have brought to incite my jealousy with?"

"This is Belladonna. Your man there made the rude assumption that I was looking to sell her." He chuckled. "He is lucky I stopped her before she could filet him."

"Yes, I received your note informing me that you did not kill this one," she smiled sweetly. "It was quite considerate of you, Viktor."

He gave her a little half-bow. "Angelique, *ma belle*, how could I forget how much you savor personally disciplining any of your people that have displeased you?"

"How true." She stood gracefully and sashayed over to the gate attendant. He flinched ever so slightly, when she trailed manicured nails down his arm. "As you can see, I have had to discipline Gerard before for his rudeness. *Mon amore*, remove your blouse and show our guests your back."

His eyes hardened, but he obediently stripped to the waist. His back bore the marks of multiple whippings. Some of the scars were old, the skin shiny and white; others were only a few days old, still red with some scabbing on the more severe ones.

"Unfortunately, Gerard seems to find my punishments quite pleasurable, since he continues to strive for new levels of rudeness," she pouted, then shot Belladonna a wicked smile. "He gets quite hard when I beat him. Too bad it is such a mediocre thing to behold, unlike your captain. Viktor is quite a *magnifique* sight."

The siren found that she actually liked this woman; an unusual experience for her. "I cannot argue that point. He is equally dangerous." She turned her attention to the vampire. "But I am puzzled as to why we have come here. I sense no great magic in this place. You are not the Sister we are looking for."

Angelique's laughter was musical. "I should hope not! Viktor, you naughty boy, did you lead this poor child to believe you were bringing her to a convent? I am no nun, although a few of my clients have paid me to dress as one for them."

"Interesting." He smirked. "But no, I did not. Belle refers to what my business with you is about. However, I am sure you would like to resolve the immediate issue of Gerard's behavior."

"Yes. He must be disciplined, but I have grown bored with the activity. Your Belladonna seems to be a kindred spirit." She turned to the siren. "Would you like to have the pleasure of disciplining him?"

"Do you require him to be returned to you alive and able to function?"

Angelique shrugged. "Do with him as you wish. If he survives, I plan to discharge him. He has proven to be untrainable and is rather disappointing in bed."

Belladonna looked over at Viktor. "Do we have time enough?"

He nodded. "I am here for information that may take some time to gather. Enjoy yourself, pet."

"Oh, I intend to," she smiled.

"*Bon*!" Angelique laughed. She clapped her hands, and two large men, dressed in the same servants' uniform as Gerard, answered the call. "Phillippe, Bertrand, please escort Gerard and our guest to my discipline chamber."

They grasped the victim by either arm and led him off. Belladonna followed with a predatory gleam in her eyes.

Once they were gone, Jon-Jon muttered, "Poor bugger."

The madam raised an eyebrow. "You sound as if you actually pity Gerard, Mr. Jon, how uncharacteristic of you."

"I've seen what she can do to a man," he replied. "It's not pretty."

"Jon-Jon is right, Angelique," Vik added. "I seriously hope you didn't want your man back. There will not be much left of him once Belladonna gets through with him."

She waved her hand in dismissal. "He has outlived his usefulness to me. Now, my handsome young pirate, what may I do for you?" She returned to the chaise, draping herself on it in a provocative pose.

Viktor smiled, enjoying the view. "As I said earlier, I am looking for information."

"I am but a simple whore. Why come to me?"

He laughed heartily at that. "There is nothing simple about you, lovely Angel. Your profession makes you privy to the entire city's secrets. I know for a fact your house's clientele includes some of the most powerful men – and a few women, in New Orleans."

She gave him her musical laugh once again. "You are correct, Viktor Brandewyne. What do you seek to know?"

"I am seeking a Sister of Power." He got right to the point. "She will be a very powerful witch."

"You didn't need to ask me for this information. There are any number of magic practitioners all along this coast."

"Ah, but this is one is different. She will be more powerful than common potion mixers or pagans. She also will be difficult to get to or find."

"I see. Do you have a name?"

"Not yet."

"That will make it more difficult. I can think of a few possibilities of who might fit your criteria. I will see to it that I can give you places to look for this witch by tomorrow, but it will cost you."

He smirked. "I can imagine it will. What is your price, Angelique?"

She eyed him up and down, a sultry smile on her lips. "Oh, I think you know what I want for the information, Captain Brandewyne, and I believe you will pay it willingly and with interest." She ran her tongue across her lips.

"If you can keep up with me, pet, I may even give you some gold to go with it." He laughed. "Mr. Jon, why don't you go and find yourself a wench?"

"Aye Cap'n!" He grinned and headed into the brothel.

Viktor turned back to the madam. "Before I meet your price, you might want to tell your people to expect my first mate to arrive before the evening is over."

She clapped her hands, summoning another servant. "I was wondering where Mr. Rigger was. How many girls will he require?"

"Jim is no longer my first mate. The Grimm Reaper sails with me now."

She did not question the change of mates. She was quite aware of Brandee's reputation and figured that his long-time friend and first mate had either fallen in battle or had become an obstacle to him. "I remember Hezekiah. He is much like you, *non*?"

"Yes," Vik nodded, "he prefers quality to quantity."

"Bertrand, have the girls prepare the gold suite and tell Babette to await our guest there." She then whispered some instructions to him about inquiries to make.

The servant bowed and exited.

Before she realized he had moved, Viktor hefted her out of the chaise and draped her over his shoulder.

"Viktor!" she protested. "Put me down! This is my brothel, and I make the rules!"

"Not tonight, pet." He swatted her rump. "You offered yourself to me, and I intend to take full advantage. I promise you won't be disappointed. Now, tell me which room is yours."

She struggled, trying to break free. "No, this is not how it works, and you know it! In my house, I am in charge."

"Oh, so you prefer to be taken in the garden. I can do that."

"No!" Her voice held a note of panic. "I just mean that I should be the one in control."

"Well then, I'll just have to break you of that habit." He laughed and carried her down the hallway. As soon as his heightened senses told him he had reached an empty room, he opened the door and went in.

"This is not my room."

"It is tonight." He dumped her on the bed, locked the door and proceeded to disrobe.

The next morning, Angelique stretched awake, moaning in pleasure at memories of the previous evening. The moan soon turned to a hiss of pain. Viktor had been much more vigorous than she'd remembered him being.

Amazingly, he was not asleep in the bed next to her. Surely, he should have been just as exhausted as she was.

She rang the bell for the chambermaid and ordered a hot bath and her blue velvet dress to be brought to the room.

Once the maid brought the clothing and filled the large tub – a feature of all the bedrooms in her brothel – with steaming hot water, she dismissed her. Carefully, she eased herself into the water. It had been a long time since she had been this sore. The water soothed but stung at the same time, especially on her inner thigh.

That struck her as odd. She had been careful to make sure the brooches had not gotten mixed in with the bed clothes. Glancing over, she saw they lay on the vanity where she had placed them the previous evening. She looked more closely at the two small wounds she found and realized they were too large for a pin to have made. She also saw what appeared to be a ring of teeth marks

Tamara A. Lowery

Chapter 6

Viktor and Grimm sat in the dining room of the brothel enjoying their second helping of breakfast. Jon-Jon was on his third. Angelique stopped in the doorway, gripping the doorframe and looking both shaken and angry.

"You bastard! You bit me!"

He didn't even look up from his food, although Grimm did. The first mate watched for the attack he knew was coming. Vik had that effect on women sometimes.

"And you were just as delicious as I'd anticipated, pet, almost as tasty as these biscuits," the vampire told her, still not paying her much mind.

With a frustrated shriek at his indifference, she ran at him, pulling something from the folds of her skirt. Grimm knocked his chair over in his haste to intercept her. He wasn't worried about Viktor's ability to defend himself against the madam. He was, however, fond of Angelique's services and didn't want to see her get killed simply because she'd forgotten exactly who the pirate she was attacking was.

He grasped her around the waist from behind, lifted her from the floor and held the wrist of the hand her weapon was in. It didn't stop her from yelling at the vampire, "Get out of my house, foul creature of darkness!"

She dangled a pearl rosary with a delicate golden crucifix from her hand. Viktor wiped his mouth, pushed back from the table, stood and slapped her lightly.

"I'll leave when I damn well please." He then lifted the crucifix to examine the workmanship. "Very pretty, but I like mine better."

He pulled out the emerald encrusted cross. Grimm had returned it to him that morning. He'd lent it to his first mate to show prospective buyers the quality of the emeralds.

Angelique's eyes were wild with fear and confusion. This flew in the face of all the legends she had heard. The crosses had no effect on him. It also dawned on her that it was full daylight, and he had been eating regular food just moments ago. Perhaps she had imagined the two puncture wounds. No, she knew what she'd seen. It was a bite, and the punctures marked that he had become a blood sucker.

"How can this be? You are a vampire."

"I am?" he grinned, plainly showing off his fangs. "How did you guess?" His mates chuckled.

"You can set her down, Mr. Grimm. I don't think she's going to give us any more trouble, are you, pet?"

"*Non.*" As soon as Grimm released her, she tried to run. When she reached the door, she almost collided with Viktor.

"Leaving so soon, pet?"

She tried to back up, but he grasped her and pulled her to him. He found her fear and struggling very exciting. Somewhere in the back of his mind, he noticed that the emerald cross must have been keeping his Hunger at bay. His excitement was much as it would have been when he had been human. He had no desire to feed on her at the moment.

The brothel madam started to relax a bit, once she realized that he wasn't about to rip her throat out. In fact, his arousal, which she was pressed up against, made her feel she was back in familiar territory. She found herself cuddling up to him.

"Since you put it like that, no," she giggled. "But I have to ask, why did you bite me? Now I'm going to have to go to a priest to be purified."

Jon-Jon almost choked on a beignet from laughing at her statement. Even Grimm smirked.

"Where would you find a priest willing to offer you absolution and purification, Angelique," he asked.

"Oh, cher, the parish bishop is one of my best customers." She winked.

Vik chuckled, "You truly are wicked, Angel."

"*Oui*. Would you like me to show you just how wicked I can be?"

"And that is why I bit you, pet. You are supposed to be finding out where I can start looking for the Sister of Power. I know you, Angelique. You will try every means to keep me in your bed for as long as possible."

"Can you blame me, Viktor?"

"I would expect nothing less." He grasped her chin and brought her eyes to his, which were glowing. She emitted a small whimper as her will crumbled under the weight of his power. His smile of triumph looked almost cruel. He found the power rush intoxicating.

"Now, pet, what can you tell me about the Sister?"

"I know of four possibilities that could be the one you are looking for. None of them are easy to get to. Their followers are very protective of them."

He frowned. It would take time to track down all four possibilities. Time was not something in great supply. He didn't want to leave his cadre unattended for too long. Uncontrolled, they would wreak havoc on the port town. He didn't care so much about the citizens of New Orleans, but he didn't want to have to take the extra time fighting off hunters. The fewer authorities that knew he was still alive, the fewer obstacles they would present to his quest.

Belladonna picked that moment to rejoin their group. She was well-fed and radiating sexual energy drawing every very male eye in the room to her.

"I can narrow that list down to one," she purred.

"You had a vision?"

She nodded. "Mostly, I saw cold, black water, but for a brief moment I saw an old crone's face peering back at me. And I have a name to go with the face. You are looking for Gloribeau."

He turned back to his captive. "Is that one of the names you know?"

"No, at least not one of the four I had for you. I have heard of an odd old woman out in the bayous living all alone, but I never heard any talk of her being a powerful witch," Angelique replied.

Grimm grunted. "That's not much help. Those bayous go on for leagues and leagues. She could be anywhere."

"Aye." Viktor nodded. "We need an idea of what area to search and probably a guide that knows the swamps well."

"You want to go to the Quarter and look for a woman named Celine Thibideaux," Angelique told him. "She is a Creole and has dealing with many of the people who prefer the swamps and bayous over living in the city."

"I know her place," Jon-Jon piped up. "She runs a little oddities and herb shop and has some girls working out of the rooms above the shop."

Viktor smiled. "Very good, Mr. Jon. Get ready to show me where the place is." He lifted Angelique's hand to his lips. "It has been a pleasure doing business with you, Angel."

Without warning, he clasped her firmly to him and sank fangs in her neck where throat met shoulder. A small moan escaped her lips and her fingers dug into his back; but she did not struggle. He drank until she went limp in his arms.

Gently, he laid her down on the floor of the dining room. She was still semi-conscious but weak from the blood loss. "Sleep, pet. When you wake remember, you will not try to get a priest to cleanse the bites. You belong to me now."

Jon-Jon led the way through the streets of the French Quarter. They eventually came to a small shop tucked in between a tavern and a dry-goods store. A few women in petticoats, corsets, and shawls leaned over the railings of the second and third floors, trying to entice business.

One of them recognized the tall, bulky pirate.

"Look Girls! It's Big Jon!"

"Big Jon! Big Jon!"

"Where you been? We've missed you!"

Viktor raised an eyebrow. "Big Jon?"

"Aye, Cap'n, in more ways than one," the second mate grinned.

"Too bad I don't have the time to show them what a real man can do for them."

They entered the shop, a small bell above the door alerting to their presence. A dark-haired Creole woman entered from a bead-curtained doorway in the back of the shop. She was smiling until she saw Viktor and Belladonna. Quickly, she ducked behind the counter and snatched up a strange bundle of herbs, beads, bones and what looked like human hair.

Crossing herself then holding the talisman out in a warding gesture, she demanded, "Willoby Jon, why you bring these creatures into my place? I've done you no evil."

"Don't be that way, Celine darlin'," he answered. "My Cap'n has business with ye. Put away yer juju."

"I got no business with the likes of him. He shines of death. No. Get out of my shop."

Viktor started to reach for the talisman, but Belladonna put a hand on his arm and shook her head. "You don't want to touch that. It would be very bad."

"You listen to her," Celine confirmed. "Now get out. I'll not let you do me or mine any harm."

He gave a half smile. "I have not come here to do you or yours harm. I give you my word."

"Ha!" She refused to put the charm away. "I don't know you. How do I know your word is any good? Just because this one calls you Captain?"

"Ah, forgive me." He bowed mockingly. "Viktor Brandewyne, at your service, *Madame* Thibideaux."

She looked shaken, almost dropping the charm. It took her two tries to get it into her pocket. "Your word you will not harm?"

In a flash of inhuman speed, he was around the counter embracing her. "My word," he smiled down at her, his eyes glowing. He lowered his head and kissed her deeply. He deliberately nicked his own tongue on his fangs. A few drops of blood beaded up before the wound could seal itself. He made sure the droplets went into her mouth during the kiss. She struggled at first, realizing what he was doing. Then, unable to stop herself, she swallowed, and the blood bond clicked into place.

"Why did you enslave me?" she asked simply.

"I was told you would be able to help me, and I do not have time for games or evasions."

"Who sent you to me?"

"Angelique."

Celine narrowed her eyes at him. "She is my strongest competitor and has tried to steal clients from me. The only reason she would send Bloody Vik Brandee to me would be in the hope that he would kill me. She would not willingly refer you to me, if she truly believed I could help you, because she knows I would try to steal your business from her."

He chuckled, "I can see why she would have that worry. After that kiss, I understand why Jon-Jon never mentioned you or this place, as well."

"If word of Celine and her girls got out, the whole crew'd be down here." Jon-Jon shrugged. "A man would have to fight for a berth with one of 'em."

"Aye, I can well believe it." He turned back to Celine. "But Angel did not have any choice in the matter. She is mine, body and soul. She had to send me where I could find the help I need."

"I do not understand."

Belle tried to clear things up for her. "The Captain fed on her. She is bound to his will for the rest of her life †and beyond. What he has done to you will fade with time."

Satisfied with that explanation, she asked, "What do you think I can help you with?"

"Angel said you have dealings with a lot of the swamp folk."

"I do."

"I'm looking for a woman called Gloribeau."

She blinked at him. "I cannot help you."

"Angelique seemed to believe you could, and she is not strong-willed enough to lie to me," he insisted, his tone deadly.

"I cannot help you," she insisted. "No one can. You don't go looking for Granny Glory. She comes looking for you."

He felt like slapping her, and Grimm saw this. Knowing he risked drawing Viktor's ire, he leaned across the counter, smiling. "Tell us, *Madame* Thibideaux, why do you say 'you don't go looking for Granny Glory'?"

"To go looking for her is to go looking for death. All who have tried have never returned. They were swallowed up by the swamp. Some say an evil spirit lurks in the black waters, guarding the way."

"I see. Then how do you get her to come looking for you?"

She laughed. "You don't. If she wants to find you, she'll come looking. If she don't, she won't. What you want got nothin' to do with it."

"Oh, but I think it does, pet," Viktor brought her attention back to him. "I have to find Gloribeau, and I do not have much time to do so. Tell me who can guide me into the swamps."

To his surprise, she tried to fight his will. She had slipped her hand into her pocket and grasped the talisman. Then he felt warmth growing against his skin under his shirt. Remembering the effect that the milky crystal had on *Madre* Dorada's magic, he decided to try it in this situation.

The crystal was almost hot to the touch, when he pulled it out. Celine cried out and turned her head away. It blazed with light, as if the full moon were contained in her little shop. Even his shipmates had to shield their eyes.

Celine dropped the talisman and tried to shield her eyes. Viktor dragged her from behind the counter by the arm. He held the crystal right in her face and growled, "Do you know what this is?"

"*Oui.*" She nodded, her eyes tearing from the brightness.

"Then you know what it is capable of." He released her arm, and she collapsed to her knees. "Never try to use your magic against me again."

She shook her head, hiding her face with her hair. "Forgive me. I had no idea the Elder was your ally. I will fight you no more."

"Smart lass. Now, tell me who I can use as a guide."

"My brother, René, can take you as far as the edge of Granny's territory. He takes supplies to a drop point once a month. No one but Granny Glory can take you any further. All that have tried to go on unbidden have never returned."

"Send for your brother."

Chapter 7

"Have you gone mad, woman?" An angry male voice carried from the back room.

"Lower your voice, René," came an answering female hiss.

He apparently complied, because Grimm and Jon-Jon could no longer follow the argument. The vampire and the siren had no trouble hearing it clearly, however.

Viktor smiled wryly to himself. From what he heard he could tell that René was both angry and afraid because Celine had asked him to guide the pirates into the bayou country. She reminded her brother that he owed her for use of her girls' services free of charge. He argued that he would start paying if it kept him from having to lead them to the drop off point. She then pointed out another major favor she had done for him, after which he relented.

"They're coming back out," Belle warned, seconds before the siblings returned to the shop.

"My sister told you, no one goes looking for Granny Glory," the short young Creole stated.

"She did." Viktor nodded.

"But you still want to try? You are a suicidal fool."

Viktor stalked two steps forward, a deadly cold note in his voice. "It seems your sister failed to inform you of who I am. I have slaughtered men for less insult than that."

"Captain Brandewyne," Celine's voice was just a touch panicked, "you gave me your word that you were not here to harm me or mine."

"So I did, pet." He held his hand out to her, a silent summons. Against her will, she went to him. He pulled her close and began unlacing her clothing.

Her brother watched with a pale face, as he realized who he was dealing with. "Word is you were dead months ago."

"I keep hearing that." He smiled, revealing his fangs. To her credit, Celine tried to fight his compulsion. He slipped her bodice down, baring her to the waist. "Be still, pet."

Her struggles ceased at his command, but she continued to tremble, fear bright in her dark eyes.

"That's better. Very nice. How are her skills, Mr. Jon?" he asked while fondling her.

"I'll wager she's just as good as Angelique," the second mate replied with a grin.

Celine emitted a whimpering moan in response to Viktor's touch. "I may have to take that wager, Mr. Jon. What are your terms?"

"Captain, we don't have time for this," Belladonna growled.

He didn't even look up at her. "Stay out of this, Belle." A deft tug loosened the waistband of his victim's skirts, allowing him to force them down past her hips. "Aye, I'll definitely have to take that bet. Name the wager, Mr. Jon."

The siren moved forward to interfere. Grimm stopped her with a hand on her arm and a shake of his head. He then cut his eyes meaningfully to the brother, who stood with a look of torment on his face.

"Your black velvet coat and a keg of rum," Jon-Jon replied.

"You're still after that coat?" Vik quirked an eyebrow up. "He must be quite a dandy you're trying to impress."

Jon-Jon scowled and acted as if he'd go for his blade, causing his captain to laugh derisively. He smiled and relaxed, both knowing he'd never actually draw on Viktor. "What do you want if she's not as good?"

"Two kegs of rum and a dozen beignets from Marie's."

"You do know I've been banned for life from Marie's."

"I know. If I recall, her father came in waving a blunderbuss after he found you and her naked and covered in flour on the kitchen floor in full rut."

Jon-Jon laughed. "Aye. All right, I agree to the wager."

"Thought you might. On your knees, pet." He used a hand in her hair to guide Celine to where he wanted her.

When she started to reach up to free him from his breeches it proved more than René could take.

He rushed forward and shoved his sister back, placing himself between her and the pirate. "Stop! *M'sieur*, I beg you, do not shame my sister like this."

Everyone turned to look at him. Viktor's smile was calculated and cruel. "Your sister is a whore, man. I doubt that she's ashamed of what she's doing. I think you are the one who is ashamed. After all, this isn't the first time she's serviced someone in front of others in order to protect you, is it, René?"

Viktor got right in the man's face. "I am neither suicidal not a fool. I have business with Gloribeau. You know how to get us most of the way there. Now, are you going to stay in line, or shall I take this little show out into the street?"

René trembled, fear, rage and humiliation warring for control inside him. The fear won out. "I will take you to the supply drop off, *m'sieur*."

Viktor clapped him on the shoulder. "Good man." He gave Celine a wistful smile. "Our sport will have to wait, pet, but don't worry. I will be back to test my wager with Mr. Jon."

Temporarily released from his thrall, she gathered up her blouse and skirts but did not actually try to cover herself. Holding her head at a defiant angle, she predicted, "Your mate will win that wager, Captain Brandewyne. It is early for a regular supply run, but I have a few items that need to be delivered to Granny Glory. I will bring them out from the back."

She turned and walked to the storeroom, still carrying her clothes. Three pairs of eyes followed her movements. Only Belle and René seemed uninterested in the show. The Creole was staring at his shaking hands. The siren was keeping an eye on him.

"If you need an impartial party to help decide that wager, I'll offer my services," Grimm commented. "Might help to have an objective comparison from someone who has no stake in the outcome."

Vik raised an eyebrow. "You just want an excuse to have 'em both without paying."

"Already told you. I never pay. They pay me." He grinned.

"Aye, to stay away, I bet." Jon-Jon laughed.

"Now there you go confusing yourself with me again, Jon-Jon." Grimm waggled a finger at the second mate.

René kept his silence. He had gotten his fear under control and was shooting disdainful glances at the three pirates. It was clear that he didn't like hearing their banter. Belladonna just wondered if it was only because his sister was the subject or if there was another reason.

Something told her not to trust their begrudging guide. He would bear close watching.

Whatever Celine was sending with them was small. She had it wrapped up in burlap, and it would have taken at least five similar bundles to fill a sea bag.

She made a point of handing it to her brother. "This is very important, René. Don't just hang it in a tree and leave. You have to make sure it finds its way to Granny's hands," she insisted. Her tone implied he had failed to follow similar instructions in the past.

He took the bundle begrudgingly. "I remember what happened before."

"As well you should," she scolded.

Jon-Jon's curiosity got the better of him. "What happened?"

René glared at the pirate sullenly. Celine answered for him, "A raccoon got into the package and ruined over half of it. Granny Glory was so peeved she hexed him. He was impotent for three months."

"You said you would never tell anyone that!" He rounded on her.

She remained unapologetic. "*Oui*, and you said you would never put me in that position again, René."

He backed down, hanging his head in shame. "I am sorry, sister."

"You best be off now. You're losing daylight."

Celine watched them leave her shop. Her true reason for giving him the reminder was not to spare her brother another bout of embarrassment in the *boudoir*. She wanted to make sure he got the pirates to Gloribeau and didn't just lead them out and abandon them in the bayou country. Such a trick might work on ordinary men, but to try it with a creature like what just walked out would get René killed.

Conversation among the group stayed minimal during the trip into the swamps. Mostly, René grunted directions to Jon-Jon as he helped him pole the flat-bottom punt through the cypress maze.

Viktor and Grimm spent most of the time taking sharp notice of the route. The canopy of limbs and moss blocked the sky, casting a perpetual gloom and making it difficult to judge direction. The captain held an advantage over the first mate on this kind of inland navigation, having grown up on the Savannah River and its surrounding marshlands. He'd also ventured inland to the cypress swamps along the Ogeechee and the Altamaha. His heightened senses helped him keep track as well.

Between the two of them, Viktor felt sure they would be able to find their way out. He knew their guide wouldn't wait for them to return from wherever Gloribeau would take them.

The only one not paying attention to where they were going was Belladonna. She kept her attention riveted on the Creole. Eventually, he noticed this. Being young and male, he misinterpreted the attention.

Both siren and vampire could smell his arousal. Belle smiled slightly, deliberately making it worse.

"Tend your navigating, boy," Vik warned. "Ogling my crew may get you eaten."

"I enjoy getting eaten as much as the next man."

"I'll be sure to remember that." The siren used her most sultry tone. Then she broadened her smile to reveal her true teeth.

René blanched and returned his attention to where he was steering the boat.

The gloom of the swamp was interrupted by a twinkling through the trees. At first it looked like fireflies, however, as they got closer, they realized the lights were steadier. Torches lit a ramshackle dock on a small hammock of an island.

"She must be expecting us," René sounded apprehensive. "Usually there's only one *flambeau*."

Viktor and his mates noticed their guide didn't seem too happy about that. The vampire found that interesting, considering how much he knew the Creole wanted to be shed of them. He must really fear Gloribeau.

He couldn't really blame the boy, after the hexing punishment. Having learned that Dorada was the weakest of the sisters, he also knew better than to underestimate or antagonize any of them.

They tied up to the dock and disembarked. Although the torches lit the area and forced the gloom back, no one was visible on the small island. The dock widened into a platform. A rickety ladder went up about fifteen feet to a smaller platform. A boardwalk of sorts led from that and winded back among the trees into the swamp.

"Where does that go?" Viktor indicated the boardwalk.

René shrugged. "Only Granny knows. No one but she goes beyond this point."

"That is not true, and you know it, René Thibideaux," a scratchy, gruff voice chided from behind them.

They turned to see the oldest woman Viktor had ever set eyes on. Mottled parchment-thin skin stretched tight over frail bones and sparse, wispy hair gave her the appearance of a scraggly, winter-bare stunted tree. She just seemed to blend into the background until she moved.

He thought that must have been how she had seemed to just appear behind them. She hadn't used magic; they had merely overlooked her. He or Belle would have sensed magic.

Viktor bowed, never taking his gaze away from the bright black eyes peering at the young Creole guide. "You must be Gloribeau."

"I am." She continued to stare unnervingly at René, who seemed rooted to the spot with fear.

"I am Vik…."

"I know who you are and what your business here is. We'll deal with that in a moment." She waved him silent. "Right now, I have business with this boy here."

She held out her hand. Finally, René was able to move. He carefully placed the small bundle sent by his sister into the old crone's hand. Then he stepped back quickly, and almost stumbled over Lazarus.

Viktor raised an eyebrow at the black cat who had chosen to materialize un-summoned. "Decided to join us, I see."

"Mrrrrrreh." The creature leapt easily to his shoulder and rubbed a velvety cheek against his ear. He smiled and reached up to scratch the cat's head.

The exchange hadn't gone unnoticed by the old swamp witch, but she didn't comment on it. "You did good this time, René. I want you to go on back home now, but you bring an extra skiff back here and leave it tomorrow," she instructed.

"An extra skiff?" He sounded confused.

"Unless you want to stay and accompany my guests."

He shook his head just a little too vigorously. The prospect of spending any prolonged period of time around the swamp witch clearly terrified him.

"Then scat, and don't dawdle bringing that boat."

"I won't, Granny. I'll start at first light."

"You do that." She nodded, satisfied. René practically ran back to his boat to leave.

She turned to the pirates, who had been waiting for her to finish with her errand boy.

"Fetch one of those *flambeaux* and follow me."

She turned and hauled herself up the ladder with her bundle and started off down the catwalk, not bothering to check if they were behind her or not.

Chapter 8

The catwalk meandered through the trees, making several turns to follow the irregular spacing of the trunks it was secured to. This made it nearly impossible to keep track of what direction they were heading.

Still, Viktor felt sure he would be able to find his way again, if he had to.

After what seemed like hours, they approached a shack perched on stilts. Some kind of light, either a candle or an oil lamp, glowed from inside. The only the siren didn't think it felt inviting.

The sheer magnitude of the swamp witch's magic lay heavy about the place. It bore enough similarity to Belladonna's own power she knew Gloribeau to be far stronger than her. Yet it felt alien enough she could not gauge the older witch's intent. Belle did not like it.

The vampire sensed her unease but did not share it. He found Gloribeau's power and scent very similar to Mother Celie's. They felt enough alike that he suspected they might be true sisters – or perhaps mother and daughter, given how much older Glory appeared to be. It inclined him to trust her.

Grimm noticed the difference in Vik's and Belle's reactions. He decided to stay extra alert.

He wanted to be ready to protect his friend and captain. He hadn't forgotten that Zeke had warned him he might have to protect Viktor from himself at times.

"Make yourselves at home," Gloribeau invited. She fished around in a small cabinet, brought out six cups, and placed them on a rough-hewn table. Then she looked at Jon-Jon, who was the tallest of the group. "Fetch me that jug down from the top shelf, if you would please."

The pirate obediently reached for the jug she indicated. A heavy layer of dust coated the vessel, and the sheer heftiness of it surprised him. He placed it on the table with a grunt of effort. Glory tsked and shook her head at him. She uncorked the jug and filled all the cups. The fluid looked like swamp water when she poured it, lifting the jug without any effort.

"I don't…," Belle started to say.

"Drink," Gloribeau's tone brooked no argument. A small flare of power accompanied the order. The old witch lifted her own cup to her lips and drank. The pirates obediently followed suit.

Belle blinked in surprise. "Mediterranean seawater? I haven't tasted that in millennia."

"Yer daft, woman," Jon-Jon protested. "This is fine Jamaican rum, and you can't be that old."

"You'd be surprised at how old I really am." The siren giggled, actually feeling a little drunk.

Viktor and Grimm exchanged a look. Some strange magic was at work here. Hezekiah tasted quality gin and was sure the captain had his own flavor in his cup. To Viktor, the drink was almost pure blood, still warm, with a hint of brandy for spice.

"Thank you for your hospitality, Granny." He nodded. "Who is the extra cup for?"

"Your other companion." She positioned the cup in front of her then beckoned to the cat. "Here kitty."

To the vampire's amazement, Lazarus hopped to the table and padded over to the old woman. He purred loudly as she rubbed under his chin, eyes slitted nearly shut in pleasure. Even more surprising, he allowed her to lift him off the table and set him on the floor.

"He's a good cat. Useful too, I imagine."

"Lazarus is invaluable to me. I am surprised he is tolerant of your handling. Normally, I am the only one he'll let touch him."

"I know," she stated. "I also know there is a question that has been bothering you since you acquired him."

Viktor bristled a bit. "I don't know what you are talking about."

"Oh, I think you do," she chuckled. "Sometimes you wish he could talk so badly you can taste it. Then he could answer your question."

"You are in dangerous waters, old woman."

Glory ignored the threat in his tone. "So it's one of those questions. It eats at you. You want to know the answer, but at the same time, you fear the answer."

"I fear nothing."

"Only a fool fears nothing. You are no fool, Viktor Brandewyne. You may not fear the answer, but it worries you. For that reason, you need to know, otherwise the worry will become so great it will impede your quest."

"What do you know of my quest?"

"In due time. Don't change the subject." She waved off the question.

Grimm and Jon-Jon followed the exchange closely, wondering where she was going with it. Both knew there was something different, even unnatural about Lazarus. He was no ordinary creature.

Gloribeau reached down to pet the cat, smiling. "I know what you are, Lazarus. I also know who you once were. It is time for you to speak."

In an instant, Jim Rigger stood, startled and naked, where the large black cat had been a moment before.

Jon-Jon stumbled back from the table, as white as a sheet. Even Hezekiah was startled, although he suspected something from the hints Viktor let drop here and there. Belladonna knew the truth all along; but she'd never actually seen Jim as a human before. She thoroughly enjoyed the view.

Rigger blinked his eyes, trying to clear his vision. A coughing fit shook him.

"What you need is in that cup, boy," Glory indicated.

He took it in both hands and quickly downed the substance. Some leaked out and ran down his chin. It no longer looked like swamp water. It was blood. He didn't set the cup down until he'd emptied it. He wiped the excess blood from his chin with the back of his hand then licked it clean.

Finally, he looked around the room, his eyes clear and vision sharper than it had been before he had died by Viktor's hand. He looked at his killer with an expression of wonderment. "Captain."

"Jim." The vampire's face revealed nothing of his thoughts. An air of waiting filled the room.

Rigger broke into a grin, revealing fangs. Vik blinked. He hadn't been expecting that.

"Wish I could've had this form back at Angelique's. There's a bevy of wenches there I'd love to have a roll with." Jim laughed.

"I just bet you would." Vik finally grinned back, flashing his own fangs.

"What's wrong with you, Jon-Jon? You look like you've seen a ghost." He winked at the bosun then turned his attention to the current first mate. "Mr. Grimm, didn't think to sail with you again."

"Likewise, Mr. Rigger."

"Glad Vik found you. He needs someone strong enough to get him out of the trouble he gets into. Lord knows, no one can stop him from finding it."

"He wouldn't be the Captain if anyone could stop him from anything." Grimm shrugged.

"Aye, he wouldn't." His smile turned to a leer. He stalked over to Belladonna. "I wonder, Captain. I know you don't share, but do you think

I could convince you to share this one, just this once?"

The siren gave him a sultry smile. "I've no objections if the Captain doesn't mind."

"Hands to yourself, pet." Viktor's voice held steel in his humor. "You don't want to dally with Jim Rigger. He'd just use you to fulfill his own pleasure then abandon you, when he's finished."

She arched an eyebrow at Viktor. "I assure you, my intentions toward him would be the same."

Gloribeau took command of the situation before the conversation could get any further off track. "Jim Rigger, do you know what happened to you?"

He nodded, "Yes. The Captain fed on my blood, killing me, then Mother Celie gave me the forms I've used since then; both the cat and the raven."

She nodded, a small smile on her face. "Do you bear him a grudge for this?"

He blinked at her as if the concept had never occurred to him. "He is my Captain, my brother and my best friend. I would and have died for him."

"You love him, don't you boy? There's no shame in admitting it."

"Yes, I do."

"Now you have to make a decision, Jim Rigger. Do you wish to keep your human form, or do you want to return to being Lazarus?"

He thought about it, looking down at a body he had not inhabited in months. He smiled when he looked back at the swamp witch, but it was solemn. "I like being a man. It allows me to enjoy many wonderful things."

"But?"

"As Lazarus, I am far more useful to the Captain. I have to go back."

"So be it." She waved her hand at him, and once more, the large black cat stood there. He leapt up on the table, knelt in front of Gloribeau, then padded back to Viktor.

The vampire reached out to stroke the cat's head and was rewarded with a rumbling purr. He surprised his companions with his next words. "Granny Gloribeau, would it be possible to give him the ability to change back to a man at will?"

"It's beyond my power to give him that gift." She shook her head.

"Very well." He scratched Lazarus under the chin. "Thank you for your sacrifice, my friend."

"Have one more cup, then sleep if you can," Gloribeau instructed them. "You're going to need all your strength in the morning."

It was Grimm who asked, "What happens in the morning?"

"I've a task that needs doing. Then, I'll be able to help your captain, Hezekiah Grimm."

Tamara A. Lowery

Chapter 9

Viktor and Lazarus spent most of the night outside the shack back down the catwalk a few yards. Belle had been about to follow him out, but Grimm had stopped her with a touch on the arm and a shake of his head. He knew the Captain needed some time to himself after the evening's revelations.

It had explained a lot. It also confirmed Grimm's long-held suspicion that anyone was expendable, as far as Viktor was concerned. He didn't hold that against his captain; it was just who the man was. He admired the ruthlessness of it all.

Hands on the catwalk railing, Viktor stood looking out at the swamp. Lazarus perched next to him, alternately looking at him and out at the night. The cat broke the silence first.

"Meh."

Vik looked down at him with a lopsided smile and scratched his head. "I should have known Mother wasn't telling me everything. She didn't have to make you what you are, and she didn't have to bring you back. You would have risen as a vampire, anyway, wouldn't you Jim?"

The cat butted his hand, urging him to scratch harder, in response.

"I guess she did do both of us a favor, though. You make the perfect spy, and the sunlight is no danger to you. Our cadre start to smolder if they come above deck in the day."

"Mrrrreh."

They grew silent once more, but it was a comfortable silence. They watched the swamp, looking with more than just their eyes. Every sense seemed hypersensitive to Viktor. It made him aware of just how alive the swamp was. He could hear the skittering of a beetle scurrying over cypress bark. He could smell a raccoon swimming through the waters nearby. He found the frog song nearly deafening at times.

When everything suddenly grew quiet, it came almost like a physical blow. Rather than try to fill the silence, he reached out with all his senses to try to discover what caused it.

He could feel eyes watching him. The sensation came not from the shack but from out in the swamp. Lazarus bristled up, growling softly, sensing it too.

Viktor shushed him, straining to detect the interloper. There, finally, he heard the faint ripple of water as something glided through it. The odors of the swamp had died away leaving an overwhelming scent of death, cold and slimy.

A flash of what appeared to be moonlight reflecting on the black water glowed pale white several yards away. Then, it disappeared. Somehow, Viktor doubted it was a reflection. The trees grew too thick to allow moonlight through.

Just as suddenly as it had gone quiet, the swamp roared back to life, as if nothing evil had passed through it.

Dawn found him sitting, leaning up against the outside of the shack, smoking a cigar. Lazarus slept stretched across his lap, limp and heavy as only a cat could be.

A look inside earlier revealed his companions all in a deep sleep. He detected no sign of Granny Glory, even though he'd never seen or heard her leave. He wondered if the jug had really contained a sleeping draught. He knew Grimm as too good of a first mate to not set a watch. Even Viktor felt more relaxed and mellow than he had in longer than he could remember.

He knew strong magic was going on when a shadow fell over him. Looking up revealed that the old swamp witch had managed to creep up on him. He frowned up at her. Viktor did not like this loss of his edge. It went against every survival instinct he had.

"Put your boy there inside with the others, then come for a walk with me."

Viktor raked the fire off his cigar and put it in a pocket then stood, careful not to disturb the sleeping cat. "There is a presence out there that I do not wish to leave my mates exposed to."

"I know. That's one of the things we need to talk about." She nodded. "The wards on my house will protect them while they sleep. They were safer in there last night than you were out here."

Whether because of whatever spell she had worked or her similarity to Mother Celie, he didn't argue further. He went in and deposited Lazarus next to Belladonna, then went back outside.

Gloribeau motioned for him to follow her. She led him down a different catwalk from the one they had taken to the shack. He thought it odd he hadn't seen it until then.

"This here walk ain't as stable as it used to be. Give me your arm and steady an old woman."

He smiled slightly as he did so. She was definitely blood kin to the old marsh witch that had raised him. He found himself not only liking her but coming close to trusting her. Though he would never admit it, even a pirate such as he got homesick from time to time.

"Knew you were coming," she spoke as they walked along. "Told 'em that you'd be along one day and bring change with you. Some of 'em listened. Some of 'em didn't."

"You mean the other Sisters? I thought that you couldn't be in the same place together."

"Never said we were. But I used to have the ability to talk with the others, when I wanted to."

"So, you can tell me where to find the other Sisters."

Gloribeau cackled. "Ain't that easy boy. Some of 'em move around. Been over a hundred years since I was able to talk to any of 'em. Even old Zeke doesn't know where exactly to look." She sobered a bit. "A couple of them change, too. Only one was supposed to do that. She'd pass her power from one body to another."

Vik nodded. "I've already had dealings with Dorada."

"I know. You've had dealings with the other one who's changed, too."

He stopped and looked down at her. "I don't think you mean Mother."

"No. You know who I'm talking about. Juma was never meant to be one of the Sisters. She stole her power. One of the tasks you were meant for is to correct that. But we'll talk more on that later. You've got a lot of things to do before you'll be ready for that." She gave a little tug on his arm. "Now come on, I've got to show you something."

They continued on for a while in silence. Eventually they came to a small island. He saw a scaffold, a fire pit with a fire laid ready in it, and an enormous cast iron cauldron on a swing arm which swiveled between the scaffold and the fire pit constructed on the swamp hammock. He also noticed a smaller platform next to the pit, presumably so someone could stir the pot while it was cooking.

"You didn't sleep last night, but you drank two cups from my jug. Your power is strong, Viktor Brandewyne, stronger than you know. That's a good thing, because you're going to need that strength."

"I haven't slept since running afoul of Juma. Just haven't felt the need for it," he said with a shrug. "I think it has more to do with her curse than my strength."

She smiled wryly. "It's a little of both. There will come a time when even you will need rest.

Now tell me, did you notice anything unusual last night?"

Viktor suspected she knew exactly what he'd experienced that night. "At one point, everything grew deathly quiet, the air smelled of death, and I felt watched. I also saw something white in the water. It glimmered like moonlight but wasn't."

"No, it wasn't. I'm surprised he let you see him."

"Who?"

"Folks around here call him the Ghostly Gator. He's an ancient demon that's been in this swamp since before time began. I fought him once, long ago, before white men came, even before any of the tribes found their way here. I almost defeated him. Just as his mortal body was dying, his spirit escaped into an alligator hatchling. His power ended up turning the critter white, but it also protected him from any natural predators. He became death, growing in size and strength. About a century or so back, there was a man we thought was the One. But he fell to the gator."

She stopped talking, gazing off into the swamp. After a few moments of silence, she spoke again. "Let's go wake your people. There's more we need to talk about, but not out here in the open."

Chapter 10

Viktor smirked at Lazarus, when he and Gloribeau reentered the shack. The cat lay on the siren's stomach, kneading her chest with his forepaws and purring loudly. She was obviously sound asleep with one arm over her eyes and her other hand resting lightly on the cat's haunches. Lazarus turned a smug cat smile at the captain and seemed to wink.

He protested loudly when Viktor removed him by the scruff. "Oh shut up. You know as well as I do she'd throw you through the wall if she woke up like that."

"Meh."

He leaned down and lifted Belle's arm from her face, giving a light tug to pull her into a sitting position. "Time to wake up, pet."

She stretched, then immediately doubled over grabbing her head.

"Damn! That hurts!" Grimm woke to the noise. "What the hell are those two yowling about?"

"They don't like being disturbed," Vik commented. "It is morning, and I suspect we've got a full day ahead of us. Wake Mr. Jon."

He scrubbed at his face, rubbing the sleep away, and got up. Walking the short distance to the second mate, he kicked the man in the foot. "Pop tall, Jon-Jon."

Jon-Jon sat up and stretched, letting out a bellow of a yawn. Belle moaned, holding her hands over her ears. The burly pirate noticed and grinned. "Looks like someone can't handle her liquor. I know a hangover when I see one."

The siren shot him a venomous glare, her eyes reverting to their natural amber but rimmed in red. "I'm sick from whatever magic she put in that jug. I do not have a hangover, whatever that is."

"Actually, our large young pirate isn't far off," Gloribeau stated. "What you're dealing with is very similar to a hangover. Both our magicks are water-based, but different enough to make the weaker magic user intoxicated or sick."

Belle only growled in response. She did not like being called weaker but could not honestly argue the point.

It was Grimm who brought their attention back to the business at hand. "What are our plans, Captain?"

Viktor nodded to Gloribeau. "You said you had more to tell me after waking my mates, Granny."

"I do," the old woman confirmed. "Wasn't safe to tell you more out there. Old Tulimanchulo was listening."

"Who is Tulimanchulo?" Grimm asked.

"Shh! Hush!" The swamp witch fluttered her hand agitatedly. "Saying that name once, inside the wards on this house, is safe, but even the wards may not protect you if you say it too often."

The vampire narrowed his eyes at her, starting to put the pieces together. "This has something to do with the ghost gator, doesn't it?"

She nodded. "Yes. That is his true name, the one he had before he took that form. That name holds power."

"What kind of power?" Belladonna reentered the conversation despite the headache. As a witch herself, she best understood how dangerously vague her kind could be. What they told you wasn't always as important as what you asked them. It helped to have the skills to ask the right questions.

"Depends on how, when, and where you use it. Those of us in this room are the only living creatures that know his name. It can draw him to you, but in the wrong setting and without the proper magic, you would be inviting your destruction. So, it is best that none of you ever utter that name aloud."

"You're warning will be heeded," Viktor nodded. "But you still haven't told me what you need from me in exchange for your aid."

She scowled at him, strongly reminding him of Celie, then she smiled. "I can see young Celie had her hands full raising you, boy. You're stubborn and not easily distracted."

"No, I am not easily distracted." He deliberately ignored her reference to his foster mother.

"That's a good thing. It'll help keep you alive. I want you to hunt down the ghost gator for me."

"Do you want me to finish what you started with him so long ago?"

She shook her head. "No, I'll finish the job. I just need you to catch him and bring him to me alive. Not here, though." She wagged a finger. "Once you've caught him, if you can catch him, bring him to the place I showed you this morning."

He stood, the others standing with him. "Then I should get started."

"Not so fast, Viktor Brandewyne. First, I have to give you what you'll need to bring the ghost gator back." She cackled at him. "What were you planning on doing, wading out through the muck and the quicksand and wrestling him by hand?"

She went over to a cupboard and pulled out the bundle that René had delivered. "You'll need this." Laying the package on the table, she opened it to reveal a fine net and a coil of braided rope.

Without waiting for permission, Jon-Jon stepped over and started examining the rope with a practiced eye. Neither Viktor nor Grimm tried to stop him or reprimand him. They both knew that he was one of the most skilled among the crew with a marlin spike and line. When he set the rope down and reached for the net, however, Gloribeau slapped his hand away. "That's not for you to handle, boy, unless you want to lose a finger or two," she warned.

"That flimsy looking thing? It doesn't even look like it would hold a minnow," he scoffed. "That's a fine rope, though."

She ignored him and handed the net to Viktor. "It may look frail, but this net is one of the few things that will hold the ghost gator. It's made from the silk of a rare spider from the far side of the world. It's stronger than anything crafted by man and almost unbreakable. It has been infused with ancient spells known only to the oldest of my kind. I made this net to bind the demon ages ago, after our first fight. The rope is just to keep him from wiggling while you bring him back."

He lifted the net and let it open out, holding it up by the edge. It didn't take him long to realize it was a form of cast net. Basically, round in shape with small stone weights ringing the edge. Taking one end of the rope, he threaded it around the edge then up through the center of the net.

"Why did you do that?" Belladonna wanted to know.

"It will let me close the net or retrieve it easily if a throw misses. The stones keep the net open for the throw. I grew up using a smaller version of one of these to catch shrimp and fish in the salt marshes around Savannah."

Glory smiled knowingly. "More 'n' more you're proving you're the One, Viktor Brandewyne. That was one of my tests. You knew the net wasn't fully rigged for use without having to be told. Of course, the fact you can handle it without suffering burns or cuts proves you are no mere mortal."

She stood and rubbed her hands together. "Now, you just need one more thing for your hunt."

"A boat." He nodded.

"Yes. That pup, René, better have gotten it to the dock by now. If he hasn't, I'll shrivel him for a year. Fool boy don't need to be spreading his seed around anyway. He'd probably just make more fool idiots."

"If he's so useless, why do you keep him on?" Grimm half smiled.

She shrugged. "Even a fool can serve a purpose. Besides, it would break his sister's heart, if anything serious happened to him. Celine is very valuable to me."

Arriving back at the supply dock, they found a small skiff tied up. In the distance, almost lost between the trees, they could see René poling his own craft back toward civilization. He looked to be making good time and wasn't looking back.

Gloribeau smirked a little and muttered under her breath, "You think you're afraid of me now, René Thibideaux? Just you wait."

Only Belladonna heard her. A quick glance at Viktor and a tentative testing of the bond they shared was enough to tell her that the vampire had not. The siren narrowed her eyes in distrust at the swamp witch. She knew a spell of some sort was at work, but she was unable to sense it.

"Boat's going to be mighty small for the four of us, Cap'n," Jon-Jon commented as he rubbed the back of his head.

"Only three of you are going on this hunt," Gloribeau declared. "She stays. This is going to be man's work."

Belle bristled. "I am stronger than any of them, save the Captain! You imply that I would be a hindrance. How dare you? I'll just swim, if the boat is too small."

"I dare plenty, you unctuous little snip! These are my waters, not yours." Glory got right in her face. "Cold, black swamp water, with not a drop of salt in it. Your magic will not work here."

"Belle." Viktor's voice held a tone of warning. "I do not have time for you to bicker with the Sister. She doesn't want you with me on the hunt. Therefore, you will not go with me."

"But Viktor, I have to go with you! I am supposed to help you!"

He backhanded her hard enough to split her lip. "You forget yourself." His voice was icy. "I need your help, but I also need hers. You are bound to my aid. She is not. I will not risk losing her aid to assuage your temper and ego. You will stay here, and you will not cause trouble."

He turned to the swamp witch and gave a slight bow. "If there are no further instructions or advice?" She shook her head. "Very well. Mr. Grimm, Mr. Jon, let's go catch that damned reptile and get this over with."

Tamara A. Lowery

Chapter 11

There was too much activity in the bayou. Tulimanchulo did not like it. First, the whore's brother had come early and brought strangers with him. Then last night two of them had been arrogant enough or foolish enough to stay outside of his old enemy's wards. The demon's curiosity had gotten the better of him.

Neither proved to be what they appeared. One seemed to be an animal but smelled of human and carried an aura of death and magic. The other looked human and even smelled of it but was more. He reeked of ancient magic and blood. He also exuded a burgeoning power that tasted vaguely familiar but remained just beyond the demon's ability to identify.

In his efforts to discern the source of the stranger's power, he had allowed himself to be sensed and seen. Tulimanchulo couldn't help but wonder if it had been a mistake. It had drawn the witch's attention, after all.

He thought for a moment earlier this morning someone had uttered his true name; the one nearly lost to a long memory far too ravaged by time. It drew him back to the area near the witch's shack.

He thought about attacking and killing the whore's brother, when the boy arrived bringing an extra boat. The brat still wore the witch's talisman, though. It wouldn't have kept him from killing the boy, but it would have brought her retaliation.

Although the passing centuries made him stronger, just as they slowly aged and weakened her body, they failed to diminish her powers. Neither he nor she was as strong as before their ancient struggle, when he'd had his true form. But he took satisfaction in the fact that he now held at least a physical advantage over her. Her body was too frail to allow her to actively come after him.

He became very alert when he saw the boy tie the empty skiff to the dock then start back the way he'd come. This was different. The witch was up to something. He concentrated on hiding his presence and settled in to watch the dock.

It wasn't a long wait. The strangers returned to the dock, and the witch with them. Though not close enough to hear their words, Tulimanchulo could easily guess what was taking place. He still remembered how the witch sent some poor fool to try to hunt him down once before. This one brought companions, but he would fall to the demon just like the last one.

The female was interesting, though. She smelled of power, but it felt shackled. Her magic tasted very similar to the witch's. If he could take her power, perhaps it would give him the final boost he needed to be able to eliminate his old enemy, Gloribeau.

He wasn't very pleased to see she wouldn't be joining the hunt, but he wasn't surprised, either. He knew the old swamp witch was too clever to allow such a tempting and useful morsel to deliver itself up. No matter: he would deal with the males then wait for the female to leave the safety of the wards. It was obvious she wasn't getting along with Gloribeau, and she was worth the risk of killing the witch's errand boy to get to.

Gloribeau frowned as she watched the pirates head off into the swamp. There was a glimmer just at the edge of her perception. Although he was trying to hide, she knew the demon was close and watching. It was just a matter of time now. Either Brandewyne was the One, and Tulimanchulo would be defeated, or he wasn't and would fall to the demon.

He had strength and a vicious mean streak that his erstwhile predecessor had not. She hoped he proved to be the One. The world was beginning to change at a faster pace. If he failed, it might be centuries before another candidate emerged, if another ever did.

"Go on, girl. Get back to the house," she ordered.

The siren glared at her. Still angry over being denied passage and humiliated by Viktor's reprimand, she was in no mood to be alone with the swamp witch for any period of time.

"Don't even think about giving me any of your sass," Glory warned. "I don't fancy being cooped up with you any more than you want to be cooped up with me."

Belle started to say something acidic and found her voice would not cooperate. It only took her a moment to figure out just how binding Viktor's will was on her. He had ordered her not to cause trouble, and she found herself unable to. The extent of his control both infuriated and terrified her. If she had been physically capable of tears, she would have cried in frustration – or screamed. But she found herself unable to do even that.

Seeing herself with no other choice, she followed the old woman back to the shack.

The men poled the flat-bottom skiff through the murky waters, going ever deeper into the swamp. The light remained a perpetual gloom. A network of vines, hung heavy with Spanish moss, stretched from tree to tree, creating an almost impenetrable canopy.

For most of the morning, they traveled in silence. By early afternoon, the air was thick and oppressive with humidity. Even the insects seemed to find it too much of a bother to stir. All three men poured sweat.

"Damn, didn't think a white gator would be this hard to find," Jon-Jon commented, wiping sweat out of his eyes. He didn't really mind the heat, but he was used to being shipboard, where there was usually a breeze.

"It's a big swamp, Mr. Jon," Grimm replied, ever practical. "These bayous go on and on for leagues. That thing could be anywhere."

"How do we really know which direction to look, Cap'n? That old biddy didn't really tell us a whole lot."

"He'll be deep in the swamp, Jon-Jon, far away from prying eyes. I doubt he'll be easy to spot, even with a white hide. Most gators won't move around during the day. They like to hunt at night; even then, most of the time only their eyes and snout are above water. If this was an ordinary gator, we could have passed him several times and not have known it."

"But he's not a normal gator," Grimm said. "According to the old crone, he's a demon."

Viktor nodded confirmation to his first mate. "Aye. That means he'll be crafty and more dangerous. I never expected this to be easy. I'm starting to think that anything easy, where this curse is concerned, is false dealing."

Grimm grunted. "It sure seems that way."

Tulimanchulo followed the skiff at a discreet distance. He was tempted to move closer, when he saw them talking amongst themselves. But he held back. It was too soon in the game, and he wanted to see what they would do. What they said was of little consequence.

No, he did not want to reveal his presence just yet.

Viktor gazed off into the swamp, not really seeing what was in front of him. He concentrated more on what his mind's eye saw. He sent Lazarus out in raven form shortly after they left Gloribeau's.

Through the raven's eyes, he could see the demon alligator following them the entire time.

More importantly, the creature seemed unaware of being watched. Lazarus kept high in the trees, and his black feathers helped him blend into the shadows.

Now the challenge would be for Viktor to make sure the demon did not realize he knew it was following behind. The temptation to turn and try to take the beast head on was almost overwhelming.

The vampire wanted to choose his own battleground, however. His thoughts about the demon were very similar to the demon's thoughts about him; let his prey think he had the advantage before springing the trap.

Near dusk, they still had not encountered the ghost gator. Although still steamy, the swamp had cooled off a bit. After the sun set, an eerie sort of fairy light seemed to surround them without really illuminating anything. It almost seemed to emanate from the water itself.

"I don't like this, Cap'n," Jon-Jon sounded a little apprehensive. "'Minds me of the witch fire you see in the rigging sometimes. That's always a bad sign."

"Stand fast, Mr. Jon. Better this light than no light at all." The order seemed to galvanize the second mate. "Now, let's make for that small island. We'll use one of the poles to make sure it's solid, then make camp."

"Aye, Cap'n."

The grassy hammock of land felt a bit spongy, but solid enough to land on. Jon-Jon was first out of the boat, taking the mooring line with him. He then pulled the boat part way up on the bank. Grimm got out to help pull the boat further up.

Just as Viktor set foot on the island, everything grew deathly quiet. He recognized it for what it was. A quick visual from Lazarus confirmed it.

"What the blue blazes?" Grimm exclaimed, wondering at the unnatural silence and spotting a quick moving form in the water. It made arrow-like ripples straight for the captain.

"He's making his move," Vik answered. He reached in the boat for the net and rope. His superhuman speed allowed him to grasp it, but only just, before Tulimanchulo plowed into him.

The blow came hard enough to knock him off his feet. The gator clamped a booted leg in its jaws and, as quickly as it had flashed up on the island, it dragged the vampire down under the black water.

The searing pain of the alligator's teeth shredding boot and breeches and digging into flesh caught Viktor off guard. It was not, however, disorienting. Pain and injury were part and parcel of any pirate's life, and Vik Brandee was no exception. He well knew that survival often hinged on not letting it slow him down or distance him from the task at hand.

He still maintained a hold on the net Granny Glory had given him. Now he needed to get free of the gator's grasp so he could use the damned thing.

The second he tasted blood, Tulimanchulo realized he might have bitten off more than he could chew. He sensed an amazing wealth of power to be had, much of it untapped. He recognized the flavor of the power as being vampire, having eaten an undead creature or three on past occasions. His demonic nature rendered him immune to the vampire's sway.

But something was different about this vampire. He was living rather than the walking dead. No matter. If he was living, then the demon would just have to remedy that. He dove deeper, hoping to drown his prey.

Viktor found that he could just make out the gator's form. The pale white hide emanated a ghostly glow despite the murkiness of the water and the dead dark of nighttime in a swamp. Though not sure, he thought the demon was dragging him down even deeper.

He had to act now, if he was to have any hope of taking control of the situation and surviving the encounter.

Using his own trapped leg as leverage, he managed to pull himself double. With all of his strength he punched the gator in the top of the head right between the eyes. He successfully stunned the creature, allowing him to pull free of the deadly jaws.

With no possible way to deploy the net underwater, he swam for the surface with all possible speed. He knew he had to get out of the water before the creature recovered.

Both pirates called out for their captain when he disappeared beneath the black water. Grimm stopped Jon-Jon from diving in after him.

"Watch the bubbles, man." He pointed. Rather than arrow away in a trail, they only went out about twenty feet or so from the shore. "They'll let us know where to watch for him to come back up."

Although the upwelling of air bubbles stayed fairly stationary, it gradually tapered down to only a few, then to none. It seemed as if hours had passed since the gator's attack.

Without warning, the water erupted with a great splash. Viktor broke the surface. The men shouted in relief and threw a line to him. He grabbed it and half swam to shore, as they pulled him in.

Once back on solid ground, he steadied his footing as best he could with the damaged leg and readied the cast net. Wrapping the draw rope several times around his wrist and forearm to secure it; he then held the net open with one side in either hand and the upper edge in his mouth.

When he tried to look through the raven's eyes to see where the demon would attack from, he found himself instead rewarded with a view of the inside of Gloribeau's shack. He saw Belladonna in one corner, curled in on herself and sulking. On the far side of the room, Granny perched on a stool, smoking a long thin clay pipe and watching the room from heavy-lidded eyes. A glitter in her eyes, a slight smile, and a wink let him know she knew he was looking at her.

He disconnected from his familiar, irritated that the witch had interfered, but resigned to the fact that he would not have use of Lazarus' aid for probably the remainder of this hunt.

"Meddling bitch," he mumbled around the net in his mouth.

"Captain?" Only Grimm heard him. A quick warning glare from the vampire let him know not to push the matter.

"Keep a sharp eye, lads," Vik ordered through his mouthful.

They didn't have to wait long, although the attack didn't come as quickly as expected. The white gator surfaced close to the same spot Viktor had. It swam back and forth for a bit, shaking its head sporadically before focusing on the small island. Then, it submerged again.

☠

Tulimanchulo was having trouble seeing. Normally, he had excellent night vision, but now everything seemed blurry. His prey was stronger than he had anticipated. The blow the vampire dealt him must have damaged his eyesight. It certainly stunned him long enough that he worried his enemy might truly escape

Finally, his vision cleared enough that he could just make out his surroundings. Three roughly human-sized figures stood on the grassy hammock nearby. He still couldn't make out much detail, but he knew it must be his prey and his companions. Marking their approximate locations, especially the one that smelled of fresh blood, Tulimanchulo submerged.

He knew they probably saw him, but he didn't want them to know which direction he would come at them from.

With the sharper eyesight of the two humans—sharper than Viktor's before he'd been cursed to vampirism, Grimm noticed the gator seemed to be injured. He saw a fist-sized indent close to one of its eyes, and that eye appeared to be bleeding.

"Looks like you hurt him pretty good, Captain," he said, when the creature sank back into the murk.

"Aye," Vik managed to reply, never releasing his grip on the net's edge. "But not enough to kill him. Keep sharp. He could come at us from any direction."

The three of them spread out to watch all sides of the islet. The swamp remained dead silent the entire time. That, more than anything, let Viktor know the demon still lurked close by. He strained all his senses, trying to pick up any sign of the demon's approach. The heartbeats and breathing of his mates almost deafened him. His leg throbbed incessantly from the tearing bite the creature had delivered. Even with the suppressing power of the emerald cross, his Hunger started to flare.

Then he heard it, barely audible, a slight ripple in the water. It came from between where he and

Jon-Jon stood. Quick as a flash, he turned in that direction, pivoting on his hips. The net fanned out into a near perfect disc, the weight of the stones holding it open in flight as he released it. A second later, the demon gator surged up onto land, near his second mate but speeding toward Vik.

The net dropped, seeming to have magically grown to match the gator's size. It covered him completely from snout to tail-tip. Tulimanchulo let out a roaring, guttural growl the moment he felt the web on his hide. He recognized it immediately, even though he'd never seen it before.

Viktor deftly snatched back on the rope, causing the net to draw closed around the gator. Although it completely encased the creature, the pirate had to use all his strength to hold the line, as the demon rolled and writhed. It almost pulled him off his feet, trying to get back to the swamp.

"Jon-Jon, Hezekiah! Don't let him get to the water!"

Grimm grabbed the loose coils of the rope hanging behind where Viktor gripped it. The latent magic in it tingled a bit at first, but then settled. He made a loop in the end and tried to get close to the gator.

"Grab his tail, Jon-Jon," he ordered. It took the burly pirate two tries before he could catch the thrashing thing. He ended up having to tackle it, and still got taken for one hell of a ride.

The second mate's weight on the creature provided enough of a distraction to allow Grimm in close. The first mate quickly slipped the loop over the gator's snout and pulled it taut.

From there, Jon-Jon got to his feet and finished trussing up their catch until it could barely wiggle. Viktor inspected the man's handiwork and approved. "I don't imagine he'll get out of that rig on his own. Never seen some of these knots before."

"Couple of 'em I came up with on my own," he puffed. "That one, there, I learned from Sniff about a month ago, though. Been itchin' for a chance to try it out."

"Aye, ol' Sniff's right mean with a line and marlin spike." Grimm laughed. "That's probably why he was still able to sign on with that bastard, Jorgen, as a rigger."

Viktor nodded then stretched. He winced a bit from the leg wound. It should have already started healing. The bleeding stopped not long before he threw the net, but the wounds remained raw and open. That wasn't good. He'd have to have Belle look at it, when they got back to Gloribeau's.

This brought up another problem. Grimm voiced it before he could, "How are we going to get him back to the old witch?"

Tamara A. Lowery

Chapter 12

"How, indeed?" Viktor looked around, peering into the gloom. The faint swamp glow already began to fade. Before long, the thick canopy would render the swamp as black as the interior of a cave with almost no light left at all. He thought he spotted a possible solution to their problem.

"Mr. Grimm, you and Mr. Jon take the skiff and check out that fallen tree." He pointed, indicating a spot about fifty yards off.

They did as ordered and discovered that the tree in question was partially hollow. "This should do the trick, Captain," Grimm called back.

He and Jon-Jon worked to free the trunk. It took some shoving and a little hatchet work, using the small hand ax Jon-Jon carried for cutting lines on board, but they finally got it loose from the nest of vines which held it upright. As they had hoped, it was buoyant.

They hauled it back to the islet. It took all three of them to lift the gator into the hollow of the tree trunk. Testing it in the water, it rode low, but it still remained high enough to avoid capsizing or sinking.

Using vines and the mooring line for the skiff, they secured the creature in the log and the log to the skiff.

Finding their way back to Gloribeau's proved tricky. Even after fashioning *flambeaux* from limbs and Spanish moss, the swamp presented a veritable maze. They ended up having to rely on Viktor's sense of smell.

Finally, by first light, they grew close. They spotted her shack in the distance. But Viktor didn't steer them toward the shack. Instead, he took a course toward the back catwalk.

Jon-Jon frowned in confusion. "Where are we goin', Cap'n?"

"Gloribeau wants this delivered to the area at the other end of this catwalk."

"What catwalk?"

Viktor frowned. The structure was plainly visible, yet it seemed the man couldn't see it. "Can you see it, Hezekiah?"

"Maybe she's put a spell on it to keep it hidden," he offered. He could see it but did not want to say as much. If there was a spell at work, the captain would want to know why he was immune to it. Uncle Zeke had warned him not to let the vampire know he had given him a fraction of his power. Grimm started to suspect keeping this secret was going to grow increasingly difficult. It already grated on him to keep anything secret from his captain.

"That would make sense, now that I think about it. I was outside almost the entire night and don't remember noticing it until she led me down it."

They continued on, following the phantom catwalk, until they came to its end. Granny Glory stood, tending a fire in the pit. The cauldron hung over by the scaffold, apparently waiting until the coals died down enough for it.

"Took you long enough," she chided without even looking at them.

"So sorry, milady," Vik's voice dripped sarcasm. "But I'm afraid our guest didn't want to come along willingly."

She cackled, finally looking up from the fire, as they tied up at the shore. "That's a poor excuse, Viktor Brandewyne. I see he tried to take a chunk out of you there. Best have your sulky little sea-witch take a look at that leg, once we finish our business here. Demon bites do some mighty strange things to a body."

The siren arrived, climbing down from the catwalk and carrying a small bag. She spared him a glare as she stalked over to Gloribeau and handed it to her.

"Uh-oh, the silent treatment," Grimm commented. "I think she's mad at you again, Captain."

"She'll just have to get over it."

Glory took the bag from Belle, who quickly stepped away from her, rubbing her arms as if cold. "That's a good girl. All right, the fire's right about where it needs to be. You boys get him out of that log and up on this scaffold," she ordered. When they didn't move right away, she snapped, "Don't dawdle! This has been started and has to be finished before the spell gets cold!"

"All right lads," Vik half-snorted, "you heard the woman. Let's move this heavy bugger."

With much grunting and sweating, they managed to get the gator moved to where the old witch wanted him. All three were glad Jon-Jon was so good with knots. If the creature had been able to move at all, it would have been nearly impossible to lift him up onto the scaffold.

Once the gator was in place, Gloribeau pulled a knife out of the bag. "This can come off now," she said, cutting the rope and net off.

"What are you doing? Do you have any idea how hard that bastard was to bring in?" Vik demanded.

"Hush up. He ain't goin' anywhere. The spells built into this scaffold won't let him, and he knows it."

As if to prove her point, the demon gator hissed, but made no move to try to escape. Unbound, he was almost too large for the structure. The wood creaked under his weight, and his tail hung off the edge, twitching angrily.

She rapped him on the snout with the flat of the blade. "You just be quiet, old Tulimanchulo. You knew this day would arrive eventually, and there's no use fighting it. Granted you've grown quite a bit since I had this altar built, but it'll still work."

She swung the cauldron on its pivot until it hung directly under the gator's head. Then she shifted her grip on the knife and drove it up into the creature's throat. With more strength than Viktor would have credited her with, she worked the blade back and forth until she had nearly sawed the head off. The spine and a bit of hide were all that was holding it on.

The gator's blood, so dark a red it almost looked black, filled the cauldron nearly to the top. Once sure the creature was completely drained, she pivoted the cauldron to hang over the fire. Then she reached into the bag again and pulled out some wicked-looking pliers. She handed these to Viktor.

"You take these and pull all his teeth and put them in the blood."

The gator's mouth hung open in death, so the teeth weren't hard to get to. Pulling them was another matter. They didn't come loose from the jaw easily. He doubted a normal human could have managed it.

He was truly tired by the time he got the last tooth free. His leg throbbed and made it difficult for him to concentrate.

He gathered all the teeth and dropped them into the pot of blood. Gloribeau stirred the blood with a large wooden paddle until it boiled.

Viktor half expected her to babble some nonsense language, but she remained silent. Given the potency of the magic he could sense, he supposed she didn't really need any verbal aides. He could see he wasn't the only one who felt it, either. Belladonna stood as far away as she could with a wild, fearful look in her eyes. Even Grimm and Jon-Jon seemed effected, hugging their arms as if cold.

Viktor boldly stepped forward to peer into the bubbling mixture. The heat of the fire had made the blood truly black. Oddly, even when it had been gushing fresh from the gator's body, he'd had no desire to taste any of it.

Finally, Glory gave a small swirl, as if trying to catch something, the same way one would try to get the last bean out of a bowl of soup. Smiling in triumph, she lifted the paddle out. Dangling on the end was a necklace made of the gator's teeth.

She held it out to the vampire. "Take it, boy, but don't put it on. No one is to wear this, ever, not even for a moment," she instructed. "You can put it in that bag the tools were in."

Obediently, he lifted it off the paddle and picked up the bag. He hesitated before putting it in, however. The wound on his leg felt suddenly on fire, the jolt of pain so intense he almost thought he was going to collapse.

He heard a voice in his head, whispering seductively, *"She's lying. Put the necklace on. Your wound will heal. You will be stronger than ever. Then you can drink her and take her power as your own."*

As if in response, his Hunger flared. He actually advanced on the old crone a step or two. She stood her ground, expression neutral, and watched him.

"Captain?" Grimm's voice broke through the fog of pain, Hunger and power-lust; bringing him back to his senses.

Viktor shook his head to clear it and found that he still held both the necklace and the bag. He sensed that he just escaped some deadly trap, but he wasn't sure what it was.

He put the string of alligator teeth into the small tool bag, cinched it shut and stuffed it into his shirt. The pain in his leg didn't go away, but it eased considerably. His Hunger simply evaporated.

Granny Gloribeau nodded, satisfied. "You did good, boy. You need to take that to Zeke. He'll know what to do with it, so you can get the help you need. But before you go there's one more thing I need you to do."

"And what is that, Granny?"

She locked eyes with him. "I need you to put me into that cauldron of demon's blood."

Grimm exclaimed, "You're mad, old woman! You'll be boiled alive!"

"He's right, Granny," Viktor stated calmly. "If you are set on having me kill you, there are much swifter, less painful ways than being cooked like a crab."

"No, you have to put me in the pot." She started disrobing. This caused the two humans to fidget nervously. Her slight and frail-looking frame sagged in places men didn't like to see a woman saggy in. Viktor didn't even blink.

"Why? I have the necklace. You said to take it to Uncle Zeke. Why do you need me to do this?"

"I don't need you to do this; you need to do this."

Belladonna piped up, breaking her sullen silence, "I'd be more than happy to toss you in."

"Heh! You can't do that girl. It's not in your power." The crone laughed. "No, the only one who can do it is Mr. Brandewyne, here."

The vampire shrugged. "If you insist, Granny, but I still would like to know why. You have done me no ill."

She peered at him, as if looking into or through him. "You don't want to, do you, boy?"

"Not particularly. It seems unnecessary. I can just take this to Zeke and get what I need."

"Oh, you could do that, but you wouldn't get what you need. If you don't put me in that cauldron of blood right now, then that necklace is nothing more than a string of teeth with no magic."

Viktor needed no further prompting. He scooped the old woman up and tossed her into the boiling blood.

She quickly sank beneath the surface without uttering a sound. Shaking his head, he turned back to his companions. It didn't take him long to realize they all stared at some spectacle behind him. Belle glowered fiercely. The men looked both stunned and as if they were starving and had just been presented with a bountiful feast.

He turned and immediately understood the reason. The most beautiful woman he'd ever laid eyes on was rising out of the blood.

Silky, straight black hair fell to her waist. Her breasts rode full but high. Her slender waist accentuated pleasantly full hips. Her fine-featured face bore a Cupid's bow mouth, a narrow straight nose, naturally arched eyebrows, and high cheekbones. Her eyes mesmerized: a striking shade of teal that shifted from blue to green to brown depending on how the light hit them.

Viktor found himself next to the cauldron, ignoring the heat of the fire. The woman smiled and held her arms out to him. His sea-weathered hands looked very dark against the white flesh of her waist, as he lifted her out of the cauldron.

"Thank you for your help, Viktor Brandewyne. You can let go now."

Enjoying the softness of her skin beneath his hands, he smiled lustily down at her, "I don't think so."

He started pulling her in closer. She held up a hand between them without actually touching him and released a small blast of power. It succeeded in blowing him back from her several feet.

He shook his head and picked himself up, then started stalking toward her. Again, she held her hand up toward him. "You mind me, boy, and keep your distance."

The tone of his answering laugh made it plain what occupied his mind. "But I don't want to keep my distance, Gloribeau. In fact, I want to get very close."

"I said stay back." The air breathed with her power. "You might think you do, but you do not want to be with me right now. I haven't had a man in so long I would tear you apart."

"Oh, I think I could handle it." He leered.

"No, you couldn't." Her voice grew solemn, her power finally breaking through his lust clouded mind. "It is not your fate to die in my bed, Viktor Brandewyne. You need to go back to New Orleans, gather your crew, and sail for Hell's Breath."

He gave her a wistful look but nodded. "You're right, Gloribeau. I do need to attend to my business."

"Aye," Grimm added, "my agent should have that deal ready on the emeralds."

Glory frowned. "I know I can't talk you into skipping that and leaving port immediately."

"No, you can't. I do have the needs of my crew to consider."

"That's what I thought. Well, you do what you have to do. But know this. You aren't the only one of your kind in that city. There are several, and they are dangerous. You stay away from them."

Viktor couldn't help but laugh. "Anybody that sails the seas knows New Orleans plays host to my kind, as you put it. They know who I am and fear me, not the other way around."

"Mm-hmm, so you say. I know who you are, too. More important, I know what you are. Now you listen to old Granny – and wipe that smirk off your face, Hezekiah Grimm. I know you, too. Just because I have this fine new body doesn't mean I'm not still Granny Glory." She huffed, then turned back to Viktor. "As I was saying, there is a bunch of your kind that is like you, but not like you. They are a very real danger to you, whether

you believe it or not. You heed me and stay clear
of them until you leave port."

Tamara A. Lowery

Chapter 13

They got back to New Orleans just after sunset. They made their first stop at Celine's. She was just closing her shop. She nearly dropped a small bottle of rare medicinal herbs when they entered.

"You are still alive," she gasped.

Viktor smiled wickedly. "I'm not that easy to get rid of, pet." He raised an eyebrow, when she moved back from his advance with a fearful look. It brought out the predator in him. He thought about using his superhuman speed but decided that stalking her would be more fun.

Celine whimpered, as she continued to back up from the vampire. She knew she would get no help from the others. They were part of his crew. She also knew she had no hope of escaping him. He finally backed her up against the wall.

He got as close as he could without touching her but placed a hand to either side to prevent her trying to sidestep him. Dipping his face down close to her, he took in her scent.

It spoke volumes to him. She was both aroused and terrified. She was also no longer under his thrall. Just a slight change of odor was enough to tell him that none of his blood remained in her. He toyed with the idea of recapturing her but decided it would serve no purpose for now.

"You are trembling, pet. Do I frighten you that much?"

She nodded, keeping her gaze off to the side. She knew the danger meeting his eyes posed.

He smiled, well aware of the reasons behind her behavior. "Don't worry, Celine, you aren't on the menu, although I do intend to follow through on my bet with Mr. Jon and see if you are as talented as Angelique."

She surprised him with a blush, something he rarely encountered from a seasoned whore. The proximity of all that blood just under the surface of her skin fired his Hunger.

With a growl of frustration, he distanced himself from her with blinding speed. "But not tonight. It will have to wait until next time. Mr. Grimm, how long do you think it will take to complete the transaction with your agent?"

"He's had time to make his contacts and broker the deal. I've just got to meet with him and set up the exchange," the first mate answered. "Should be done no later than high tide tomorrow afternoon."

"Good. Mr. Jon, find the crew and let them know to get their fill of wenching and drinking tonight. I want them back on the ship no later than midday."

"Aye, Cap'n."

Belle, leaning against one of the counters, crossed her arms and asked, "Do you have any orders for me?"

"As a matter of fact, I do. I need you to recruit some additions to our larder."

She smiled slightly. "That task suits my mood."

He shot her a venomous glare. "I am so happy for you. I am going out to hunt."

Celine crossed herself and pulled out her small talisman, kissing and rubbing it, as the vampire and his mates exited her shop. He did frighten her, but what frightened her more was the desire he stirred in her. She almost felt sorry he hadn't stayed to complete his bet with Jon-Jon. Unfortunately, she didn't think any kind of magic existed to protect her from herself.

Hezekiah Grimm spent close to an hour watching the area around the building he'd set up his meeting in. Cautious by habit when dealing with contacts in the black market, he had been doubly so since signing on with Brandee. While grateful to be sailing again with his old friend, he didn't want to repeat the experience that had led to their reunion. Although many still believed Vik to be dead, lost at sea, Grimm was still on the lists of known and wanted pirates.

He watched his contact arrive alone, as instructed. A few minutes later, he spotted the man's lookout arrive and position himself. He smiled to himself. Charlebois was even more paranoid than him.

When no one else showed up to lurk around, Grimm decided it was safe enough. He harbored no worries about Charlebois leaving before he showed himself. The man might be paranoid, but greed fueled him. He wanted those emeralds.

Belladonna found her task both enjoyable and strangely troublesome. She always enjoyed a good hunt, but she was unaccustomed to hunting multiple prey. Add to that the frustration of having to take them alive.

Of course, she knew how to keep prey alive for extended periods. She liked playing with her food, especially to relieve the frustration and aggravation of dealing with Viktor on a daily basis. The damned vampire had yet to come to her bed. The siren, a very sexual creature, found his persistence in denying her irritating beyond belief.

Belle forced those thoughts aside and concentrated on singling out the men on the docks who best suited her and Viktor's mutual needs for sustenance. The victims had to be healthy.

Jon-Jon spent the better part of the night making the rounds of every tavern and brothel he could find in New Orleans. He would have liked to spend some time at some of them, but his captain gave him the task of finding his crewmates.

Several hours after midnight he finally completed the errand. He was ready to find a bottle, a bed, and a whore, not necessarily in that order. Recognizing his own fatigue, he decided it best to take whatever girl he found back to the ship with him. He didn't want to risk sleeping ashore and missing cast off.

If the girl overslept and got stuck on board, oh well. Jon-Jon didn't mind sharing with his crewmates. He might even get some coin out of them for it.

Viktor headed the opposite direction from Belle when they left Celine's shop. He wanted to hunt alone. The siren was too much of a distraction in his current state.

He avoided Angelique's and the other brothels for the same reason. At the moment, he needed blood more than sex, and he really didn't have the kind of time he would like to enjoy both.

He prowled the Quarter, senses heightened, as he searched for a likely candidate. Just as he spotted his prey, he sensed a vaguely familiar presence. It took a moment to identify it, so he held back, keeping his prey in sight.

The underlying scent he picked up smelled like one of his vampires, but it wasn't one of his. There was no psychic connection with this creature. After a few moments, he pinpointed it.

The strange vampire crouched on a rooftop and seemed to be watching the same victim he had targeted. Out of curiosity, he decided to see what the other predator would do. He could always find other food.

He didn't have to wait long. The vampire dropped three stories to the alleyway without suffering any apparent damage. He seized the drunkard as the man staggered into the alley. To Viktor's amazement, the vampire then flew with his victim back up to the rooftop. Finally, he realized *Madre* Dorada had not been just spouting silly superstition, when she had accused him of flying off with her apprentice.

Heeding Gloribeau's warning about others of his kind, since he now understood that she meant this, he bided his time waiting for the vampire to finish feeding. He had no intention of avoiding him completely, however. He wanted to learn how the creature was able to fly. None of his cadre had exhibited that talent.

The arrival of a second vampire, female and petite, surprised Viktor yet again. He had not sensed her presence at all. Even her scent nearly eluded him. He could only surmise she was the more powerful of the two and was shielding herself. It made sense to him that she wouldn't want to make her true nature obvious to her prey.

The two vampires held a heated, but hushed, argument over the dead drunkard. Then the female turned and looked directly at Viktor. Aware that he had been discovered, he stepped out from his hiding place.

She seemed to flutter down from the rooftop as graceful as a bit of dandelion fluff. Smiling, she approached the pirate, daintily sniffing the air. He made no attempt to flee, nor did he smell of fear. He did smell of blood, however, mostly dried, but there was fresh in the mix, and it smelled very rich.

Now that she stood near, he finally picked up the faint odor of death under her expensive perfume. He also detected a brush of power as her grey eyes started to glow faintly. She was trying to bewitch him.

Viktor smiled, amused. Though powerful, the power of so many other beings from his recent dealings dwarfed hers with ease. He knew for a fact that Belladonna was more powerful.

The vampire's smile wilted, and she cocked her head, puzzled. "How is it that you resist me, human?"

Viktor laughed, but didn't reveal his fangs. "I'll tell you, if you tell me how you are able to fly, pet."

Rather than answer him, she blinked then redoubled her efforts to bespell him. He raised an eyebrow, a half-smile on his face, and boldly met her gaze. Then he upped the ante, bringing his own power into play.

He felt a thrill of triumph as she fell to him. "Now you will tell me how to fly.""

Please, I cannot teach you how," she pled, panicked that this stranger not only could resist her power but was actually able to take her will. "I just do. I do not know how."

That actually told him more than she realized. He thought about it. He hadn't actually tried to fly. Maybe it was just as simple as merely doing.

"You are different, human." She reached up, wrapping arms around his neck. His height forced her to levitate a bit to do so. Unlike her typical prey, he did not bend to meet her embrace.

"You are strong," she purred. Viktor had relaxed his mental hold on her while he mulled what she had told him. She intended to take full advantage of the distraction. "And I am Hungry."

If he had been truly human, he wouldn't have even seen her strike coming. But Viktor had reflexes now that he never could have matched before he was cursed.

With some effort, since the vampire was much stronger than she appeared, he forced her off before she could bite. Snarling, she leapt at him again. He caught her by the throat and held her at arm's length. She lashed out, unable to get leverage. Frustrated, she kicked, catching him in the gut by sheer chance. He grunted from the blow but did not release his grip. Rather, he tightened the stranglehold to the point of nearly crushing her windpipe. The vampire continued to struggle, trying to get into a position where she could get a bite on him.

"Be still!" He put his full power behind the command. The vampire obeyed, eyes wild with fear and Hunger. Her fear doubled, as he revealed his own fangs. "You aren't the only one who is Hungry, bitch. But I don't find you very appetizing."

He only had a split second to react to a warning scent. He needed no more.

Maintaining his stranglehold on the vampire, he drew his sword with the other hand with a practiced fluidity. Swinging it with his full strength in an upward and out arc, he decapitated the male as he leapt from the roof. The body and head dropped to the ground; thick, almost black blood oozed from the neck.

Viktor wrinkled his nose at the stench of rot coming from the corpse. Usually, bodies spouted fresh red blood. But this? Not so much as a spray marked the death. If not for the throbbing leg wound, his Hunger would have been completely suppressed.

The female let out an ear-piercing keen. Viktor flung her from him, fully expecting her to attack again, but she lay where she had landed, continuing the shrill wail.

"Stop that infernal noise!" he barked irritably. The wail ceased immediately. He looked at her in disgust. She resembled a starved feral beast more than a human, with wild eyes grown wide, lips pulled back from her fangs, and her entire body seemingly shrunken in on itself.

"I don't have time for this. Go on, get out of here."

In a flash, she darted up and disappeared into the night sky.

Grimm arrived at the boats in time to see Belladonna dragging a burly, but limp man toward him. He noticed something of a pile of bodies hidden in the shadows between boats pulled up on the mud.

"Are they…?"

The siren grinned and shook her head. "Not dead, just paralyzed for the moment." She glanced back to see several of the pirate crew straggling in. "Just in time. Some of these boys will be stirring soon. I didn't want to use too much venom. Dead blood is no good to the Captain."

Grimm took the hint. "Mr. Murph! Mr. Bland! Get some of the lads there to help get these new recruits into the boats, before it gets too light."

"Aye." "Aye."

The two pirates turned to the others. "You heard the man," Bland barked. "Heave to!"

"Where do y'want 'em when we get 'em on board, Mr. Grimm?" Murph asked.

"Captain's larder."

Bland shook his head. "Poor buggers."

"Aye," Murph agreed, "but better them than us, Chuck."

By dawn, all of the crew had returned to the *Incubus*. They ensured Belle's catch was safely locked in the hold set aside for Viktor and his cadre's blood stock. After finishing off the last one of the earlier prisoners, the small group of vampires turned in for the day. The siren, of course, stashed the body in her cabin for later disposal.

Jon-Jon snored away in his cabin, two working girls with him. Grimm thought about rousting the girls and putting them off the ship but decided against it. They still looked to be fairly fresh, and he wouldn't mind having a go with one of them, once the second mate had finished.

Only Viktor's failure to return kept the ship in port.

Grimm and Belladonna stood at the railing, watching for him, with a boat at the ready to bring him aboard. Behind them, the crew readied the ship to sail with the tide.

After an hour, the tide almost at its peak, Viktor still remained unaccounted for.

"Maybe we should go look for him," the siren suggested. "This port has quite a nest of local vampires, some of them very old and powerful. I had to abandon one of my victims to three of them hunting in a group. I hope he didn't run afoul of any."

"Actually, I did." Viktor stepped up behind her. "But it was nothing I couldn't handle. Thank you for your concern, though, pet." Before she could react, he clasped her to him and kissed her deeply.

Belladonna looked a bit dazed, when they broke from the kiss. She enjoyed it but felt she really ought to be mad at him for being so presumptuous.

Grimm laughed. "You're in a good mood. How did you sneak back on board?"

He released Belle and clapped his first mate on the shoulder. "I am in a good mood, Hezekiah. I am well-fed, and I have learned a new skill."

To prove his point, he hovered a foot above the deck. Satisfied with the reaction this got, he returned to solid footing and gave the order. "Mr. Grimm, weigh anchor. We make for Hell's Breath."

"Aye, Captain. All right you scurrilous sea dogs! You heard the Captain. Let's get this bitch under way! Move!" Grimm barked.

Chapter 14

Vik surveyed the increased activity of his crew. Confident they would manage well under Hezekiah's watchful eye, he grabbed Belladonna by the wrist and headed for his cabin.

The move caught her off guard, and she nearly stumbled. "Hey!"

"I have business with you that cannot wait, pet."

The siren smiled slyly. The night's hunt had put her in the mood for some sport. The kiss and now this led her to believe that he was, as well. It was about time, as far as she was concerned.

He released his grip, once they were in the cabin with the door shut. He then started stripping out of the musty, shredded boots and trousers he'd been wearing sine before they'd gone into the swamp to search for Gloribeau.

Belle took this as her cue to start disrobing as well.

"Not that I'm complaining of the view," Vik commented when he noticed, "But what are you doing?"

She stopped in mid-strip and looked at him, confused. Her shirt already lay on the floor, and she had her breeches half-off. "Why? Did you prefer to undress me yourself?"

He gave her a half-smile, seeing that she had mistaken his reasoning for bringing her to his cabin. "A tempting proposition, pet, but that isn't why you're here right now."

Her face darkened, not in embarrassment, but in irritation. Viktor Brandewyne was, perhaps, the only man who could drive her to angry frustration so quickly. With jerky motions, she pulled her breeches back up and cinched them then retrieved her shirt from the floor and slipped it back over her head.

As she pulled the garment down, Vik flashed to her side and placed a gentle hand on her shoulder. It stopped her more effectively than a show of force would have.

"Don't be angry, Belle," he started. The admonition had the opposite effect. Her temper flared full force.

"Don't be angry? You practically drag me here to your cabin then start getting naked. But when I start to join you, I get told no! You drive me insane!"

Viktor stood, looking down at the furious siren and had to admit she had a point. He also realized his senses were hypersensitive. When he'd told Grimm he was well-fed, he'd meant it. He'd come across the remains of a tavern brawl and finished off three of the unconscious combatants in the back alley they'd been dumped in.

Now he grew keenly aware of the way the fabric of her clothes clung to her lush curves. He could hear the cloth move against her skin as she breathed. Her heartbeat mesmerized him, and her scent held not only anger but an underlying desire.

"What?" Belle asked with some apprehension. His scrutiny became unnerving, and she felt unsure of what he might do. He looked at her like the predator he was. He was too close. If he attacked, she knew she wouldn't have time to get away.

Her involuntary squeak, when he clasped her to him made him chuckle lustily. That she actually struggled against him some only increased his lust. She wasn't using her talons, so he knew she didn't really want to get free.

Using one arm to hold and lift her for better access, he buried his other hand in her hair. She closed her eyes, a small moan escaping her lips. Her scent grew even muskier with her arousal. With a growl, he kissed her possessively, reveling in the feel of her body's surrender to him. One word went through his mind.

Mine.

He set her on the edge of the table to free up his arm. Then he slid his hand up under her shirt to cup a breast. With a practiced flick of his thumb, he brushed and teased her nipple, feeling the skin of the aureole pucker as it swelled and hardened under his touch.

She moaned into his mouth and raised her legs to wrap around him. In the process, her foot brushed the backs of his bare calves.

"Damnit!" Viktor broke the kiss with a hiss of unexpected pain. It was violent enough, that he had to brace himself against the table to keep the leg from collapsing under him.

"What?" Belladonna asked. When he didn't answer her right away, she asked again, "Viktor, what happened? What's wrong?"

"Fucking leg," he growled, as it continued to throb.

She tried to twist around to see, but her position on the table, between his arms, made it difficult. "Let me see."

Her wriggling was starting to distract him from the pain. He leaned into her, trapping her even more and started nibbling at her ear.

"Viktor, I need to see your leg."

"But there's something else I'm just aching to show you, pet." He proceeded to nibble down her neck to her shoulder. His hands moved to knead at her hips where they bent to join her legs.

Her body couldn't help but respond to his touch. She even sighed in pleasure, but she was not as easily distracted. As much as she was enjoying this, she knew his leg needed attention. His enhanced metabolism should have already healed the wound.

She did the only thing she was sure would stop the current seduction long enough to allow her to examine the gator bite. She dug her heel into the damaged area.

"Bitch!" he roared at the renewed pain and forcefully shoved her across the table, away from him. She grunted, as she hit the deck after tumbling backwards off the far edge.

"If that's what it takes to get you to cooperate," she grumbled, picking herself up. "It's been over a day. You shouldn't be having any trouble with that bite by now. Lay down on your stomach so I can get a good look at it. That is the reason you brought me in here, isn't it?"

"It is," he admitted. Knowing she was right; he walked over to the bed and lay down. "I wish you'd make up your mind. I thought you wanted some sport," he grumbled.

She took a moment to admire the view of his backside, frowning a bit at the fact that he still had his shirt on. "I do, but this is more important right now."

Viktor had to laugh, uncomfortably aware of his arousal, since he was lying on it. "And you say I drive you insane."

Belle ignored him and forced herself to concentrate on the wounded leg. It showed some sign of healing. She saw scabbing and puckering, but she also saw fresh blood where she'd reopened it with her foot.

"Well?" His voice jarred her back to the moment. She'd been mesmerized by the blood, to the point that she started leaning down toward it. She shook her head to clear it.

"I don't see any tearing. It must have bitten to hold only. Doesn't look like it shook you."

"No, he didn't shake. He just took me under."

"That's good. These are only punctures. There was no shredding of the muscles, so you shouldn't lose any use of the leg. It has started to heal, but barely faster than a similar wound on a human would heal."

He looked over his shoulder at her. "Do you know why it is healing so slowly?"

She bit her lip, not liking the choice before her. "I have a suspicion, but there is only one way I can be sure."

He frowned, sensing something was bothering her, but growing irritable and impatient as his leg continued to throb. "Well?"

Sighing, she gave him a resigned look. "I have to taste the blood in the wound."

Now he understood her apprehension. To do so would also bind her that much closer to him. He knew she feared losing herself completely to his will. He was mildly surprised, when she knelt beside the bed and placed her mouth over one of the larger punctures.

Ever so gently, she probed the wound with her tongue. She sealed her lips around it and sucked to draw more blood to the surface. Viktor moaned as she forced her tongue deeper into the puncture then started stroking with it. He found the sensation both painful and highly erotic. He gasped when she withdrew.

Belle threw her head back and took in a deep, shuddering breath. Her eyes closed; she meticulously licked every bit of blood from her lips. When she opened her eyes, they glowed their true amber gold. She let out a shaky, nervous laugh.

She felt so tempting to have another taste. She found the power rush intoxicating. She almost didn't mind that she was in danger of completely enslaving herself to the vampire.

Looking at his leg again, she noted that the puncture she had tasted was now nearly healed. "Interesting."

"What, pet?"

"There is maleficent magic in the wound, but it is weak, and I think I've figured out how you can speed the healing process up," she told him.

He rolled to his side and propped on his elbow to look at her. She couldn't help but look back, since the change in position allowed him to expose himself fully aroused. She had to bite her lip to force her concentration back to the problem at hand.

"You said you fed well last night?"

"Aye," he nodded. "Three men's worth of blood. But that didn't heal the bite."

"It started it, though," she pointed out. "If you had been an ordinary man, that leg would be black and rotten by now, going by the demon's residual magic. Plus, you weren't really hurting until I accidentally bumped it."

"True, now that I think about it. In fact, it wasn't hurting at all while we were playing, until you kicked me again."

Belladonna nodded to herself, but she also looked perturbed. "That's what I thought. Feeding helps, but sex speeds it up even more. You need to do both."

Viktor liked the sound of that. He reached for her but frowned in confusion when she shied away from his touch. "Now what?"

She wouldn't look at him. To do so could prove fatal to both of them. "You weren't listening, Viktor. You have to fuck and feed to heal this. You can't feed on me. Just a taste of my blood can kill you."

"Damnit!" he roared in frustration. "So I have to let this heal slowly, or reverse course back to New Orleans!"

"No, actually, you don't," she corrected. "Hezekiah said Jon-Jon had a couple of girls in his cabin."

"Oh, did he now?" Vik raise an eyebrow. He reached out along the line of power that linked his crew to him until he found his second mate.

Jon-Jon yawned and stretched, then, sat bolt upright, suddenly fully awake. He didn't know how, but he knew his captain's attention lay heavy on him. The captain knew he had whores aboard. He also knew somehow that the captain wanted one of them sent to his cabin.

He rubbed the back of his stubbly scalp and looked at the two women still sleeping in his bed. Not sure which one his captain would prefer, he figured he better take them both. He was through with them anyway. All he really wanted at the moment was a bottle. He was feeling entirely too sober.

"Time to wake up, me lovelies," he gave them each a slap on the rump.

"Pet, stop pacing," Viktor ordered the siren. She obeyed but gave him a glare of anguish and frustration.

"I never thought I would ever wish I'd been born human," she growled.

"If you were human, you wouldn't survive what I'm about to put one of those girls through," he pointed out.

"I don't care."

"Well, I do. You are worth more to me alive and as the siren you are, than you would be as food." Then he surprised both her and himself. "Go down to the larder hold, Belle. Pick yourself out a playmate. You can even finish him off, if you like."

She stared at him, stunned. He had made it painfully clear that he didn't like for her to play with her food, or the idea of another male sharing her bed. Now, he was offering a selection from his own larder as a bedmate.

"Who are you, and what have you done with the Captain?"

He smiled wryly. "Oh, I still don't like the idea of you with another man. But I know the one you choose will soon be dead, if not by your hand, then by mine. And I would not deny any other member of my crew a little pleasure."

She blinked and arched an eyebrow at him. If she had been human, she probably would have been offended by that and hurt. Belle was not human. She knew this was a rare offer, and she was not about to pass it up over an imagined insult.

"Very well. Thank you, Viktor." She turned and left before he could change his mind.

As Jon-Jon and the two whores approached the captain's cabin, they saw Belladonna heading the other way very fast. The second mate wondered but knew better than to ask where she was going.

"Who is she?" one of the girls asked.

"Never you mind, darlin'," he told her as he knocked on the door.

The other girl huffed, "She's probably another one of us that these pirates have kidnapped, Jeanette. You told us you would take us back to shore this morning, Big Jon. Now the ship has left port, and we're stuck on board."

"I don't know why you're being such a bitch about this, Theresé," Jeanette chided. "I'm sure the captain is a reasonable man. Between the two of us, we should be able to convince him to either take us back home or drop us at the next port."

Jon-Jon hid his smirk. *"Let the little fools think what they liked."* He knew Vik Brandee didn't do anything unless he wanted to or there was a profit to be had. He also knew his captain wouldn't hesitate to kill anyone who annoyed him, male or female.

"Enter."

Viktor had removed his shirt after the siren left. He now stood completely naked and unabashed. Jon-Jon closed the door behind them. Both of the women stood momentarily speechless; a fact which revealed them as relatively new to their profession.

The vampire stalked forward and circled the women, inspecting. "They're very fresh, Mr. Jon. Are you sure you've even tried them yet?"

"Wore 'em both out last night, Cap'n." He puffed up.

Vik couldn't resist teasing him. "I don't know. They don't look worn out to me. Maybe you just brought them back then fell asleep before you could enjoy them. This one," he indicated Theresé, "doesn't look very happy to be here. I don't think you satisfied her."

The girl in question flinched at his touch and darted her eyes nervously. She didn't know why, but she a sudden fear overwhelmed her. She didn't like boats to begin with but had allowed her companion to talk her into joining her and the tall pirate behind them. Now rather than proving her hope of return to shore, this pirate captain eyed her as if she were a banquet.

When he stopped in front of her and inhaled deeply, taking in her scent, it was more than she could stand. "Please, *sil vous plait, m'sieur*," she whimpered. "I just want to go home."

"Of course you do, pet." His smile looked more predatory than gentle. Her fear appealed to him greatly. Without looking away from his chosen prey, he instructed, "That will be all, Mr. Jon."

"Aye, Cap'n. What do you want me to do with the other one?"

"I'll only need one, I think. Why don't you see if Hezekiah will trade you a bottle of that gin you're so fond of for her, if you're through with her."

"Aye, Cap'n!" Jon-Jon grinned, grabbing Jeanette by the wrist and heading for the door. She had other ideas, however.

Pulling against the second mate, she protested. "Theresé is too scared to be good, *m'sieur*. I could be so much better."

Viktor slowly looked over to her, his eyes already glowing. His smile definitely turned predatory now, as he made no attempt to hide his fangs. "If you wish to take her place, pet, I will be more than happy to accommodate you."

She screamed in terror. Theresé crumpled to the deck in a faint. Jeanette clung to Jon-Jon, crying and shaking her head. He had to nearly carry her out of the cabin, she was so frightened.

As the door shut, Viktor laughed. "That's what I thought." He bent and lifted his prey effortlessly, dropped her on the bed and proceeded to undress her.

He could have saved time and ripped the clothes away, but the dress was too well-made to ruin. He could always find a use for it or sell it in the future.

Belle arrived at the hatch to the hold designated as the vampire's larder. It was the same space that would have been used as a brig, if this ship had made it to its intended Royal Navy commission.

Although she didn't really need the protection, she allowed a couple of armed pirates to escort her inside. The prisoners greeted her with a mixture of lust and fear. Which emotion was stronger varied depending on how drunk or sober each man had been, when she'd captured them.

She looked them over in silence before singling one out. "You'll do." She pointed. "Come with me."

When he hesitated, one of the guards goaded him forward. Reluctantly, the man shuffled forward, heavy leg irons hobbling his movement. Belle grabbed the chain connecting the shackles on his wrist and jerked him forward, off balance. Reaching up with her other hand, she grasped his hair and pulled him down into an almost violent kiss. It didn't take long for him to return her fervor.

Finally, she broke the kiss with a lusty, deep-throated laugh. "Oh yes, you'll do nicely." She looked him over once more. "You even look a little like him."

"Like whom?"

"Don't worry about it."

She just hoped he would have enough stamina to allow her the fantasy of being with Viktor.

Though probably ten years younger than the captain with brown eyes and clean-shaven, his coloring and build were strikingly similar.

She got the spare key from one of the guards, unlocked the leg irons, but left the wrist shackles on him. "I'll take those off when we are in my cabin." She smiled seductively at him.

When she turned and stalked off, she threw a tantalizing sway into her hips. The prisoner followed like a lamb to slaughter.

Chapter 15

Aboard the *Shining Star*, the quartermaster knocked at the door of the captain's cabin.

"Come in."

The man entered the cabin to see his captain bent over a table spread with charts. He waited patiently for him to look up.

"Ah yes, Mr. Bainbridge," the captain, a much younger man than the quartermaster, acknowledged his presence. "What is the report?"

"The new course is set, Captain Brumble," he answered. "A few of the newer men are grumbling about going so far out of the trade lanes, but they're following orders. If I may speak freely, sir?"

"You know how much I value your input, Mr. Bainbridge. There's no need to stand on formality."

"Aye, Captain. I still believe we should have contracted more gun boats, at least until we could get past the Turks and Caicos. The pirates always get more active this time of year in that area."

Zachary Brumble went to his cabinet and returned with a couple of glasses and a decanter of port. He poured, then handed one of the glasses to Bainbridge. "That is precisely why I did not want extra gun boats for the convoy, George," he replied. "Their presence would have marked us as a rich prize."

"Hadn't thought of that, sir," he ceded. "I'm glad you took my advice about studying the tactics of known pirates as well as naval commanders. I dare say you've kept up with them better than I have lately."

Brumble grinned, "A little too closely for my father's taste, actually. He'd probably fire me and take away my ship, if he knew how tempted I've been to turn pirate."

"He would have you locked up and flogged until you were crippled," Bainbridge confirmed. "You know too much about his trade business and other less public ventures."

"I know." Brumble took a long pull on his glass then topped it off. "He's terrified that Thom or I will turn on him one day and bring him to ruin. Father has not forgotten, nor will he let us forget, what happened to the Chapelwaites, when their son, Grayson, went bad."

"Aye, Mudstick went bad long before he finally turned on his family's business, though. I remember him as a lad, and he never was quite right."

"Too true. Wouldn't want to cross his path. That's for sure. From what I've heard, he and his crew aren't too particular about who or what they bugger – or eat." He shuddered a bit.

Bainbridge finished his glass and set it down. "So, what is your plan?"

Brumble returned to his charts and pointed to his indicated course. "We'll swing around the eastern end of Puerto Rico and head due north for Bermuda. That should avoid most of the sea lanes that are known pirate haunts. The homing pigeon message that was waiting for us at our last port confirmed the signal our contact would use. It also brought news that my brother and his entire crew have gone missing."

"That would explain why all the changes then." Bainbridge nodded his understanding. "With one shipment of emeralds lost, it would be vitally important to your father that this one makes it through."

"Aye, George. Things are tense back home in Boston. Father would probably be lynched by some of those hotheads, if they knew where his loyalties lay. He can't afford to have this venture fail. His backer in the Royal Navy may be needed to see him and my sister safely out of the city, if things go the way they seem to be headed."

"Let's hope it doesn't come to that, Captain."

With the *Incubus* over two weeks out of New Orleans, no sign of Hell's Breath presented itself. The fact annoyed Viktor, but it did not surprise him. The full moon was still a week away. If the island did not appear on its own by then, he would use the crystal to try to summon it. He knew that spell might not work, but it was the only viable option he had.

He and Hezekiah stood on the bridge, discussing how to keep the crew occupied for the time being.

"It's the right time of year for the spice trade to be at its peak," Grimm observed. "The majority of the harvest is in, and the convoys will want to make the crossing before the storm season gets bad."

"Indeed, and spices always bring a good price," Viktor agreed. "I wouldn't mind acquiring some cinnamon for our rum stores, either."

Grimm took a puff on his pipe. "Does add a pleasant taste. Oh, and Stitches had mentioned needing to lay in a fresh supply of clove oil. Says it helps the lads with bad toothaches."

"Well, we can't disappoint Dr. Coffin, now, can we?" Vik smirked. "Mr. Bland," he called to the helmsman, "head us due east. I want to check the fishing north of the Windward Islands."

"Aye, Cap'n!"

Looking over the activity on the deck and in the rigging, Viktor had an unexpected sense of vertigo. He shook his head and gripped the railing hard enough to leave hand imprints in the wood before realizing what was causing the disorientation. He closed his eye to concentrate on the images Lazarus sent him.

He saw a convoy of ships sailing north with a large landmass port and aft of them. Even as he wondered what the location was, Lazarus sent him memory images of the nearest port. Viktor smiled to himself, grateful that the creature retained Jim Rigger's knowledge of what information he considered pertinent. He clearly recognized the port of San Juan.

It also told him why that particular convoy caught Lazarus' attention. They weren't sticking to the regular trade routes. His thoughts sent the raven circling in for a closer look. He wanted to know what they were carrying and which ship to single out.

Taking care not to draw notice, the raven landed low in the rigging of the lead ship and quickly morphed into his feline form. None of the ship's crew gave him a second glance. The black cat made quick work of inspecting the cargo bays, then flitted to the next ship in the convoy.

He went through the entire convoy this way, even investigating the two small gunships. Once he had all the information Viktor required, Lazarus' form dissipated into smoke. He rematerialized aboard the *Incubus*.

"It's about time you returned to me, old friend," Vik chided, stroking the cat's fur. "Were you that unwilling to leave Gloribeau's?"

"Meh." Lazarus remained noncommittal. The vampire had to chuckle.

"You did well, Jim. That's just the thing to keep the lads busy and happy." He turned his attention to the helmsman. "Mr. Bland, steer us a course for open water past the Caicos Islands. There's a convoy making for Bermuda from San Juan that I want to intercept."

"Aye, Cap'n." Bland didn't even think to question the captain on how he knew about ships neither spotted by them nor rumored in any port. A keg of rum, tainted with a few drops of Viktor's blood had been distributed among the crew a couple of days earlier.

As usual, Grimm, Belladonna and the small cadre of vampires had been the only ones exempted from the distribution. The six vampires were his creatures. The siren had accidentally bound herself permanently to his will months ago. Hezekiah was the only man, other than Jim Rigger, that Viktor had ever trusted.

That evening, shortly after sunset, a knock came at the captain's door. "Enter, Mr. Brumble."

The fledgling vampire obeyed his maker's command. "You called me, Captain."

Viktor sat at his table, a bottle of blood-brandy and two glasses before him. He quickly noticed how the young vampire's eyes went immediately to the bottle. He smiled to himself.

"Have a seat, sir." He motioned to the chair opposite him. As Brumble obeyed, Brandee poured one glass only. He recorked the bottle and lifted the glass, sniffing the contents then holding it up to admire the color and viscosity of the liquid. He took a calculated sip, making a show of savoring the flavor.

Brumble's pupils dilated so much his eyes almost looked black. His lips parted to reveal the tips of his fangs. His nostrils flared to catch even the faintest whiff of the blood-brandy mix.

Viktor smiled at him, set the glass down, uncorked the bottle and poured a second glass.

"This is an excellent batch – almost pure blood. The brandy isn't bad, either."

When Brumble reached for the second glass, Vik's hand was just on his wrist, stopping him short. The young vampire gave him a look of pleading and confusion. Why would his captain taunt him with such rich fare only to deny him?

Viktor smiled gently, yet sternly, like a father with an impatient child. "Not so fast, Thomas. You must earn your reward."

"What is your order, Captain?" He replied, eager to please.

Just what the older vampire wanted to hear. He sat forward and steepled his fingers, elbows on the table. "We need to discuss the signals your family uses with your connection in the emerald trade."

Thomas told him everything he knew without hesitation.

The spice convoy about reached the halfway point between Puerto Rico and Bermuda, when sails were spotted on the horizon. Zachary Brumble remained wary but did not sound the alert. After all, it could be a packet blown off course or a Navy ship on patrol.

As the ship neared, the sight of the agreed-upon signal flying from the interloper's mizzen surprised him. He wasn't expecting to rendezvous with his connection until after leaving Bermuda. Still cautious, he wouldn't give the word to break formation until he was able to get a good look at the other ship's lines.

"Mr. Bainbridge, give the order to break from the pack and approach the incoming ship."

"Do you want one of the gun boats to accompany, Captain?" his quartermaster asked. "This is nowhere near the designated rendezvous point. They could be pirates."

Brumble handed him the glass. "Look for yourself, Mr. Bainbridge. They're flying the signal we agreed upon."

"Aye, that they are. Actually, looks to be a ship-o-the-line. I see Royal Navy uniforms moving about on deck. Odd name for one of His Majesty's ships though; *Incubus*?"

Brumble gave a wry smile. "Maybe her captain is proud of his prowess with the women."

"Heh, maybe he is, Captain."

Grimm and Viktor stood watching over the ship and keeping an eye on the convoy. Most of the men on deck wore uniforms, although that is where their resemblance to Navy sailors ended. Some of the uniforms had been among the original stores on board, when Belladonna originally delivered the ship to Hell's Breath Island. Others were pieced together from smaller military craft pirated in recent months.

Viktor always saved items like that. He knew well the value of playing a little dress-up to throw his prey off guard. Not that he minded a good skirmish, but the less attention he drew from the rest of the convoy, the easier this prize would be taken and stripped.

"They took the bait." He smiled when he saw the *Shining Star* change course to intercept them.

Within the hour, the two ships floated alongside each other. Sails were furled, and sea anchors were dropped. Finally, a boarding plank was extended between the vessels.

Viktor made full use of the information Thomas gave him. The correct call and answer codes had been exchanged. Therefore, Zachary Brumble and George Bainbridge were completely unsuspecting, when they crossed the plank and were welcomed aboard the *Incubus*.

Hezekiah Grimm, trying not to show how uncomfortable the uniform made him feel, escorted them to the captain's cabin. Viktor rose from his chair behind the table and walked around it to shake hands with the two men. "Welcome, gentlemen." He offered them a genial, but close-lipped smile, careful to not show fang. "Would you care for some refreshment before we get to business? I've some fine hundred-year-old Italian brandy and quality cigars."

"You are gracious, sir." Brumble inclined his head. "Thank you."

At a nod, Grimm poured the brandy and passed the humidor. Their guests had not seen that the glasses handed them had contained a few drops of blood in the bottom.

Of course, Viktor was aware of when his blood took effect. It felt like a little click in his head as the two men's wills fell to his. Smiling, he sat back, savoring his own cigar. Blowing a smoke ring, he watched it rise and dictated, "I want the emeralds delivered within the hour, along with half your spice cargo and provisions."

"Only half?" Brumble asked, not batting an eye. Deep inside, a little voice was screaming warnings at him, but the siren song of the vampire's blood drowned it out.

Viktor nodded, "Aye. That is all I require for now. I've other business to attend to, or I would take as many of your convoy as I could to fill my holds." As an afterthought, he added, "Oh, and you will be remaining as my guest, rather than returning to your ship, Mr. Brumble."

"Captain Brumble," Bainbridge corrected automatically.

"Not anymore."

Once the requested cargo was transferred from the *Shining Star* to the *Incubus*, Viktor gave some parting instructions to his "guests."

"Mr. Bainbridge, you may return to your ship. I also want you to take a message to your employer. Let Tobias Brumble know that I have taken his sons and his emeralds as partial payment of the debt he owes for the vile treatment in the past of one Jim Rigger. Jim was a good friend of mine."

"And what name shall I give him, sir?"

"Tell him Viktor Brandewyne sends his regards."

The *Shining Star* had returned to its convoy and was almost out of sight of the *Incubus*, when the vampire's blood spell wore off. George Bainbridge was a very strong-willed individual, and he'd only received a small dose. Viktor never intended to keep him in thrall for long. It would have spoiled his plan.

Bainbridge felt as though he were waking from a dream. He remembered everything that had taken place, but it seemed surreal. Had they really just handed over the emeralds without question or a fight to pirates?

He went to the captain's cabin and knocked but got no answer. Entering, he saw that Captain Brumble was nowhere to be seen. The cask containing the smuggled emeralds was missing, as well. A quick trip to the cargo holds showed that spice and provisions were gone, too.

Still, he wasn't entirely sure. He stopped the second mate and asked, "Did we just encounter another ship? Where is Captain Brumble?"

The man looked at him as if he were daft. "You must have been out in the sun too long, Mr. Bainbridge. We undocked from that ship-o-the-line not two hours ago. The Captain stayed with her to conduct business or some such. We even gave them half our cargo and provisions. Good thing we'll be making Bermuda in a few days, else we'd have to ration."

"Damn! Signal the gun boats to join us. The rest of the convoy is to stay on course. We're going after that ship!"

"Sir?"

"That was no ship-o-the-line, Mr. Warding. That was Viktor Brandewyne, and he's taken the Captain hostage."

Warding stammered in fear and disbelief, "Are you sh-sure, sir? I thought he was reported dead. And they were all dressed as Royal Navy."

"Don't be dense, man. Somehow, the bastard has gotten ahold of a warship. The uniforms were probably stolen." He continued, more to himself than to Warding, "We never should have accepted that brandy. His man must have slipped some potion into our glasses. It would explain why we just handed the goods over to them without question or payment, and why I was feeling so addled."

Noticing that Warding was still standing there, he barked, "Get moving, man! We have to try to stop them."

Zachary Brumble came to his senses in an unfamiliar cabin. Trying the door, he found it locked tight. A small port hole revealed the cabin sat close to the waterline of the ship he was in.

The cabin contained a table, a chair, and a hammock. The table was bolted down, but the chair was not. In a pinch, it could be used as a weapon, although he didn't know where he could flee to if he overcame one of his captors.

His memory of how he got there was still a little fuzzy. He remembered heady brandy and cigar smoke – and something about the emeralds.

Just like that, the entire encounter came flooding back. He had been duped, drugged, and had fallen into the clutches of one of the most feared pirates to sail these waters. Obviously, the report of Vik Brandee's death had been incorrect.

He suffered a moment of despair, knowing his father would never pay a ransom for him. But he shook it off. It had never been his nature to give up. He would find some way out of this, or he would make the best of his lot.

The *Shining Star* and the two gun boats had almost caught up to the *Incubus* as dusk neared. Bainbridge and Warding thought it best not to let the three crews know exactly who they pursued. It could very well have led to a mutiny, given Brandee's reputation.

Bainbridge hoped to be able to rescue his captain, but knowing his employer, he was more worried about recovering the emeralds. A second failed mission would not sit well with Tobias Brumble's partners in this venture and would probably result in a few heads rolling – literally.

Just as they came within range, a thick fog rolled in, obscuring the *Incubus* from view and making visibility between the pursuers almost non-existent.

Amazingly, the fog didn't last long. Just as quickly as it appeared, it dissipated.

The *Incubus* was nowhere to be seen.

Jon-Jon brought their pursuers to the captain's attention. Viktor laughed, "So they want to play. Have the lads get ready. I'm sure they'll be glad of a good fight."

Belladonna had come on deck after they had parted ways with the *Shining Star* earlier. She gazed curiously at the three approaching ships. "You aren't going to outrun them? I know for a fact that this ship can do so."

"Where's the fun in that, pet? If Mr. Bainbridge is so keen to give us the rest of his cargo and commit suicide, who am I to say him nay?"

An odd shift in the wind caught their attention. It carried a familiar shiver of power. Belladonna recognized it first.

"I don't think Zeke is going to let you play."

"Damn." his voice held mild annoyance. As a thick fog enveloped the ship, blocking his view of the surrounding ocean, he thought the old wizard's timing left something to be desired.

Night found them at anchor in the same cove Viktor had first seen the ship in. An almost solid wall of fog circled the island but did not actually touch land. The night sky remained fully visible with a full moon riding high.

Zachary Brumble peered out his port hole in consternation. He could not for the life of him figure out how they came to be in harbor. There were no islands anywhere near where they had been. Even if there had been islands, they wouldn't have been barren, rocky things like this one. The whole situation felt unnatural.

A soft sound from beyond the door put him on the alert. For the past few hours, he had gotten no response to his pounding or demands. He grabbed the chair and held it, ready to swing at whoever came in.

"Thomas?" he stopped in mid-swing, as the other man entered with a tray of food.

"Hello brother," the fledgling vampire smiled. "Welcome to Hell."

Tamara A. Lowery

Chapter 16

Viktor and his mates made their way to the rocky dell. The fire was there, but Uncle Zeke was not. The group stopped short in confusion. Even Belladonna was puzzled.

"Where is he?"

"Maybe he had to relieve himself," Grimm suggested with a shrug.

The siren shook her head, frowning, "No. this has never happened before in all the centuries I've known him. Zeke has always been here by his fire or waiting on the shore every time I've been on the island."

Viktor grunted to himself, turned around and started climbing the rise going out of the dell.

"Where are you going?" Belle wanted to know.

He looked over his shoulder at her. "To look for the old man. Gloribeau said to give the teeth to him, and I don't feel like waiting around for him to decide to show up. It's already been close to a month."

"Heh! Boy, you need to learn some patience."

Zeke sat by the fire, poking it with his stick and holding his pipe. None of them had seen him arrive. He looked as comfortable as if he'd been there the whole time.

The vampire growled under his breath and stalked back to the fireside.

"Temper, temper," Zeke chided. "I believe you said you have something for me." He held his hand out expectantly.

Vik reached in his shirt and pulled out the bag containing the necklace. He hesitated before handing it to the old man. He frowned at the unexpected reluctance in himself. Zeke opened the bag and poured the string of alligator teeth into his palm. They seemed to shimmer in the firelight.

"Save it!" a voice whispered desperately in Viktor's mind. *"He's going to destroy it, and you'll never get the magic that you need from Gloribeau! They are trying to cheat you and keep you trapped by your curse."*

Zeke spoke and shattered the mesmerizing spell of the necklace. "So, she was finally able to dispatch old Tulimanchulo."

"With some help," Grimm pointed out.

"Heh, I'm sure. The years weren't kind to Glory, though I bet you wouldn't know that to look at her now." The old man actually leered.

Vik returned the leer. "No, she's quite a sight, now."

"I know that look, boy. You want to be careful around Gloribeau."

He nodded, "She warned me off, or I would have bedded her on the spot. Said she'd been without a man so long she'd probably rip me apart."

Zeke raised an eyebrow at him. "She must like you. Glory would make a dangerous lover. She's a wonderful ally, but you don't want to make her mad."

"How does that make her different from any other female?"

He held up the teeth. "Tulimanchulo was her last lover."

"She said he was a demon that she fought long ago."

Zeke nodded. "A right handsome demon, too. He seduced her, learned the secrets of her powers, then tried to steal them. He partially succeeded, too. That's how he escaped into that gator's body, when she killed him."

While Viktor digested that bit of information, Zeke tossed the necklace into the fire.

"What are you doing?" Vik tried to catch it, before it went into the flames, but even his speed wasn't enough.

"Purging the demon's soul and separating it from her magic that he stole."

He blinked. That explained the voice. The demon was looking for a new host body. As if to confirm the thought, a deep, guttural scream rose from the flames. The fire suddenly grew to twice its height, an angelically beautiful face suspended in it.

Just as suddenly, the fire died down to embers, barely a flame to be seen in the dull glow. Zeke seemed to be the only one not disoriented by the relative darkness.

He produced a large conch shell, stuffed with dry coconut fibers. He poked through the embers with his stick, separating them, until he had a white-hot one singled out. Using his stick, he worked it to the edge of the fire and rolled it into the shell. Placing a handful of the fibers over the ember to protect it, he handed the conch to Viktor.

"Do not let this ember die. Only you can carry it, no one else is to even touch the shell. Go back and give this to Gloribeau. It contains the magic stolen from her which she will give to you," he instructed.

Viktor looked at the shell containing the ember. "If this is the magic she would give me for my quest, why should I have to take it back to her? She told me I would get what I need if I gave you the necklace."

The old man nodded, "True, you could just keep the ember and go looking for the next Sister. But it will not be easy to keep the ember alive. If it goes out, the magic will be lost forever, and you will not be able to complete your quest."

He looked at Zeke, an annoyed yet wry look on his face. "Of course. Nothing can ever be simple or easy with you people."

Zeke grinned back. "Nope. Wouldn't be very potent magic if it was, now, would it? Now you scat on back the Glory's. I'm sure she'll make the magic a bit easier to carry than that is."

☠

Zachary moved forward to embrace his brother. "Thomas! I was sure I'd never see you again! We'd gotten word that you had been taken by pirates."

"Aye, brother." Thomas endured the hug. Rather than comfort him, it made him acutely aware of his brother's heartbeat and all that blood just under the skin. "Given the way things are now, I had hoped we would never meet again." His voice held a note of sadness.

Zach pushed him back and looked at him. "How can you say that? Thom, you're a prisoner, just as I am. I know Father would never ransom either of us, but together we should be able to find some way of escape."

Thomas shook his head. "No, Zach. There is no escape for me. Ever."

"What are you talking about? Are you worried about being tried for piracy? You're no more a pirate than I am, Thom. I'll testify as much."

The young vampire laughed at that, "Then we'll both get hanged."

"No. We won't."

"Yes. We would. Think for a minute, Zach. You gave up the emeralds without a fight. The pirates knew the signals, because of me, granted. Father will assume that we've both turned against him. He'll never believe the truth."

Zachary sat down hard. The hope seemed to drain out of him. "You're right. And, even if he did, he couldn't afford to back us up. It would make it look to his partners like he was conspiring to cheat them. He would be forced to turn against us."

Thomas edged the tray of food toward him. "Eat, Zach. You'll need your strength."

"I'm not hungry. It's probably drugged, like that brandy or the cigars."

"It isn't drugged. I prepared it myself, since I knew that would be one of your worries. But the brandy and cigars you had with the Captain weren't drugged, either."

Zach glared at his brother. He could tell Thomas had thrown in with the pirates, and it made him not want to trust the younger man anymore. "You're lying. I don't know why, but you are. I'm not surprised at you turning against Father. I've been tempted to turn on the brutal bastard myself, but it hurts me that you would betray me, as well. Were the signals how you bought your life?"

"I haven't betrayed you, brother."

"Prove it! You eat the food!"

Thomas' eyes filled with sorrow and regret. "I can't."

Zachary backhanded him or started to. With amazing speed, Thomas caught his hand. Snarling, he made sure his fangs were clearly visible. He'd been trying to hide the truth from his brother, but he saw there was no point to it.

"I can't eat food anymore, brother, and I didn't buy my life with information. I didn't buy my life at all. I have been dead since shortly after I was captured! If I was going to betray you, Zach, I would have torn your throat out and drained you of your blood the minute I entered this cabin."

The elder Brumble brother stumbled back when the younger one released him. His face drained of all color. "What did they do to you, Thom?"

"The Captain killed me."

Zach shook his head in disbelief. "But you aren't dead! You're standing here talking to me! How can you say that?"

"I assure you, brother, I am dead." His smile was almost cruel. He stalked toward the other man. Zachary's fear aroused is Hunger. He didn't really want to feed on his brother, but if they both didn't gain control of themselves quickly, it was going to happen.

"I only exist to feed on human blood and serve my Captain, who created me. You weren't drugged; you were bespelled, brother. The Captain is not human. He is a blood-drinking creature of darkness," he tried to explain.

"Is that why you gave him the codes and signals?"

He nodded. "The Captain demanded them. I had no choice but to obey. His will is mine."

"And is he commanding you to attack me?" Zach found himself backed up next to the port hole.

"No, but he has not forbidden it, and you are behaving like prey. I do not want to feed on you, Zach. My control is not strong enough to keep me from killing you, if I do. Then you would become what I am."

Zachary braced himself for an attack that never came. In the blink of an eye, Thomas stood back by the door. He hadn't seen the fledgling vampire move.

"Eat the food, Zach. I swear it is safe. I need to go feed." He opened the door and stepped out. "I have to lock you in. It's for your own safety. Brother, be careful and be wary. I don't know when, but the Captain will call for you and decide what he wants to do with you."

"Enter," Viktor answered the knock at his door. He sat brooding, chin-in-hand, staring at the conch shell and ember.

Grimm came into the cabin and closed the door behind him. "The fog is starting to clear. We've already lifted the anchors. The soundings show the island is long gone."

"Very good. Have the helmsman set course for New Orleans," he answered, distracted. "Any idea what we have on board that will be good tinder to keep this thing lit? It's going to take close to a month to get back to Gloribeau's at this time of year."

"It might not take as long as that, Vik."

That got his attention. "What do you mean?"

Grimm shrugged. "Going by the stars and the color of the sea, Hell's Breath transported us to within a day's sailing of New Orleans."

Viktor raised an eyebrow. "Interesting. Maybe the old man is trying to help us out a bit."

"Maybe. One of those bales of pipe tobacco we took off Brumble might work. It seemed to have a good consistency, not too moist, but not too dry. Should burn good and slow without dying out."

"I'll give it a try, then. Thank you, Hezekiah."

"I'll have Anvil bring it up." Grimm nodded and left the captain's cabin.

Several hours after Thomas left the food with Zachary, it still sat uneaten. He just couldn't bring himself to trust the creature that had once been his brother. He was beginning to think he was going mad.

He was finding it harder to keep from giving in to his stomach, however. Even cold, the food was obviously fresh and smelled good. He was so hungry.

It startled him when a large black cat yawned and stretched, as it got up from where it had been sleeping under the table. Odd, he hadn't noticed the animal in the cabin until that moment.

"Hello, where did you come from?" He started to reach down and pet the cat, but thought better of it, after the baleful glare the creature gave him.

The cat leapt onto the table and proceeded to wash its face. Then it looked at the prisoner, decided he was no threat, and sniffed at the food. After a couple of moments, it started eating.

Zachary watched the cat, bemused. When it began eating the food his brother left, he watched it even more closely.

It seemed to be suffering no ill effects from the food. In fact, it began eating with greater gusto.

Unable to fight his hunger and finally convinced the food was safe, he snatched the plate away from the cat and finished the meal off. He suffered a bit hand for the theft.

He never noticed the cat turn to smoke then vanish from the cabin while he was eating.

Chapter 17

They dropped anchor close to what both Viktor and Grimm felt would be a good sea entrance to the bayous. They agreed it would be best to bypass the port city for this errand. They knew where they had to go to find Gloribeau.

Or so they thought.

The waters ran deep enough, and they found a clear channel to get from the ship to the docks they originally left from to find the Sister. From there, they could see that it wasn't going to be as easy as they thought it would be.

"Looks like a bad storm came through, Cap'n," Jon-Jon commented, scratching his head.

The dock was a shambles. Some still survived, but most had been reduced to broken pilings and planking splintered beyond repair. They found two flat-bottom skiffs still tied to one of the pilings; one half submerged with a piece of planking piercing it, the other intact and afloat. It even had a load of supplies. A tarp had been secured over them and had protected them from the weather.

Grimm raised an eyebrow at that. "Must be close to time for René to make a supply run to Gloribeau."

"Aye," Vik nodded. "I don't feel like waiting for him to show up, though. There's room for all of us in the skiff. Our boat is too deep a draft for some of the swamp passages."

"What about the supplies?" Belle asked.

Viktor grinned at her. "Never knew a female that didn't like for a man to bring her something."

Two hours into the swamp, Viktor noticed that the shell didn't feel as warm. Pulling it out of his shirt, he saw that the tinder surrounding the ember was nearly consumed. He took a good handful of tobacco from the pouch on his belt and gently stuffed it in around the ember.

Oddly, it didn't seem to burn his skin. It glowed brighter when his fingers were close to it, too. It had shrunken some, however, the edges dissolving into a fine ash. He tucked the conch shell back into his shirt to keep it close to his skin. The ember seemed to fare better when he held the shell in his hand, he had learned, but it just wasn't practical.

Frowning to himself, he wondered if maybe they should have gone to find René Thibideaux before entering the bayou. Storm damage had changed the landscape significantly. Even the scent clues he had memorized from their first trip in had been altered.

They should have arrived at the drop point where they'd first encountered Gloribeau, by his calculations.

Looking over at the siren, who was huddled in on herself, he asked, "Belle, can you sense the Sister's presence?"

She didn't answer right away. He assumed she was seeking some trace of Glory's magic, when she closed her eyes. After several minutes, she opened them again and looked at him blearily. "What?"

He growled in irritation. He hated having to repeat himself. Any crew member that made him do so usually ended up maimed or dead for it. Yet where the siren was concerned, he found himself being a little more tolerant.

"I asked if you could sense Gloribeau's whereabouts."

She shook her head, but her movements were sluggish, as was her voice. "No, nothing. Not even your power."

She shivered uncontrollably. "So c-c-cold. Quiet, too. Is this what it feels like to be human?"

The men looked at her in confusion.

"Pet, are you well?"

"No. I don't know. I don't feel any magic. Not the Sister's, not yours, not even mine. Everything smells strange, too. Not so sharp. Even what I see seems dull and fuzzy." She sounded tired and scared. "I don't like this black water."

He definitely did not like the sound of that. Shrugging out of his coat, he leaned forward and draped it around her. He wasn't sure why she was cold. He found the climate to be on the warm side, almost too much so for the coat, in fact.

Belladonna gave him a weak smile in thanks for the coat. She hated not only that Viktor saw her weakness, but so did the two humans. It was never good for potential prey to see a predator at a disadvantage. Still she couldn't seem to find the energy to hide the sudden feebleness or the fear it engendered.

As she pulled the dress coat tight around her, she noticed her senses seemed to clear a little bit. The garment felt huge on her. It also was very strong with the vampire's scent, even to her currently dulled senses. For reasons she couldn't explain, it made her feel safe.

Viktor was bemused by how delicate the siren looked, wrapped up in his coat. Given her ferocity and forceful personality, it was rare for him to notice how physically small she actually was in comparison.

Grimm noticed the slight smile on his friend and captain's face, as he gazed at the siren. Wisely, he kept it to himself, but he wondered if maybe Viktor did love her on some level. It would be a first, in his experience. For all the years they had known each other, Viktor had been with countless women, but he had never loved any of them or even cared about them beyond what they could do for him.

Jon-Jon was too busy watching the waters ahead of the skiff for cypress knees and submerged trees to notice anything going on in the boat.

It was nearly dark, before they found any land at all. It didn't look familiar to any of them. They saw no sign of any sort of man-made structure on the islet.

"Should we light the *flambeaux* and keep going in, Cap'n?" Jon-Jon asked for instructions.

Part of him wanted to continue, but all the *flambeaux* would do was magnify the darkness. "No. There's been too much storm damage. I don't want to get anymore off course than we already are. We'll camp here tonight and continue at first light," he decided.

They pulled the skiff up on the islet far enough to make sure it didn't drift away in the night. Enough dry wood lay around for Grimm to build a small fire. He lit it using the flint striker he kept for his pipe.

"I will take the first watch, then wake Jon-Jon for the second," he told Viktor.

The vampire shook his head. "No, Hezekiah. I need both of you well rested in the morning. I do not sleep anymore. I will keep watch tonight."

Grimm understood the reasoning. He thought about staying up to keep his friend company but respected him enough as his captain to obey. It was unclear now how long it would take to find Gloribeau again. He and Jon-Jon ate and shared a flask of gin, then bedded down for the night.

Once sure his mates were asleep, Viktor moved to where Belladonna sat huddled in on herself. She sat far enough from the fire and the two sleeping pirates that she seemed almost lost in the shadows. She still wore his coat.

It worried him that she was not her usual, annoying self. But he didn't want to show too much concern in front of his men. He was Captain, and he would not readily behave in a way that they could perceive as weakness. If he pretended to care for some wench, he knew they would recognize it as just playing her. Belladonna was not just some wench, however, and he really did care about her wellbeing. He told himself that it was because of her value to him in his quest to find the Sisters of Power, but deep down, he wasn't sure that was the only reason anymore.

"Are you still cold, pet?"

She looked up at him with a start. Real fear shone in her eyes. Could it be she hadn't heard him approach?

She nodded, whether in answer to the spoken question or the unspoken one, he couldn't tell. Testing the bond they shared, he found her magical presence dull, almost non-existent. Something was very, very wrong.

"Why don't you move closer to the fire? It would be warmer."

She shook her head violently. Her voice came out as barely a whisper. "I am a creature of the sea. Fire is not my friend."

"Nonsense, Belle. The fire won't harm you. Here, let me help you up." He held out a hand to her. The hand she gave him felt almost as cold as a corpse. "Damn! Pet, you're freezing!"

The only way the fire could truly warm her would be for her to practically stand in the flames. She needed body warmth. He just didn't like the idea of her snuggling up with either of his mates.

"Lazarus, come forth."

Obediently, the cat materialized. "Meh?"

"Belle is ill, old friend. I need to stay with her. I trust you to stand watch."

Lazarus blinked and nodded. He gave the siren a sniff, blinked again, then rubbed his cheek against her leg. Turning, he trotted to the other side of the fire and sat, looking out into the darkness.

Viktor led Belladonna to a tree closer to the fire. She clung to him, eyeing the flames fearfully. He could smell her terror and did not try to get any nearer. Instead, he sat them down and propped against the tree.

"I'm frightened, Viktor."

Pulling her close, he replied, "I know, pet. I will keep you safe. Rest."

Over the course of the night, he had to refresh the tinder for the ember three times. Proved awkward to do the first time, since Belladonna used his chest for a pillow. She later lay down with her head on his thigh, which made tending the ember easier.

Lazarus shifted around the perimeter hourly. He also periodically checked on Viktor and the siren.

Grimm woke just before dawn. He stretched, got up and went to the water's edge to relieve himself. Then he went over to the captain.

Viktor motioned for him to be quiet. "Don't wake her."

He nodded his understanding, wondering if Vik even realized he was stroking Belle's hair. "Is she any better?"

Viktor shook his head. "I don't know what has happened to her, Hezekiah. Even her scent is weaker. She almost smells human."

Grimm didn't really know how to respond to that comment. Although Vik had told him about his enhanced senses, he really couldn't get a solid grasp on the concept. He had to just accept it as being magic.

"The quicker we find Glory, the better for Belle, there," he whispered.

That got the vampire's attention. "Explain, Mr. Grimm."

"I think she needs saltwater. Back on the Isle of Youth, when we were looking for Dorada, she seemed mighty uncomfortable about being so far from the sea."

Viktor mulled that over. "She did say something yesterday about not liking this black water." He nodded toward the swamp. The second the words left his lips, the siren shuddered, as if in the grip of some nightmare. She then began sobbing, although no tears flowed.

"Wake Mr. Jon and douse the fire," he ordered. "We need to get moving." As Grimm went to follow his instructions, he gently shook Belladonna awake. "Come on, pet, wake up. You were having a nightmare."

She blinked blearily up at him. Recognizing him, she smiled. Then her eyes grew wide, and she scrambled to her feet, as she realized she had been lying in his lap. It was so much like the reaction he sometimes got from virgins or ladies from respectable society the morning after he had seduced them that he had to chuckle. "Your honor is intact, m'lady," he teased. "I did not take advantage while you slept."

She glared at him then asked a question so typically her, it gave him hope that she would recover her powers quickly.

"Why not?"

He smiled and gave her a look. "You hardly seemed to be in any shape for it, pet. Where would the sport have been in that?"

She threw a stick at him, which he easily dodged.

"Looks like she's feeling better," Grimm grinned, when he saw the exchange.

"Aye," Vik returned the grin.

"Stop talking about me as if I'm not here!"

All three pirates laughed at her outburst. Her growling scream of frustration turned to a gulp of surprise, as a clammy hand brushed her ankle.

Grimm and Jon-Jon went instantly on alert, drawing their weapons. Viktor was even faster. He placed himself between the siren and the prone man, a blade at his throat with an inhuman speed. The unfortunate creature rolled onto his side, trying to crawl away from the sword tip, but lacked the strength. If the vampire had been slower, the man would have skewered himself, when he collapsed back onto his face.

Sheathing the sword, Viktor knelt down and rolled the unconscious man over. "René," he identified him. His mates moved to his side, looking down at René. The boy looked as if he'd fought with a wildcat and lost. He was naked, muddy, cut up and bloody. What clean patches of skin that remained visible looked almost corpse pale. His eyes were sunken with the skin around them dark.

"Damn." Jon-Jon whistled. "Looks like he ran the gauntlet a few times in a row."

Grimm nodded in agreement. "Aye. What is he doing out here, though? Do ye suppose whoever beat him thought he was dead and dumped him in the swamp?"

Viktor's senses told him otherwise. Even through the swamp muck, he could smell recent sex, and he saw how raw the skin on the boy's privates was. "No, Mr. Grimm. He's suffered something more sinister than attempted murder."

As if to confirm this, a female voice, seductive and sultry, lilted in the distance. "René, where are you, my lover? You can't run far from me."

"Who?" Jon-Jon asked.

"What." Grimm corrected.

"Gloribeau," Viktor and Belladonna answered in unison.

The swamp witch soon appeared, gliding more than wading through the black water. Her glossy black hair seemed to blend into the black silk chemise she wore, which in turn, seemed to blend into the swamp water. In her element, her restored youth and power made her a force to be reckoned with.

All three men felt the pull of her body, even more so than when she had first been reborn. Viktor's steel will kept him from rushing to embrace her. It also kept Jon-Jon rooted in place. The fraction of power Uncle Zeke had granted Grimm protected the first mate, since the Elder's power trumped all of the Sisters' power. Viktor was unaware of its presence in his first mate and attributed the man's resistance to his own adamant nature.

Belladonna felt nothing but fear. In her weakened state, nothing, not even her charge to protect Viktor, could make her face off with Glory.

The Sister smiled seductively, taking in the scene before her. "So, this is where René got off to. Hello, Viktor Brandewyne."

"Hello, Gloribeau." He cut his eyes down to the boy then back to the swamp witch. "Is this why you warned me off?"

She stepped up onto the island, her dress and bare feet showing no sign of having been wet. Her swaying, stalking gait was equally as seductive as the siren's. Stopping just inches from the pirate captain, she looked up at him. "Yes. I needed someone to take the edge off. René has done that, and he has whetted my appetite, as well. Now, I can take the time to fully enjoy my lover without such an urgent need to rut."

Viktor's smiled wryly. "There is much to be said for simple rutting, even though it doesn't take any real skill. But it is much better to prolong and savor the experience with a talented partner."

Her smile was both wicked and angelic. "I'm glad you see it that way, Viktor Brandewyne. But you will need to be at full strength to take me on, boy. I want you to take René back to his sister. It was for her sake I restrained myself and didn't just use him up completely. Once you've done that, take a few days and feed well. Then you can come back to me."

He lifted her hand to his lips, kissing the palm. His smile just as wicked as hers. "It will be my pleasure, Gloribeau – and yours."

She laughed; a dark melodious sound rich with promise. "Of that, I am sure. Until we meet again."

All of them, even Viktor, fell sway to her magic as she simply vanished.

Chapter 18

George Bainbridge sat at the captain's desk mulling his course of action. It wasn't the first time he'd sailed in the captain's seat, but he was not happy about the circumstances that placed him there this time. He genuinely liked Zachary Brumble.

Having personally served under his father, Tobias, he knew the young man was a better captain. Where the father was stern to the point of being abusive to his crew, the son was stern, but fair. Much like his brother, Zachary believed in keeping his men well-fed and gave them ample rest periods. He still managed to bring his cargoes in on time and make a respectable profit.

Now Bainbridge puzzled over how to break the news of recent events to the elder Brumble without making the younger look like he had double-crossed his father. He had to admit that the circumstantial evidence looked bad. He was sure that he had been drugged. He was almost sure that Zachary had been drugged, as well. What he couldn't explain was how the imposters had known the correct signals. That one fact was the most damning.

It also did not look good on him that he lost the pirate ship in that freakish fog bank. The way the fog came up so quickly and vanished just as suddenly was unnerving enough. But that the ship vanished with it smacked of witchcraft.

Bainbridge sighed and shook his head. Tobias Brumble was perhaps the least superstitious former seafarer he knew. Even with the captains of both the gun boats backing up his story, it would be hard to convince his employer.

A knock came at the door, followed soon after by the cabin boy.

"Captain Bainbridge?"

He started to correct the boy, but the title was correct. "What is it, Edwin?"

"Sir, the helmsman said the lookout reports a ship on the horizon."

"We're nearing the shipping lanes again. I'm not surprised."

"Captain, he said to tell you it's flying the same signals as that pirate ship that took Captain Brumble."

Bainbridge stood so fast he knocked his chair over. Grabbing his hat, he headed for the helm.

Looking through the glass, he could tell it wasn't the same ship. It had only been a brief whisper of hope it might have been. Realistically, he knew the pirates wouldn't be that foolish. Their captain claimed to be Viktor Brandewyne. Reports were that he was supposed to be dead, but reports had been wrong before. The stories and rumors he had heard about Bloody Vik Brandee told him he should count himself lucky to still be alive and free.

It was yet another reason his employer probably wouldn't believe him.

He frowned as they got closer to the signaling ship. The sails puffed out fully rigged, but the vessel moved erratically, as if no one manned the helm. Another look through the glass revealed no movement in the rigging. He would be willing to bet it was derelict.

"Signal the convoy to steer clear. Send one of the gun boats over to investigate. She appears to be abandoned, but it could be a trap," he gave the order.

The gun boat gave the all-clear. As the *Shining Star* approached, men could be seen going aloft to furl the sails of the interloper.

Bainbridge went over to the strange ship as soon as they tied up alongside her. A grim sight indeed greeted him. Bodies littered the deck, some headless and some with gaping wounds in their chests. Oddly, he saw very little blood, as if someone had cleaned it up or killed the ill-fated crew elsewhere and staged the corpses.

"Captain Bainbridge, over here." The captain of one of the gun boats gestured. "We've found a survivor. It's all right, boy. No one is going to hurt you now."

He nudged a scrawny boy who looked to be no older than twelve forward. The lad held his arm to his body awkwardly and darting frightened glances between the two men. "Had to break his arm to get this pig-sticker away from him." He held out a long knife.

Bainbridge looked around at the carnage again then back at the boy. "If he saw all this happen, you're lucky he didn't gut you before you could disarm him, Captain Perkins."

"No worries there, he couldn't have done this. He's not big enough, and there's not the first drop of blood on him."

"In case you haven't noticed, Perkins, there doesn't seem to be a drop of blood anywhere," Bainbridge pointed out.

"She took it all," the boy muttered.

"What was that lad?"

The boy's eyes held a horror he'd never seen in one so young. "She took all the blood. She killed everybody and took all the blood."

Bainbridge and Perkins exchanged a look. There was no denying the boy had witnessed an unspeakable horror, but both found it hard to believe that a woman was responsible for the carnage.

"What is your name, lad?" Bainbridge asked.

"Robin Jones, sir."

"Mr. Jones, I am Captain Bainbridge, and this is Captain Perkins. You see that man over there?"

The boy nodded.

"I want you to go with him. He will take you to my ship, make sure your arm is set properly, and find you some food. Later, I want to talk to you in my cabin about what happened on this ship. Do you understand, Robin?"

Once again, the boy nodded. Bainbridge motioned the sailor over and instructed him to take care of the boy.

No sooner had they taken care of that business, than another sailor alerted them to the discovery of two more survivors. They had just hauled the two men on board. Apparently, the men had tied lifelines about their waists and hidden over the side of the ship.

Both were battered, bloody and waterlogged from being dragged along by the ship. The vessel was in sore need of careening with barnacles visible almost a foot above the waterline. One of the men was unconscious. The other crouched on his knees on the deck heaving out seawater. Clearly both had lacked the strength to climb back aboard once it was safe.

Bainbridge ordered them taken to sickbay to have their wounds dressed. He and Perkins decided that the ship would be towed to harbor and sold. It wasn't really worth the effort, in his opinion, but it would serve as evidence for the report he would prepare for old Brumble.

The unconscious sailor never woke up. He died within a couple hours of being rescued and was buried at sea along with the slaughtered crew of the derelict ship. The other man lay sick with fever, but the physician held the opinion he should recover with a couple of days of rest and food.

That left Bainbridge with only the boy, Robin, to question about what had happened. He had the boy brought to the captain's cabin.

"Ah, Mr. Jones. I see your arm has been properly set."

"Yes sir. Thank you, Captain Bainbridge."

"Now that you've had time to calm down and been fed, perhaps you can tell me what happened aboard your ship."

Robin paled visibly. The nightmare he had witnessed was still all too fresh in his memory. Still, the Captain had been kind and was treating him like a man rather than a child. He shook himself and began to give his tale of horror.

"About two days ago, a strange ship began approaching us. Captain Hermosa ran up the special signal flags, because he was expecting to meet up with another vessel for some private business. The captain was very put out that this ship was so far ahead of schedule and not where he was expecting them."

"The other ship didn't run up any kind of signal in answer but kept sailing toward us. The captain said to keep our flags up, so it wouldn't look strange to the other ship. He figured they were a merchant or a packet probably wanting news."

"The winds shifted, and they didn't reach us until sundown. They hailed us and got leave to send a boarding party. There were four of them; three men and a woman. I think one of the men was the captain."

Bainbridge interrupted him, "Can you tell me what the captain looked like?"

Robin blinked at him. Try as he might, he couldn't seem to fix an image in his mind of any of the three men. Finally, he shook his head. "No sir. I can't remember his face. I remember the woman, though. She was very pretty, and I think she was rich."

"Why is that Mr. Jones?"

The boy fidgeted and blushed. "I know it's not right and proper for someone like me to even look at someone like her. She was a lady. She didn't wear rich clothes or lots of jewels, but she acted and moved like she was a queen or something. Even Captain Hermosa acted like she was. He was all proper and polite, nothing like he was around women in port."

Bainbridge nodded encouragement to him to continue. He understood how the boy's captain's behavior could lead to that assumption. "And then what happened?"

"Well, they went to the captain's cabin and talked while I waited on them. The lady didn't eat or drink anything."

"Do you know what they spoke about?"

"No sir. They were talking in a language with lots of sounds in it like one of the ship's cats with a hairball. The only part of what they said that I understood was the name, Viktor Brandewyne. The lady seemed very intent about that. Why would a lady want to know about such a vicious pirate?"

"I would like to know that myself, Mr. Jones. Hopefully, your shipmate will have some answers, when he recovers some. Now, what happened next?"

Robin hugged himself. "Things went real bad, Captain Bainbridge. The lady got mad at what Captain Hermosa told her. Her voice got so cold I swear I could see my breath. Her face changed, too. She was still beautiful, but she looked evil. Her teeth got sharp and long. Before I could even think to stop her, she lunged at Captain Hermosa and tore his throat out with those teeth. Then she drank the blood, making horrible slurping, sucking sounds."

"When she was finished, the captain was dead. One of the men chopped his head off. I grabbed a knife to defend myself. She laughed at me with her bloody mouth and glowing eyes. It scared me so bad, I wet myself. She said something to the men with her, and they laughed. Then they all left the cabin. I locked myself in the cabinet, in case she came back. I heard the crew fighting and screaming for a while, then I didn't hear anything after that."

By the time he'd finished his account, Robin was crouched on the deck, rocking back and forth, hugging his knees to his chest with his good arm.

Bainbridge retrieved a blanket and wrapped it around the boy's shoulders. He had a hard time believing the lad's story, but he could see the lad believed it. Some people just couldn't handle the horror of battle and bloodshed. It was probably easier for the boy to believe some unholy demon had murdered his ship's crew than to believe that men could slaughter each other over an argument.

He hoped the rescued sailor would have a more coherent account of what had taken place on the derelict ship.

A rap came at Bainbridge's door. "Captain?"

"What is it?"

A sailor poked his head in the door. "The doc sent me to ask you to come to the infirmary, Cap'n. The man we pulled up is asking for you."

"He's coherent?"

"Aye."

"I'll be right there."

The ship's doctor gave Bainbridge an indifferent frown when he reached the infirmary. "Sorry to bother you, Captain. I told him he needed to rest, even tried to give him a sleeping draught, but he insisted he had to talk to you first."

"It's all right, Roger." He clapped the man on the shoulder. "I would like to get his version of events, before his fever gets worse and while it's still fresh in his mind."

"Very well." He led him over to the bunk. "Captain Bainbridge, allow me to introduce Samuel Warren." He brought over a stool and left the two men alone.

Taking the seat, Bainbridge looked at the rescued sailor. "So, Mr. Warren, what was so urgent?"

Warren coughed and clutched the blanket the doctor had given him. "They told me the boy is the only other survivor."

"Aye. The other man pulled up with you died not long after being brought aboard."

"Check the boy for bite marks, not rat bites, human bites but with two punctures like from a couple of small nails."

"What are you talking about, man?"

"If that devil-bitch or the blood-sucking bastard with her bit the boy, he can't be trusted. I first heard about that kind of demon years ago, when I was starting out as a powder monkey under a German captain. They're evil creatures of darkness, and there's some kind of venom in their bite that will make a slave of even the strongest man."

"I will bear that in mind," he assured the sick man. He was of the opinion that the man had swallowed too much sea water, but he kept it to himself. "Can you tell me what happened aboard your ship?"

"Aye. I was second mate. We foolishly let the bitch and her companions aboard, even after Captain Hermosa determined they weren't the ship we were supposed to meet up with, greedy bastard. He thought to hold them ransom, as if the primary trade mission wouldn't be enough."

"You mean the emeralds?" Bainbridge interrupted.

Warren narrowed his eyes at the man. "Who told you about those? It couldn't have been the boy. He didn't know."

"We were the ship you were supposed to rendezvous with."

"Oh. Well, anyway, I wasn't able to follow the whole exchange, since my German is rusty, and I didn't recognize the dialect, but they were asking about Viktor Brandewyne. The female seemed irritated when Hermosa told her Brandee was dead by all reports. Now that I know what she is, what she said makes sense."

"Why? What did she say?"

"She said, 'I know he's dead. What I want to know is where he is now.'"

Bainbridge took a while to digest that bit of information. He was starting to develop a theory about what had befallen his employer's smuggling operation. If he was right, it would exonerate both Zachary and himself.

"So, this woman was looking for a notorious pirate."

"Aye. The bitch turned real nasty when Hermosa told her he was probably at the bottom of the ocean. She flew into a rage and tore his throat out. I tried to pull her off, but she threw me through the cabin door. One of the men with her attacked the first mate. I ran to warn the crew. I had barely rung the bell once, when that she-demon and her companions boiled up on deck. She and the other demon were soaked from chin down in blood. The other two were spotless, but armed. The blood suckers cut through the crew with a speed like I'd never seen before. Only a few of us had time to tie lifelines on and go over the side."

"We only found two of you attached to lifelines," Bainbridge pointed out.

"Aye. Barnes and Stockard didn't tie their knots tight enough. They held on as long as they could, but the seas got rough just before dawn and they were washed loose," Warren answered. "About that time, a thick fog came up. It muffled sound and sight. A shadow passed us and pulled away. I think it was our attackers' ship. The fog seemed to last forever, yet it vanished just as quickly as it came up. I tried to pull myself back up, but the ship was moving too fast, and I just didn't have the strength left in me."

Bainbridge nodded, giving the man a sympathetic smile. "Understandable, Mr. Warren. Your information has been very helpful. I will have the boy checked for the type of bite you described," he added to placate the man. "Now sir, I suggest you cooperate with the good doctor and take that sleeping draught."

He nodded to the physician as he left the infirmary.

Chapter 19

Celine's shop was shut up tight, when they arrived back in New Orleans. This proved mildly puzzling and more than a little irritating to the pirates. Obviously, the worst of the storm hit the swamps and spared the city, for the most part.

Hezekiah rapped at the door and pulled the chain for the bell to alert those in the apartments above. There was no answer. He rapped harder. Still, no answer came.

"Maybe they fled to a safer place for shelter," he guessed.

Viktor shook his head. "No, they are all still here, but not entertaining clients. They are hiding."

"How...?" Jon-Jon, who was carrying René, started to ask.

"I can smell them, Mr. Jon. There are five women in the upper apartments, no men. I also smell fear."

Belladonna, relieved her full powers had returned, noticed something else odd. "Whatever it is that they're hiding from isn't human. I sense several wards on all the windows and doors."

Vik frowned, sniffing the air. "The magic feels weak to me. The place reeks of garlic, though. I don't think the wards will affect any of us. Will they?" he asked Belle.

The siren confirmed his supposition, "They shouldn't. They seem to be targeted at vampires."

"If they are targeting vampires, then why did you say they shouldn't affect us? Have you forgotten what I am, pet?"

"Never. But you have proven immune, so far, to every weakness of regular vampires. Why should this be any different?" she pointed out.

Mentally, he shot back along the link they shared, *"I am not immune to your blood, pet. Are you absolutely positive that this seemingly innocuous warding will not strike me down, as well?"* Even in front of his first and second mates he was determined not to voice that weakness aloud.

Catching the hint, she thought back at him, *"If the wards work on you, they will only prevent you from entering. They won't actually harm you."*

Not in the mood for games, Viktor decided to put an end to their waiting. "Celine Thibideaux, I know you're in there. Open up and let us in," he demanded.

A female voice answered from behind the shutters of the second floor, "Go away, *m'sieur*. We are closed for the night. Come back in the morning."

"By morning, your brother will be dead. He needs care now. Besides, who ever heard of a brothel that closed at night?"

"My brother is already dead. He was caught out in the storm. Go away."

"I don't have time for this," Vik growled. "We're coming in, whether you open the door or not, Celine." With that, he kicked the heavy oak door completely off its hinges. They heard the sound of shattered glass, as it crashed into the shelves on the opposite wall inside the shop.

Viktor felt a mild tingle as he crossed the threshold. It reminded him vaguely of the feeling when circulation returns to a hand or foot that has gone to sleep. He heard frightened whispers and cursing. The sound of footsteps running down the back stairs soon reached his ears. A few moments later, Celine appeared in the doorway brandishing both a crucifix and a pagan charm. She froze in place, as she recognized the intruders.

"You. You have been back to see Granny again," she breathed.

"Aye, but I don't think the title 'granny' suits her anymore. Just ask your brother." He drew her attention to the young man that Jon-Jon carried.

"René? He is alive? What happened to him?" she cried, running to check on her brother.

"Barely alive," Jon-Jon answered. "Gloribeau got ahold of him, poor bugger. Where do ye want me to put him?"

There were questions showing in her eyes, but she kept her wits about her. Her brother needed tending. The questions could wait, but she gave Viktor a glare that left no doubt she was determined to get answers.

"The big room on the third floor," she replied curtly. "It is best suited for tending to what needs to be done for him. You know the room, Big Jon."

He nodded and carried René upstairs. Celine motioned for the others to follow. "Come with me. It is no longer safe here. I don't have time to repair the ward on the door right now. The inner wards will have to do. I have to talk with you, Captain Brandee, once I've gotten René settled in."

After about a half hour, Celine joined the pirates in her second-floor salon. Viktor had toyed with the idea of leaving to hunt, but he wanted answers that would be easiest gotten from the Creole beauty.

She noticed that the vampire was watching her with a predatory posture. He was ensconced in the plushest chair in the room, leaning back and appearing relaxed. But she had enough experience in her profession to read the subtle cues of his body language. Her connection to Gloribeau and recent events in the port city had kept her psychically on guard, as well. The look he was giving her made her feel like prey. The sensation terrified her yet, on some deep level, it also thrilled her.

To calm herself, she clutched the pagan amulet in her pocket tightly and prayed she lived through the night. For safety's sake, she would play gracious hostess to these home invaders. They had returned her wayward brother, after all.

"May I offer you something to eat or drink?" She forced a smile.

Belladonna shook her head. Grimm and Jon-Jon nodded. "Some of Melina's cooking would be appreciated," the second mate told her.

Celine's smile faltered a bit. "Melina is gone. Perhaps I could have Suzette heat up the gumbo."

"That'd be fine with me. What about you, Mr. Grimm?"

"I have no objections. Some rum would be good, too." Unlike Jon-Jon, he noticed the reaction to the missing girl's name. But he was only mildly curious.

Celine clapped her hands, signaling a younger girl. She gave her instructions then turned to Viktor, before sending her off. "Was there anything you wanted, Captain Brandewyne?"

The entire time, his eyes had never left her form. Currently, his senses were very acute. He could smell her fear and found it intoxicating. His Hunger was growing, but he didn't want to feed from her. He still needed Gloribeau's help, and it wouldn't be good to do damage to one of the Sister's minions.

"I will hunt later."

Celine relaxed just a tiny bit, her fear lessening. He wasn't going to attack her. She sent the girl to the kitchen and returned her attention to the pirates.

"You are not like other vampires, Captain Brandewyne."

"No, I am not. I thought we had already established that fact."

She nodded. "I should have realized that the wards would not be effective against you. I remember that you wield the Elder's Stone."

He didn't move, but his green eyes emitted a faint glow, and a dangerously calm tone colored his voice. "Were you trying to ward against me, *Madame* Thibideaux?"

"No," she answered honestly. "I did not expect you to return so soon."

"Then who or what were you trying to keep out?" Belladonna demanded.

Without taking her eyes from the seated vampire, she answered the siren. "Shortly after your departure, my business dropped off drastically. Something was killing off customers, at first after they left, but increasingly before they could get in. The attacks were always at night. I suspected the source of the attacks, but it was not confirmed until shortly before the storm came through."

"Vampires." Viktor made it a statement rather than a question.

"*Oui*. Something or someone has stirred up the nest. It has hurt business all over the Quarter and around the docks. Oddly, the only place outside of these areas similarly plagued has been Angelique's."

"That would explain why the streets seemed so deserted. Tell me, Celine, how were you able to verify that the attacks were by vampires?" he asked.

She hugged herself, taking her eyes off Viktor, seeming to look inward at some haunting memory. "Four nights ago, one of Melina's regular clients showed up. I was finishing up with one myself, or I would have caught the warning signs and forbidden him entry. She was always too trusting."

"Warning signs?"

"He didn't come straight into the shop. Instead, he stayed outside by the bell and called out to her. The man was frequent here and usually just came right up without knocking, ringing or even announcing he was coming in. Both Melina and I had chided him often about his rudeness. But this time he called out, and when she answered from the window, he asked her if he could come in – and she invited him up." A single tear escaped to slide down her cheek.

Viktor raised an eyebrow. "Odd, becoming a vampire didn't change my behavior or that of my cadre."

That clearly confused Celine. "You mean you first entered my shop without an invitation? I thought Willoby Jon asked you in."

"I have always gone where I wanted to. I require no invitation."

"And your cadre? They can enter a dwelling uninvited as well?"

He could smell her fear returning. "In truth, I do not know. I've never let them off the ship except in battle. Was Melina the only victim?"

She nodded her head. "I heard the scream and used my juju to drive the creature out. He was newly turned and not fully in command of his powers or his Hunger. Melina's throat was torn wide. She died in my arms. I set the wards to prevent the bastard from returning, since she would not be able to revoke her invitation." Her voice grew softer as she relived something she could never un-see or undo. "After she died, I cut off her head and cut out her heart. I burned the heart in the fireplace and had René take the ashes with him into the swamp."

Viktor nodded his approval and understanding. Too many vampires concentrated in one area could decimate whole communities within days, he imagined. He admired her fortitude and ability to do what was necessary to keep the dead prostitute from rising as undead, although the removal and burning of the heart seemed to be overly cautious.

He noticed that a spot near his side was growing cooler. Cursing under his breath, he took the tobacco pouch from his belt and opened it. The amount inside looked dangerously low. He needed to find some more tinder, if he wanted to keep the ember alive long enough to return it to Gloribeau.

He had to open his shirt to get at the ember and the conch shell containing it. The shell had slipped around almost behind him. He emptied the ashes of the old tinder into a nearby spittoon, then, he put what tinder he had left around the ember being sure to pack it loose enough to let air get to it. The shell grew warm again, so he put it back inside his shirt.

It was only then that he realized Celine and Belladonna were watching him with almost identical expressions of hunger and fascination. The girl, Suzette, had returned with food and would have been staring as well if Jon-Jon hadn't deliberately placed himself between them, blocking her line of sight. He'd learned long ago to take such precautions. A young serving wench had given him a lapful of hot mulled ale once, because she'd been staring at the Captain.

Viktor smiled a little smile. Even if he hadn't seen the looks on their faces, their scents told him he could have either of them at that moment. He'd almost wager he could have both at once, if he wasn't so sure the siren would not willingly share his favors with another female.

Celine found herself suddenly drawn to the vampire. She plunged her hand into her pocket and clasped the talisman. Its magic soothed her, yet she still felt her lust growing. Maybe there was some truth to all the rumors she had heard over the years about the pirate's prowess in bed. Stories like that, in her experience, were usually just bluster and braggadocio. Seeing the unconscious grace of his movements and the masculine beauty of his muscular chest and stomach, she was itching to test the stories for herself.

She also remembered the kiss.

Emboldened, she approached him, using all her skills to make her every move seductive. Grimm elbowed Jon-Jon and nodded with a wry smile to the Creole madam's behavior.

"Looks like you're going to be losing Celine's business to the Captain."

"Aye," Jon-Jon sighed, shrugged then leered down at Suzette. "But I'm sure this lovely lass will more than compensate for my loss." The girl giggled as the large pirate caressed her thigh.

Viktor looked up smugly at the woman standing almost over him. "Was there something you wanted, *Madame* Thibideaux?"

She lifted her skirts enough to straddle his knees, placed her hands on the arms of the chair and leaned down, making sure he had a good view of her cleavage. Her voice held a dark, honeyed laughter. "Wasn't there a wager you needed to settle with your Mr. Jon?"

He raised his hand, but rather than grabbing her breast, as she had expected, he tucked a strand of her hair behind her ear. Then he trailed fingertips down her cheek, brushing his thumb lightly across her lower lip. "I do believe there was, pet." He smiled. "What say you, Mr. Jon? Do you think you'll still be up to taking on Angelique after that slip of a girl gets through with you?"

"I'll just be warmed up by then, Cap'n." The pirate grinned.

Belladonna stood abruptly and stalked toward the door. It was Grimm, not Viktor who asked, "Where are you going, Belle?"

The siren's eyes flashed amber with barely suppressed emotion. "Out."

"I can't let you do that, lass. The Captain would never forgive me if I let something happen to you."

"I don't need your protection, Mr. Grimm. I am not some fragile human female. Any vampire foolish enough to attack me will find out just how deadly I can be."

"Let her go, Hezekiah. Belle can take care of herself," Vik ordered. "I imagine she needs to go hunt, anyway."

Belle shot him a look that was both angry and hurt. He always seemed to elicit warring, almost human emotions from her. She wanted to stay with him, but she really didn't want to listen to him bed another. He was right, too; she was nearly ravenous from her weak spell back in the swamp. She wouldn't survive another trip back in, if she didn't feed soon.

Without a word, she turned and left.

Tamara A. Lowery

Chapter 20

The next morning Viktor left an exhausted Celine's bed. Grimm met him in the hall outside her room looking like he hadn't gotten much sleep. His clothes looked like they'd been thrown back on in haste, and his hair was unkempt.

"You look like hell this morning, Hezekiah. How many girls did you go through last night?" He teased his first mate, knowing how fastidious the man usually was, when there were facilities to take advantage of.

"Just the one, Vik. I know you don't sleep, but damn, it's obscene how not tired you look. Maybe I'm getting old."

"Never. How come you didn't groom, man?"

"Finally heard things get quiet in there and figured you must be stirring. I wanted to be ready, Captain."

Viktor had to admire the man's loyalty. "Go clean up, Mr. Grimm." He clapped him on the shoulder. "I'll roust Jon-Jon. I want to visit Angelique's and settle this bet. I'm also curious to see how much attention the local vampires have been paying to her place."

"Aye, Captain." Grimm gratefully returned to his room for a wash and a shave.

Approaching Angelique's, they noticed dense black smoke billowing up from the direction they were headed. As they got closer, the streets got more crowded. They found themselves having to force their way through in places.

"I don't like this, Vik," Grimm muttered.

"Nor do I." Viktor grabbed a man near him and demanded, "What has happened?"

The man shook his head, "Haven't been able to get close enough to see. They say one of those fancy houses burned down."

"Aye," another passerby added with a nod. "One that'll be missed by many with gold to jingle. Just came from there. It was the finest whorehouse in New Orleans."

"Angelique's?" Grimm asked.

The stranger nodded. "That'd be the one."

Viktor began plowing through the crowd, Grimm and Jon-Jon following in his wake. Suddenly the crowd seemed easier to pass through, even though it had grown denser. Men were instinctively getting out of the vampire's way. Before long, they reached the site.

Several men formed a bucket line. But rather than trying to douse the blazing remains of the main house, they instead wetted down the outbuildings and the nearest houses. In fact, it looked like the neighbors' houses had been protected longer than the fire could have been burning.

The three stood staring at the destruction of an establishment which had served some of the most powerful and wealthiest men in southern Louisiana.

"Damn," Jon-Jon whispered. "I'll forfeit the wager, Cap'n."

"That won't be necessary, Mr. Jon," Viktor answered, not even looking at him. "She's not here. From the smell, though, not all of the girls made it out." Without another word, he turned and led them away from the scene.

Watchful eyes from a rooftop a safe distance from the light of the fire were the only ones that took notice of the raven coalescing from the smoke and gliding over to fly ahead of the three pirates. Noting the direction they went, the watcher ducked back inside the attic access to alert his masters.

The two pirates were unsure of their captain's destination, but they recognized his mood. This day was not going to end well for some unlucky soul. Although he would never admit a need of it, they were going to make sure they had his back.

Viktor forged ahead, Lazarus circling over his head, and kept his attention focused on some point straight ahead. Grimm and Jon-Jon walked fast to keep up, but they kept a watchful eye on their surroundings. They drew a few glances from passersby, but no more than were normal in most ports they visited.

That they were able to keep from barreling into him, when he stopped without a warning, was a testament to the battle readiness their years of piracy had given them. They found where they stopped puzzling, however.

"A boneyard, Captain?" Grimm had to ask.

"She's here somewhere, hiding. Lazarus, seek."

Obediently, the raven flew out among the crypts. Viktor closed his eyes, searching the necropolis through his familiar's eyes. Finally, he *saw* what he was looking for. "He's found her." he smiled. It was not a pleasant smile.

With inhuman speed, he ran through the graveyard until he came to an ancient, weathered crypt that for some reason sported an obviously new door. Lazarus perched above the crypt, still in his raven form. He watched Viktor with shiny black eyes, awaiting further orders.

"Go lead Hezekiah and Jon-Jon here. You've done well, old friend."

The bird cawed once and flapped off to find his shipmates.

Not waiting for them to arrive, he tested the door of the crypt. It moved a bit but seemed to be latched from the inside. With a sigh, Viktor ran his hand through his hair and retrieved the dagger he kept sheathed at the nape of his neck. Sliding the narrow blade between the door and the stone, he located the hasp and adroitly worked it up and off the latch. Once he accomplished this, the door swung freely open.

Rather than the expected ledges and coffins inside, he saw another door a few feet inside the entrance to the crypt. It confirmed what the inner hasp and latch had already told him. Vampires.

Why else would a crypt be locked from the inside?

Closing the outer door most of the way first, he slowly opened the inner door. At first glance, the burial chamber seemed completely quiet and lifeless. Mostly empty ledges lined the crypt walls. Only a couple held old, nearly decrepit coffin. One had partially rotted away to reveal a skeletal hand and forearm. A slight skittering sound in the corner betrayed a rat. He knew Angelique was in here. He could sense her because of the bite he'd given her. He could even smell her. He was about to open the other coffin, when the rat scurried again, slipping through a narrow space under the blank back wall.

He recalled the aerial image he'd gotten from Lazarus of the crypt. Even with the space taken by the false entrance, this chamber should have been longer. The question now was if he could find a way past that back wall to the remainder of the crypt, or was there a separate entrance from the other end? He doubted the latter. Why go to the trouble to make this side so hard to get into from the outside?

Examining the wall revealed no seams or any pivot point. He stumbled a bit on the second pass. Looking down, he could just make out an uneven stone in the floor that was slightly smoother along one edge, as if from frequent handling. Testing it, he found his fingers just fit between it and the flagstone next to it. Hidden out of sight beneath it was a hand hold carved out of the side.

He lifted the stone with some effort, enough in fact, to tell him it would be very difficult for an ordinary man to move without tools. The hole beneath held a ladder leading down into darkness.

"Captain?" Grimm and Jon-Jon had finally arrived at the crypt.

Viktor used his inhuman speed to exit the crypt before either man could enter. Some instinct told him that the less they knew about the interior, the better it would be. Danger was a daily part of their lives as pirates, but he was not one to needlessly endanger any of his crew.

"Stand guard out here. If anyone approaches, send Lazarus," he ordered. "On no account enter this crypt. This is something I must do alone."

He encountered icy cold water before he reached the bottom of the ladder. Thankfully it only came about two feet up his legs once his feet found the floor. The near total darkness rendered even his enhanced vision useless. He thought about going back up for a torch or lantern but didn't really want to take the time. He sensed and heard no current in the water, so fear of a blind drop didn't seem likely. Still, he decided to tread carefully just in case of a flooded pit. Using his hands, he discovered a passageway before him with a low ceiling, forcing him to stoop.

A short way into it, he ran into a dead end. This began to get seriously annoying. It would help if he'd brought a light. He ran his hands over every surface, searching for some sort of latch. He found nothing.

He grew increasingly irritated. The water covered his boot tops, soaking the footwear through and making them squishy. He found the space cramped for his six-foot-three frame. His Hunger began rising. Angelique's nearby scent was maddening. The conch and ember seared his side, and an itchy warmth grew around his neck and upper chest.

The last reached an almost intolerable level and distracted him from his efforts to find a way to continue. Reaching his hand in his collar to scratch, he snagged on a familiar silver chain. He pulled it out, and the burn and itch immediately ceased. The milky crystal pendant hanging from it flared to life with an almost blinding glow.

With a disgusted sigh, he realized he had his light. Somewhere in the back of his mind he could picture the damned old wizard sitting by his fire and laughing at him.

Allowing his eyes to adjust, he then held the glowing crystal up to examine the three walls around him. Still there was no latch to be found. Looking up, however, revealed a narrow space between the ceiling and the dead end. Looking down, the water merely reflected the light back at him.

On a hunch, he bent down and plunged the crystal beneath the surface. There, at the bottom of the end wall, he saw hand holds notched into the stone.

The stone door slid up into the ceiling with amazing ease and quite silently. He guessed it must be on a counterweight system.

On the other side, the passage continued a few feet then took a sharp turn. Now he faced a new dilemma. Straight ahead he spied a stairway.

Another turn at the base of it led off in yet another direction. His nose told him to go up the stairs, although the other passageway teased his curiosity.

Once at the top of the stairs, he realized he stood in the other half of the crypt, behind the false wall. He put the crystal away. Several sconces of candles lit the chamber, blackening the ceiling with soot. Four well-appointed coffins sat on raised platforms. A multitude of pillows and cushions were piled in one of the corners.

Sleeping or unconscious on the cushions lay three women and two men, Angelique among them.

None of them stirred when Viktor approached. Unexpectedly, he actually felt relieved that she appeared to be unharmed. This emotion warred with a flare of possessive anger at finding her in situ with these others. He recognized the women as a couple of her girls. He had no idea who the men were. The one thing he was sure of at the moment was that he wanted Angelique out of that nest.

In answer to his unspoken command, the madam sat up and crawled over to him. She then curled back up at his feet. Raising an eyebrow, he squatted down and gently rolled her over. This action rewarded him with a soft snore. He realized she had never woken.

Testing his hold on her, he silently willed her to stand up. With a slight whimper, her body obeyed. Still asleep, she swayed a bit. He toyed with the idea of walking her out but didn't think she looked steady enough. He didn't want to rouse the others. None of them had stirred when she'd left them.

Scooping her up, he carried her back down the stairs. Making his way through the corridor, he realized he wasn't going to be able to shut the false wall behind him. He wasn't too concerned about it, though. The vampires he'd scented were in their coffins and dead to the world. The humans were apparently in some kind of stupor and wouldn't be aware he'd even been there.

The ladder back up into the crypt was going to be a problem, however. The hole was too narrow to carry her up draped over his shoulder. He was going to have to wake her up.

Placing a hand over her mouth as a precaution, he willed her awake. It took a bit more force of will than he expected, irritating him with whichever vampire had bespelled her. He was glad he took the precaution with his hand. Once she came fully awake, Angelique let out a muffled shriek.

"Hush, pet. We don't want to wake the others."

She rolled wild, frightened eyes up to his face. The fear melted away to relief, as she recognized him. She nodded her understanding when he pointed at the ladder then up.

Once they were back up in the front of the crypt, he slid the flagstone back in place, concealing the entrance to the vampires' lair. Then he pulled the crystal back out. Its glow wasn't as bright as before, but it was adequate for his purpose.

Rather than wasting time arguing the whys and wherefores, he willed her to stand spread eagle. He then used the glow of the crystal to inspect every nook and crevice of her body. She wore one of her sheerest negligees, which made the task easier.

"What are you looking for, *mon amor*?" Angelique asked nervously. The pirate captain's odd behavior and their surroundings made her very uncomfortable.

"Looking to see if any of them bit you. Why did they bring you here? Which one of them bespelled you? Did you fuck any of them?" That last question betrayed an underlying fury.

Angelique had been her own madam for several years and took offence at his tone and treatment of her. "No one has bitten me but you, Viktor Brandewyne. They said they brought me here to supervise a couple of my girls for a private party, which was in a much nicer place than this dank crypt, even if the décor was a bit odd. I don't know why you had me in those horrid tunnels or brought me here."

She got on tiptoe, having been released from his hold for the moment, and tried to stare him down in her own fury. "As for whether or not I fucked any of them, as you so crudely put it, that is my business and not yours. I bed whoever I wish, provided they pay my price. You do not own me!"

Viktor grinned, admiring her fire. "Actually, pet, yes, I do." He clasped her to him, lifting some, and kissed her thoroughly. Both his Hunger and his lust fired, as she wrapped herself around him, her body surrendering to his touch.

Finally breaking from the kiss, she threw her head back with a soft moan. "Not here, *mon amor, sil vous plait*, take me back home to my *boudoir*."

That put a damper on his ardor and returned his cold, deadly anger. "I cannot do that, pet. Your home no longer exists."

She blinked at him in confusion. "What do you mean?"

"It was burned this morning. Some of your household may not have escaped," he said bluntly. "No other structures were damaged however, which makes me suspect it was burned deliberately. Do you know who may have planned it?"

Angelique continued to cling to him out of shock. "I didn't think he'd go through with it."

"Who?" The demand held steel that would not be denied.

"Bishop DePardeaux. He saw the bite scar during his monthly visit and demanded that I have it cleansed. When I refused, he swore he would see my house purged of this 'evil infestation,' as he called it."

At last, Viktor had a target for his rage – and Hunger.

Outside, he bade Grimm to loan his coat to the madam. She was small enough, in comparison to the first mate, that the garment covered her nearly to her ankles.

"Not that I don't appreciate the view, pet." Vik smiled. "But you would draw too much attention on the street in that gown. I don't think it's wise to let any of the bishop's minions know you still live. Mr. Jon, take her back to Celine's. She should be safe there from both the bishop and any other vampires."

He gently held her chin, capturing her mind with his eyes. "Forget your grief for your girls for now, pet, and under no circumstance invite anyone into Celine's home. You will be a proper and polite guest there. Your life may depend on her mercy and hospitality."

"I will behave *mon cher*."

"Also, I have an outstanding wager with Mr. Jon, which you can help settle. I want you to give him your best performance ever."

She looked over at the towering pirate, who'd been assigned to escort her. "It's not like you to share, cher. It must be a very expensive wager. I love a challenge." Her smile was at its most seductive.

"More so to me than to the Cap'n." Jon-Jon eyed her greedily. "A keg of rum and his black velvet coat against two kegs and one dozen beignets from Marie's that Celine is just as skilled as you are."

Angelique threaded her hand around his arm and chuckled throatily. "I hate to inform you, Mr. Jon, but you are going to lose your bet. I'm much better."

"If that's true, it'll be worth it."

☠

Grimm stood, leaning against the front of the crypt, arms crossed, giving Viktor a knowing look. A half-smile tugged at the corner of his mouth.

"What is it, Hezekiah?" The vampire grew irritated with the scrutiny.

"I know you, Vik." He pushed off from the wall. "Are you sure you wouldn't just be stirring up a hornet's nest going after a bishop?"

"Possibly. Probably not, though. I imagine there are at least three priests just waiting for the bastard to die, so one of them can step into the position," he said with a shrug. "Go back to the ship, Hezekiah."

"Vik?"

He fixed his first mate with a hard stare that brooked no argument. "Belle is hungry and doing her damnedest to block me out. I don't trust her not to feed on the crew."

"Aye, Captain." Grimm understood the reasoning, even though he didn't like leaving Viktor without backup. As he turned to go, he gave a parting shot. "Remember to keep the coal alive."

Viktor rolled his eyes and laughed, "Yes, mother."

Bishop DePardeaux had just finished attending to his morning business. Having been up most of the night, he'd called the parish priests to meeting early, to get it out of the way. He'd also made arrangements for a substitute to deliver the evening Mass.

Now, as soon as his meal was brought in, he could be left alone and catch up on his rest. It was too bad about Angelique. Over the years, she was the best whore he'd ever used, but he counted himself lucky to be free of her taint. He couldn't believe that she would willingly consort with the unholy demons who infested this city.

At least the fire should have freed her soul of the bloodsuckers' foul influence.

A knock at the door announced the arrival of his food. "Come in."

The sight of a tall stranger carrying the tray rather than one of the neophyte priests surprised him greatly.

"Who are you? What is the meaning of this?"

The stranger set the tray down. "The name's Vik Brandee." He crossed the room with inhuman speed and grasped the bishop by the throat, lifting the shorter man up to eye level. "Angelique sends her regards."

The following morning, the cloister woke to blood-curdling screams. Rushing outside to find the source, the neophytes were horrified to see what was once a man bound to the cross atop the chapel roof, burning alive.

Chapter 21

To fight off despair, Zachary Brumble spent his time planning his escape. It helped keep boredom at bay, as well. No one on board spoke to him except his brother. Different pirates brought his morning rations every time, and none of them made any attempt to converse.

He finally, slowly started to accept what Thomas claimed had happened to him. Of all their family, only their sister readily accepted the existence of anything supernatural or spiritual, for that matter. Yet many times she seemed the most practical of the siblings and least subject to emotion-driven actions or decisions. In truth, it was mostly for her sake that he was determined to escape. He couldn't bear the thought of Samantha having to endure their father's company and temper alone.

Given the limited resources in his cabin and the fact that the feeding routine ruled out bribing one of the crew, he'd settled on a somewhat desperate plan. When his morning rations were delivered, he would use the chair to brain whichever pirate brought it. He'd not seen any others nearby through the door when food was brought and felt it worth the gamble. The view through his porthole let him know they were near shore, although he had no idea which shore. With my luck, he'd be able to make it up to deck and over the side.

The sun was coming up. He knew it was nearly time. Taking the chair, he readied himself behind the door, out of sight.

Voices came from outside the cabin, something he was not accustomed to.

"Where do you think you're going, lass?"

"In there."

"I don't think so. We're only to bring him food. His brother is the only one allowed to visit him."

"I'll take the food in. Don't worry, Stubby. I promise not to eat him."

"But…."

"Stubbins, the Captain didn't say I couldn't talk to the prisoner, did he?"

"Well, no. But…."

"So, it's all right, see?"

The door started opening. Zachary quickly amended his plan. Setting the chair down, he seated himself at the table. The most beautiful red head he'd ever seen brought the plate in and set it on the table. The fact that she dressed in men's clothing told him that she was either part of the crew or perhaps Brandee's bed wench. The pirate captain struck him as the kind of man who would allow himself such an indulgence.

As she set the cutlery down, he said, "Thank you."

"You're welcome."

He stood and offered her the chair, banking that she wasn't used to such consideration from any of the crew. "Please, join me. It's been some time since I've shared a meal with such a lovely lady."

Belladonna smiled demurely. This human would suit her purposes even better than she thought. His attempt at seducing amused her.

"No, thank you. I fed before returning to the ship. But I will keep you company."

Only briefly did he wonder about how she'd phrased her reply. Her exotic accent was unfamiliar to him. He thought it a safe bet she wasn't colonial. It was immaterial to the fact that he thought she would make a good hostage.

Snatching the fork from the table, he grabbed her hair and held the sharp tines to her throat. "Nothing personal, miss, but I need to get off this ship. Now." The last was directed to the pirate guard still in the corridor.

The man started laughing so hard he nearly doubled over. The red head even surprised him by remaining calm and unruffled.

"This is no joke," he snarled. "I will kill her, if you do not put me ashore."

"Mate, you'll be lucky if she doesn't kill you," the pirate chuckled. "Of course, if she doesn't, Cap'n Brandewyne probably will."

"You can go ahead and lock the door, Stubby. I'll be fine in here." Belle smiled. "I even promise not to damage Mr. Brumble, here."

Zachary pressed the tines hard enough into her flesh to draw blood. "Don't be foolish, miss. I will do what I have to do."

"Sorry, mate." Stubbins shook his head, as he closed the door. "You're on your own with that one." He clicked the lock in place.

Sniff haled Grimm when he boarded. "Yo, Mr. Grimm! Welcome back. Cap'n and Jon-Jon not with ye?"

"Ho, Sniff! No, they've still business ashore. Captain Brandee sent me to check on the crew. Belle ran off in a huff, and he doesn't want her to eat any of them."

The legless rigging rat lowered himself with a rope to hang at eye level with the first mate. "She came aboard at dawn and headed below. Not long after, Stubby came up from feeding the prisoner laughing so hard he wet himself. Didn't have anything better to do than sit up in the crow's nest teaching me dick to yodel, so I dropped down to hear the joke. Seems that fool Brumble tried to take the bitch hostage."

If the situation hadn't been so dire, Grimm would have laughed, himself. Viktor had always been particular about any prisoners he took, even when he was human. He preferred to decide how they were used or disposed of.

"That's one way to commit suicide," he sighed irritably. "I better get down there and see if I can salvage the situation. If either of them has damaged the other, the Captain will be damned angry."

The noises emanating from the prisoner's cabin made Grimm quicken his pace. It wasn't until he almost reached the door that he realized the sounds he heard was not that of them killing each other. The inarticulate cries spoke highly of the siren's skills. If he didn't know Vik would probably kill him for it, he was tempted to try her out himself.

He raised an eyebrow at Brumble's staying power. It was nearly midday. *"If they had started shortly after dawn...."*

Fishing out his own key for the lock on the door, he unlocked it then banged hard on the door before opening it, also.

"Go away, Hezekiah Grimm!" Belladonna snarled before he'd even gotten the door halfway open.

"Get dressed and get out, lass. It's going to be a job, as it is, to convince the Captain not to punish you – or not to kill him." He nodded to the man she currently straddled.

"Ha! What would he do to me?" She was defiant.

Grimm shrugged. "My suggestion would be to give you to Sniff for a week."

Belle stopped in mid-thrust and gave him a look that could curdle milk. "You would, too, you cold-blooded bastard."

He merely smirked evilly.

With a growl of frustration, she climbed off her willing victim. Zachary just lay there nearly spent for a few moments. At that minute, he didn't care if the pirate skewered him where he lay. He'd never been bedded by a woman like Belladonna, and he was sated and deeply in lust, if not love.

He actually sighed, as she finished getting dressed and started to push past Grimm. The first mate grabbed her arm to stop her. She glared at his hand. He ignored it and grasped her jaw, forcing her to bare her throat. Two tiny punctures crusted with dried blood marred the pale flesh.

"How did that happen?"

"Zach threatened me with a fork."

"Take a quick swim, lass." He loosened his grip and whispered low. "If Vik sees you marred, he will kill the man."

She nodded and left the cabin. Grimm looked over at the drowsy prisoner. Then he looked around at the cabin's furnishings. "No more cutlery for you, I think, Mr. Brumble. You'll just have to eat with your fingers. I'm going to have Mr. Murph send a lad down to secure that chair to the deck. Things have a tendency to shift about too much on this deck in high seas. Wouldn't want it banging about hurting someone."

Satisfied with his decisions, he left and locked the cabin once more.

"Bugger me," Zach grumbled at the locked door.

☠

The following morning, Grimm woke to find Lazarus sitting patiently outside his cabin door. He found the demon cat even more disquieting now that he knew who it used to be. Lazarus just stared up at him with golden eyes.

"Checking up on me, Jim?" He smiled, trying to mask his discomfort.

The cat cocked its head, then stood, twitched his tail and walked away. A few feet down the corridor, he stopped and looked back. Grimm hadn't moved. Lazarus stalked back to him, stretched one paw out and latched claws into his trouser leg. He gave a small tug and a little growl then retracted his claws and stalked off once again.

"I can't believe I'm taking orders from a cat," he muttered, following the creature.

They stopped in front of Belle's door. Grimm knocked. "Go away!" came from inside.

"She's mad at me as well as at the Captain," he told the cat. "Open up, lass. We're being summoned."

"Bugger off!"

Lazarus laid his ears back, growling low in his throat. The cat grew amorphous, drifting like vapor beneath the door. He must have rematerialized inside the cabin, because Grimm heard him yowling loudly and constantly from inside. The tactic worked. Within minutes, the siren yanked the door open and stomped through it.

"Shut up already!" she snapped at the cat.

"Come on, lass." Grimm fought not to chuckle. "I think Vik wants to see us."

"Meh," Lazarus confirmed.

Taking raven form once they returned to shore, Lazarus led them back to Celine's. Jon-Jon leaned in the doorway, smoking a cigar, waiting on them. He looked too relaxed for the Captain to be in a foul mood.

"Took long enough." He smirked. "Cap'n is in the parlor waitin' on ye." He pushed away from the door frame as they stepped up off the street.

"Where are you off to, then?" Grimm raised an eyebrow.

"To fetch some beignets."

"Lost your bet, then?"

Jon-Jon shrugged and grinned, "We both thought it a tie. Those wenches can definitely hold their own with each other. But ceding to the Cap'n gives me an excuse to sample Marie's sweets again."

Belle remembered a detail from the wager. "What about this Marie's father, and there's the matter of the rum you humans seem so fond of."

"Cap'n said we'll split the bet on the rum, and he may loan me the coat from time to time. I'm not worried about her father. Rumor among Celine's girls is he took ill a year ago and died."

With that, he swaggered off, humming to himself and enjoying his cigar.

The palpable hostility in the parlor caught Grimm off-guard after hearing Jon-Jon's report. Angelique and Celine occupied opposite sides of the room staring daggers at each other. Belladonna's entrance with the first mate merely augmented the animosity, making it tri pronged.

Viktor sat in the plushest chair in the room, his feet up on an ottoman, enjoying his own cigar and a snifter of brandy. He seemed impervious to the feminine ire.

"Good morning, Hezekiah." He greeted the pirate amiably. "Pour yourself some of this brandy. It's an excellent vintage."

Grimm fought the urge to cup himself as he walked between the women. Helping himself to an empty snifter and the decanter, he chose a seat a safe distance from all three of them.

"Morning, Viktor. I take it things went well with the bishop?"

"Indeed. We had a long conversation. He experienced Hell's fires here on earth this morning."

Celine rounded on him. "What did you do? Was it not enough you endangered my house by bringing her here?" She jabbed a finger toward Angelique.

"Quiet, woman," Viktor warned. "I made sure you are in no danger from any of his parishioners. As for what I did to him, let's just say I converted him then made sure he had a good vantage point from which to watch the sunrise."

"Where was that?" Grimm asked curiously. "Tied to the cross atop his favorite chapel."

Angelique looked at him, both pleased and frightened that he would go to such lengths for her. "Thank you, cher."

He waved a hand dismissively. "I protect what is mine."

"Well, aren't you magnanimous." Celine sneered, hands on her hips. "I still say you've endangered my house. I was up all night guarding my girls against the vampires that were sniffing after her!"

"You were in no danger, *Madame* Thibideaux. I ensured that Angel could not answer their call."

That did nothing to abate the Creole's fury. "I had to stuff their ears with cotton so they couldn't hear the creatures, *m'sieur*! I've already lost one girl to them; I will not lose another. Janine had to be tied to a chair and gagged to prevent her from inviting one in."

She stalked over and snarled down at him. "Perhaps you do not understand something about the vampires here in New Orleans, Captain Brandewyne. Most of them are very, very old, some over three hundred years old. They can be very persuasive. Even without seeing their eyes, just hearing their voice can bespell. My wards prevent the one that killed Melina from reentering or inviting others in, but that doesn't prevent the stronger, older ones from trying to seduce their way in."

Viktor set the snifter down and stubbed out the cigar but made no move to rise. Expressionless, he gazed up at his hostess. He could smell her fear and frustration as well as the anger overriding it all. That she was brave enough to face him without backing down, knowing who and what he was, spoke volumes. Just as he protected what was his, she was trying to protect what was hers.

He respected that.

As the vampire continued to stare up at her, motionless, Celine's anger began to lose its edge. The fact that he wasn't reacting unnerved her. Gradually, fear became her dominant emotion.

Just as she was about to back away, he sat up and grasped her hand faster than she could see. Although she couldn't suppress her involuntary gasp, she froze rather than tried to jerk free. She'd be damned if she was going to act like prey.

To her relief, Viktor made no move to attack. Gently, he kissed her hand and stood, still holding her hand. "Thank you for showing Angelique hospitality, *Madame* Thibideaux. I know the two of you are rivals, and you hold the advantage now that she has been burned out. I will take steps this evening to ensure that neither of you need fear the city's vampires. I also have a proposition for you both."

"What?" Celine's tone belied her mistrust.

He smiled. "A partnership. Rather than competing with each other, join forces and split the profits. You both have impressive client lists. If you're not forced to undercut each other to keep business, you can have more control over the fees for your services. There are, after all, very few other whores in the city that can hold a candle to either of you."

She blinked as he released her hand. The idea of a partnership had never occurred to her.

Looking over, she could see Angelique hadn't thought of it either. Both wondered if they could trust the other. From a business standpoint, it made good sense.

"Would you be willing to try it?" she asked her rival.

The blonde shrugged. "Why not? I have nothing further to lose."

Celine turned back to Viktor. "How do you propose to get the vampires to leave us and our business alone?"

"I suspect I am the reason you have been of interest to them. I intend to let them find me tonight. Then we can satisfy our mutual curiosity."

"Are you insane?" Belle nearly screamed. Grimm agreed with her, but he knew he could never get away with talking to his captain like that in front of others.

"Hardly, pet." He flashed a decidedly evil smile. "You are going to go hunting with me today and will accompany me tonight."

She crossed her arms, one eyebrow raised. "And why is that? You don't need my help to catch your prey. Nor do I care to meet any of the local vampires."

In a blink, he stood with one arm around her waist pressing her to him and his other hand buried in her hair. Her eyes dilated and her pulse quickened as her body reacted to his touch whether she willed it or no. She parted her lips expectantly as he leaned down toward them.

"I know. I need you to dispose of my leftovers. I am trying to make peace with the vampires, for now, not to antagonize them further. You are also my secret weapon. You can pass for human, so they will not find you threatening, but we both know what you are capable of," he whispered into her mouth.

"You have no idea what I am capable of, Viktor Brandewyne," she answered before rising to close that last gap between them.

Belladonna's mental barriers against him shattered during the kiss. Viktor growled, his grip tightening, as her thoughts and emotions became open to him.

To his surprise, he saw that she loved him. He also sensed her gratitude and pride that he was demonstratively choosing her over the two human females in front of them. Then he caught a glimpse of her recent activities aboard ship.

As if realizing she had revealed too much, Belle tried to start shutting him out again. He sent a psychic slap that made her wince and try to pull free. He wasn't having it, however. As he had done with Celine, he deliberately nicked his tongue, a much deeper wound this time since the siren's will was much stronger.

He held her immobile in his arms until she had no choice but to swallow the blood he forced into her mouth. Once she did, he released her.

She huddled in on herself, not daring to meet his eyes. "Who was she with, Mr. Grimm?"

Hezekiah didn't know how Viktor knew, but he answered truthfully. "I found her locked in with the prisoner. Had to threaten her with Sniff to get her off the lad.”

“Was he damaged?”

“No, although he may walk funny for a while. She’d been riding him most of the morning, yesterday.”

“I’ll decide what to do with Mr. Brumble after my business on this shore is complete. You, pet, are not to touch him again,” he warned.

She nodded her obedience. She would rather have been forced to spend time with that disgusting little lecherous troll than have this deeper bondage to the vampire’s will. That would have been temporary. This was much more permanent. Even though she loved him, at that moment she hated and feared him even more.

Chapter 22

They both fed well that day, but the siren found no pleasure in her meals. She preferred to eat in the water. Although she didn't mind her master's leftovers, she really would rather make her own kills. Stale fear just didn't compare to fresh, quivering flesh flavored with terror.

She did have to admit to herself that city and farm fed humans tasted much different from sailors. She just wasn't sure if she liked the difference.

It wasn't until after their third victim that afternoon that Viktor noticed her behavior. Her feeding was efficient, but mechanical.

"What is the problem, Belle?"

She glared at him. "You have to ask?"

"No. I could just let you pout, but I do not ask a question unless I expect an answer."

"You deny me what I crave! You forbid me to enjoy my food as I wish! You won't even let me take a lover, and you steal more and more of my freedom!" Her eyes reverted to their natural golden color with her frustration. "And then, you insult me by picking those human bitches over me! Why? Do I repulse you that much?" If she could've shed tears, she would have been sobbing at that point.

Without a word, he grabbed her wrist and started pulling her along. His grip was gentle, so she could pull free if she wanted to. She made no attempt to, although her silence spoke more of hopeless resignation than sullenness. Viktor sensed this and hoped he hadn't broken her completely. As much as it aggravated him, he had grown to look forward to her defiant and independent nature.

Casting about, he finally spotted what he was looking for. Grasping Belle about the waist, he flew them up to a secluded balcony over an alleyway. The shadows were long from the imminent sunset, and none of the traffic on the nearby street took any notice of them. It did take the siren by surprise, however.

Motioning for her to keep silent, he quietly opened the French doors to a bedroom adjacent to the balcony. Quickly checking inside to assure the room was empty, he pulled her in. He then locked the interior door and turned to face the confused siren.

Viktor let his lust show in his eyes, as he stalked toward her. It didn't take long for her to figure out his intent. She allowed him to back her up until the backs of her legs bumped against the edge of the bed. Her laugh sounded both nervous and anticipatory.

"There is nothing repulsive about you, pet." His voice carried heat, as he lowered her to the bed.

They had each other half-undressed, when a voice behind them broke the mood. "I see you like to play with your food."

Belladonna felt like screaming. If the intruders had been human, she would have, destroying their minds in the process.

Four vampires stood outside on the small balcony; among them the female Viktor had encountered before. He felt sure she was the one who led the others to him. She knew his scent.

The interruption displeased and frustrated him as much as it did Belle. His lust was up, and it took a supreme effort of will to both keep it from translating into rage and to hold the siren's temper in check. For the moment, he felt it best not to reveal that the siren was not food. If it came down to a fight, she and her toxic blood were his secret weapons.

Standing and re-dressing, he couldn't keep the irritation out of his smile. "I like to work up an appetite. Hello again, pet." He made direct eye contact with the one he recognized. She did not answer or flinch, but a slight, almost human tremor ran through her body. She feared him.

The knowledge increased his confidence, but he sensed he should proceed cautiously. The fact that she was trying to hide her fear from her companions told him that they could be forces to be reckoned with.

"I understand that you and yours have been seeking me."

A male, who looked to be younger than the female, answered him. "You have proven quite difficult to find. You made quite an impression on our Memnette, Mr. …?"

"Viktor Brandewyne, Captain." He made a flourishing bow and stepped out onto the balcony.

One of the other vampires raised an eyebrow. "I've heard of this one, master. There has been talk of a pirate known as Bloody Vik Brandee around the docks for a few years. Latest rumors were he'd been stricken from the lists as lost at sea, presumed dead."

"So, you are new to our ranks, and you obviously were not made here."

The statement intrigued Viktor. "How can you be so sure?"

The supposed teenager's power flared. It felt quite impressive, but Viktor was by no means cowed. He'd dealt with beings recently whose powers dwarfed this vampire's. He felt he was at least this one's equal.

"If you had been made here, you would know who I am."

"There is that," he conceded. "Which reminds me; you have yet to introduce yourself. It is the least courtesy you could do me, since you saw fit to interrupt my sport."

The vampire laughed, amused by the neophyte. "How rude of me; I am Jeorge, and I am the master of all Louisiana. No vampire is made inside my territory without my knowledge or my blessing. If this law is broken, there are severe repercussions for the fledgling and its maker. But you," he paced forward and circled Viktor, lips parted, scenting and tasting the air around him, "you do not taste of my kiss. None of my vampires made you."

Viktor held his temper at the scrutiny. It reminded him much of the way he sized up prisoners, but he reminded himself he wanted to make an ally of this vampire. He really didn't want to battle every time he visited New Orleans. Not that he minded a good fight every now and then, but it would make things tedious.

Jeorge cocked his head up at the taller man. "In fact, there is something very different about you. I have never met a vampire with your scent, not even a newly made one. Memnette was right. You do smell like you are still alive."

"That would be because he is." Belladonna finally broke her silence. She felt a mental rebuke from Viktor, but replied, "Don't be angry with me, Captain. I have dealt with vampires before, and the older ones have a habit of talking everything to death before getting to the point. I don't think anyone really wants to sit here all night."

"I see your pet is experienced as well as attractive." The vampire raised an amused eyebrow.

Belle started to protest being called Viktor's pet but obeyed his silent warning against it.

"Yes, and she's rather outspoken, sometimes at inopportune times," he growled.

"She is not human, master," the previously silent member of the foursome spoke. "She smells of the sea and her blood runs cooler than a woman's."

The siren sat, still half-naked, and stared calmly at the vampires. Viktor remained silent, as well.

Finally, Jeorge spoke, "You intrigue me, Captain Brandewyne. Come; hunt with us. Later we will talk in a more secure location at our leisure."

"I and my companion accept your invitation, sir." He bowed graciously.

Shortly after midnight, they ended their hunt and went to a house very near the cemetery Viktor had retrieved Angelique from. He didn't think it a coincidence and suspected the building connected to the unexplored tunnel.

The house was well-appointed. The furniture was all mahogany and velvet. Gilt adorned many of the architectural flourishes. Yet the over-all impression was of understated and tasteful opulence.

Viktor eyed it with a pirate's mind, almost subconsciously taking inventory of all the valuables and cataloguing where best to sell them and for how much.

"Are you thinking of looting my home, Captain?" Jeorge smiled at him.

"Occupational hazard. I may still be new to vampirism, but I have been a pirate all my life."

Jeorge laughed. "You are still young! It has been centuries since I have thought of my existence as my life. My mortal life was so brief and so long ago I barely remember or think of it anymore." He moved to the most comfortable chair in the room and motioned Viktor to the seat next to him. Memnette sat on a cushion at Jeorge's feet and laid her head against his knee like a lap dog. Belladonna sneered at this behavior and took up a position behind Viktor's chair.

"Is she your pet or your bodyguard?"

"Both, sir. Belladonna is quite useful in a variety of ways," he answered.

"Indeed. I imagine she is especially useful in disposing of your leftovers." He watched the pirate carefully for his reaction.

"So that is why we were revisiting places I had hunted earlier." He didn't seem surprised.

"It is not my usual manner to be blunt, but then, I rarely deal with the newly made anymore. Realizing that you still think like a mortal, I shall be direct in my questioning."

"That is good. I prefer directness."

"Your pet is definitely not human. What is she?"

"Belle is a siren." Viktor decided to be concise, since Jeorge was obviously not going to play any further mental games. He wanted the vampire's assurance that Celine and Angelique would no longer be threatened by his people. He figured the best way to get that was to give him what he wanted.

"I see. That would explain why there were none of your marks on her lovely body. However did you manage to tame such a wild creature?"

"I am not tamed!" Belle's eyes flashed gold.

Memnette blinked up at Jeorge. "Master?"

"Yes?"

"I do not understand. I have heard that sirens are quite strong in magic. Why would he not want to feed on that?"

Jeorge patted her hand as if she were a simple child. "Sirens have cold blood. It is toxic to our kind. A single drop can snuff out even the oldest, strongest vampire."

"You seem familiar with my species, sir," Belladonna observed.

He nodded. "I owe my current status to a siren. The bastard who made me was recruited, along with another, to murder a siren once. They succeeded but were destroyed by the blood they took."

She blinked, realizing that she was indirectly responsible for Jeorge coming to power. She had been the one who had arranged for the assassination of her sister by vampires. Of course, she had been equally ignorant of the effect siren blood had on vampires at the time. She'd merely seen them as the best tool for eliminating a rival.

Viktor carefully hid his irritation at losing what he had hoped would have been an edge.

"I am curious about something your siren mentioned earlier this evening. She said that you are still alive, yet you are clearly vampire."

"She spoke out of turn, but she is correct. I am vampire, but I am not dead. No vampire made me. A very powerful, very angry witch cursed me."

The ancient vampire found that revelation very intriguing. He had never heard of such a thing. It made Viktor Brandewyne an unknown, which could make him a danger. Until he could determine this strange vampire's strengths and weaknesses, and whether or not he posed a threat to his kiss, it would be wise to keep tabs on him.

Smiling, Jeorge offered, "You are welcome to stay here during the day."

"Thank you for your hospitality, but I have business to attend to this morning."

Jeorge's hand was on his arm almost too fast for him to see. He realized that the seeming teenager would be a true challenge in a fight. "You can move about in the sunlight?"

"Yes." Viktor tolerated the contact. He knew this was a dangerous game he was playing. "I understand this is unusual. The witch I went to for an explanation of what had been done to me told me some of the basics of vampirism, and the vampires I have made do not fare well with sunlight."

The vampire's grip tightened. "You have made vampires in my territory?" His tone was dangerous.

Viktor showed no fear. "I was referring to my cadre: six of my crew I turned. I have restricted them to my ship except for in battle. However, I have made one vampire in this city. He tried to destroy something of mine, so I destroyed him."

"You destroyed him?"

"I did. He orchestrated a fire that burned down a favorite whore house in an effort to destroy a woman who belongs to me. I turned him, starved him for his first and only night as a vampire, then left him for the sunrise to dispose of tied to the cross of his own chapel." He showed no remorse for the torture.

Jeorge released his arm and gazed at him for some time. Viktor returned the gaze, unflinching. The siren and the vampires watched them both, waiting to see what judgment would be passed.

Finally, Jeorge spoke. "You speak of the whore, Angelique, and Bishop DePardeaux. That zealot has been a thorn in my side for nearly three decades. Perhaps the means of his death will serve as a message to his successor. I congratulate you on your creativity and will take your unknowing boon as thanks for my unknowing salvation of your human pet. She and some of her employees were my guests, when her house was burned."

"I also am beginning to understand how she disappeared from my custody during the day. I had thought your siren had retrieved her, but that flew in the face of what I know of such creatures' natures. It is a marvel you have kept her from destroying any other female you've come in contact with. I've heard they're quite possessive."

Viktor laughed. "So, I've learned, but no less so than I am. For the most part, Belle knows her place and has not needed restraint, however. Thank you for providing an unintended haven for Angelique. I am curious as to why she was in your possession at the time."

"As a test and a lure for you, sir. I must admit you surprised me by coming for her in the daylight. I wanted to see if you would be responsible for any of your potential Children."

"To my knowledge I've sired no bastards on Angel."

"I was referring to her. You've fed on her but did not kill her. Even if you do not deliberately make her, she will turn when her mortal life ends, regardless of when or how that happens, unless you take her heart or head. If you had not come for her, I had entertained the thought of completing her siring myself."

Viktor's voice held a note of deadly calm. "Angelique is mine. I protect what is mine."

Jeorge nodded. "I understand and respect that. In fact, it is fortunate that you do. I do not tolerate vampires in my territory that sire indiscriminately or fail to clean up after their feedings. Drawing undue attention from the humans tends to bring hunters and endangers every vampire in the city. I, too, protect what is mine, Viktor Brandewyne."

"Then we understand each other."

Belladonna relaxed slightly, seeing that the two vampires had reached some sort of an accord. Males had an odd way of interacting sometimes, as far as she was concerned.

Viktor had not forgotten his main reason for wanting to meet with the local vampires, however. "Jeorge, I have a favor to ask of you, and I am not in the custom of asking favors."

Jeorge considered the pirate for some time before replying, "No, I can see you are not. You may ask. I will, of course, expect something in return, if I decide to grant the favor."

"I would expect no less. The favor I ask is your guarantee that none of your vampires ever trouble Angelique, Celine Thibideaux or any of their girls again. My business takes me from port to port, and I cannot protect them when I am not here."

Jeorge steepled his fingers, peering over them. "I understand your concern for your future child. Why do you seek to protect *Madame* Thibideaux?"

"Celine is in the service of a witch I must have dealings with. She has already lost one of her girls to one of your vampires. I suspect that her house was stalked because my scent led you there. Now she has to keep wards up for protection. Her business has suffered as a result of feedings and attacks focused on it, also she has agreed to combine her business with Angel's, since I asked her to harbor her former rival."

"I see. Very well, I will grant your favor. Any of my kiss who goes against my will on this shall find their existence forfeit. Now I will tell you what I want from you in return."

Once Viktor and Belladonna left to fulfill the pirate's end of the bargain, Jeorge summoned his lieutenant. "I want that creature watched every moment he is in my city. If he truly is able to move about in daylight, I want confirmation and at least two of our watchdogs shadowing him." He made reference to the more trusted humans enthralled to them to provide daytime protection when necessary. "I want one of our kiss to get close enough to earn his confidence, also."

"That one will be difficult to track, master. I've checked around the docks. His reputation as a human was quite impressive, if even half of it is to be believed. I don't think he is one who will trust lightly or easily."

Jeorge peered at the large vampire over his steepled fingers. He stood patiently awaiting his master's next words. He had learned over the centuries that the longer the silence the worse Jeorge's mood. Gratefully, he didn't have to wait long this time.

"I have taken that into consideration, Andre. I will leave it to you to select the humans. There is only one vampire I wish to entrust this task to. Tomorrow night, when he returns to us, introduce him to Guillaume."

The choice puzzled Andre. "Guillaume? He is young and fractious. You have had him punished at least three times just in the past two years, master."

"*Oui*, I am aware. This will be his last chance to prove his loyalty. Make sure he understands that. But he is of a nature that I believe will appeal to our Captain Brandewyne. Oh, and Andre…."

"Master?"

Jeorge's smile was chilling. "If it proves true that the creature can move about in daylight, I want to know how and by what enchantment."

Andre's smile matched his master's. "I didn't believe the tale of a witch's curse, either. He has been keeping company with witches, though. He reeks of magic, strong magic."

"Indeed. He is an unknown and may be a threat. I do not like that."

"If he proves to be a threat?"

"Eliminate him. Either way, I want to know what magic aides him and how I can harness it for myself."

Chapter 23

Once well away from Jeorge's house, Belle rounded on Viktor. He could sense she was about to open fire and quickly put a damper on it. Catching her completely off guard, he grasped her face gently but firmly in both hands and kissed her deeply. She stiffened at first, then relaxed and surrendered to the embrace.

He spoke to her through the bond they shared to avoid being overheard. His mental tone was nowhere near as gentle as his touch. *"I will brook no mutiny, pet. I know you are angry and why. You will not give any outward indication of this while we are in the open. Save it for Celine's, where it is still warded. We are being followed, and I cannot afford to give the appearance of any weakness to Jeorge's spies."*

The siren extended her true teeth just enough to prick his tongue but not enough to draw blood. *"I am not your pet,"* was her mental response.

Viktor deliberately forced his tongue against the needle points, forcing her to retract them or taste his blood. He knew, as well as she, that she didn't want to be bound any closer to his will.

"Think what you like." He released her from the kiss with a smirk and headed on down the street.

Belladonna looked after him for a few moments, confused by her own emotions. She was angry, afraid and aroused by his behavior. Realizing that he wasn't going to stop or even look back, she hurried to catch up with him.

Grimm raised an eyebrow when they entered Celine's parlor carrying an armload each of Spanish moss. The siren looked less than pleased with her burden and quickly dumped it on the nearest table. She then began brushing furiously at her arms and clothes while standing close to the fire.

"That stuff is crawling with insects!"

Viktor ignored her outburst. He set his own armload down and removed a handful from the pile. Then he reached in his shirt and removed the conch shell. Carefully, he shook out the ashes of the old tinder then packed the moss around the ember. Grimm could see that it had shrunken some since they'd left Hell's Breath, but not as much as a natural ember would have in the same time frame.

"Wouldn't have thought of using the moss for tinder."

"Mother Celie used to use it to wrap fish in to slow bake them. I just remembered it on the way here. Hadn't thought about that in years," he replied. "Where are Celine and Angelique?"

"Upstairs with clients. The one with Angel wasn't too happy about having Mr. Jon in the room while being serviced." Grimm chuckled.

Viktor frowned at that. "I left no order for him to do that."

"It was Angel's idea. She's still spooked about the fire, and we all thought it suspicious that one of her regulars found out she was alive and here so quickly. She insisted on having a bodyguard present and charged the bastard double." He shrugged. "I'm not interested in voyeurism, so Jon-Jon got the job."

"Hmph. Bugger must've been starved for it to pay double and have to get it up with a leering, lurking behemoth in the room. The man has balls." Vik laughed.

Grimm stood and headed for the door. "Think I'll find the local tobacconist. Between you and old Zeke, I'm out of smoke. Most of the girls are still free if you don't feel like waiting for or interrupting Angelique or Celine."

Viktor pulled his own tobacco pouch out and stuffed it tight with moss then returned it to its resting place. "I've other business to attend to today. While you're there, fetch as many extra pouches as he has. When you bring them back, Belle can stuff them with the rest of this moss," he ordered.

"I can do what? I don't think so! I'm going with you," she argued.

He gave her an emotionless stare. "No, you are not," he finally said. "You will stay here and do as you are told. For what I have to do, you would be a hindrance. I should be back well before dark and have time to deal with you, before completing my bargain with Jeorge."

He didn't give her time to argue further, leaving to acquire what the ancient vampire had asked for.

"Lazarus, come forth." The command came as a bare murmur.

"Mrrraeh?" The cat appeared as summoned.

Smiling, Viktor scratched behind his ears, eliciting a rumbling purr. He knelt down to whisper, "I need a little bird to fly to the Lord Mayor's house and keep an eye on it. But don't let anyone see you leave for there. Two of Jeorge's pet humans are following me. I don't want word of you getting back to their master. I trust you in this, Jim."

He stood and turned to walk up the street. Lazarus rubbed against his leg then bounded off to the courtyard of a nearby house. He made a show of crouching and stalking an imaginary bird in an oak tree. Once in the tree and hidden by dense foliage and moss, he shifted to his raven form. He burst from the tree, playing the escaping prey, and flew off to find the mayor's mansion.

Viktor had to make a few stops before he embarked on his errand in earnest. There were preparations to be made. There was not enough time to return to the ship for a change of clothes. What he currently wore was neither clean enough nor appropriate for blending in among the folk he would soon have to deal with. Fortunately, a few of the previous day's victims had been well coined.

Finding a clothier and tailor's shop that supplied what he had in mind, he entered and conducted his business.

One of the watchers assigned to the strange new vampire signaled to his partner in a panic. He'd lost sight of their quarry. He still had enough freedom of thought left to question his master's claim that this creature was a vampire. It had been full daylight for a few hours now. Still, it would not fare well for him or his partner if the man eluded them.

His partner signaled back that he had lost sight, as well. This was not good. They both scanned the area, desperate to catch sight again.

When he looked back to see if his partner had reacquired, the man was no longer there. His panic started to deepen to true fear.

An unexpected shadow was the only warning of the attack.

The two men came to at about the same time. Viktor was glad of that. It meant he only had to spell things out once.

"Afternoon, lads. I thought we ought to have a little talk, before this farce goes any farther." He smiled amiably.

Both men reached for their weapons only to find them missing.

Viktor tsked at them and held up a couple of wicked looking blades. "Looking for these? Sorry, you can have them back later, if you can find them." He elicited cries of dismay as he tossed the blades off the roof to an alleyway below. "They wouldn't have done you any good. But I just bought these clothes and I'm not ready to have them ruined just yet."

"Now that I have your attention, you have had mine since you started following me when I left your master this morning. You lads are good at what you do, but not as good as you thought you were. In all fairness, I expected to be followed and was looking for it."

"How did you spot us?"

"You smell of vampires. If I had been human, it would probably have taken me a few more hours to pick you out from the crowd. But I still would have. You're not the first to try to track me, and probably won't be the last. You are, however, the only ones I have allowed to live."

He let that sink in for a few moments before continuing. "I need you lads to hang back a bit further than you have been. What I'm about to do has to be handled delicately, and I can't afford either of you being detected and throwing suspicion on me. I want those guarding my prize to keep their guard lax for as long as possible."

The lead tracker balked. "You've been difficult enough to keep up with as it is. If we lose you, our master will not deal kindly with us."

Viktor growled irritably. Normally, he would've killed them and been done with it, but he was trying to make an alliance with Jeorge, not start a war. If he hadn't encountered Memnette, he wouldn't have to be dealing with any of this. He should have heeded Glory's warning about "his kind," but what was done was done.

"I have to go pay a visit on the Lord Mayor of this port and his family. Neither of you would blend into that crowd; I've neither the time nor the inclination to do what it would take to change that fact." He hated having to take the time to explain himself. "You will give me the space I need to do my task, or you can explain to Jeorge how you prevented me from getting what he asked for."

The trackers both blanched. They realized that they were going to have to trust this so-called vampire. While their punishment for losing him would be great, it would be unimaginable if the master suspected them of hindering any task he'd assigned to another.

"You leave us no choice, then. We will stay out of sight."

Once satisfied that his shadows were nowhere near, Viktor proceeded on to the Mayor's manor. He knew it would take more than the foppish clothes to get him inside. Regardless of how he dressed, even the servants would know not to let the notorious pirate on the grounds, let alone in the house.

So instead, one Thomas Brumble came to call on the Lord Mayor with a shipping and trade proposition from his father, Tobias Brumble of Boston. Viktor/Thomas gambled that the mayor suffered the affliction of avarice as strongly as most politicians he had encountered. The gamble paid off, not only gaining him entry to the main house, but an audience with the mayor, himself.

Viktor found the alias to be ideal. Apparently, the Brumble & Sons shipping company enjoyed an excellent reputation among those acquainted with the trade. It also afforded an excuse, in case Viktor seemed a little rough around the edges at times. After all, if one spent months at a time around coarse sailors, it was difficult not to pick up some of their language and habits.

The bogus negotiations had reached the glass of port and cigar stage, when a commotion in the hallway drew their attention. Lazarus, in feline form, darted into the room closely followed by a young woman. Something shiny could be seen dangling from his mouth as he darted in and out among the furniture.

"You thieving little beast! Come back here!" the woman demanded shrilly, trying to catch the cat.

"Melanie! What is the meaning of this?" the mayor blustered.

"He has my favorite pendant," was the only answer she gave.

Viktor had to admit the girl was quick. She managed to corner the cat under a small writing desk but was unable to reach him. Lazarus growled, never releasing his prize, and swatted at her hand, careful to keep his claws sheathed.

"Give it back!"

Chuckling, Viktor knelt by the desk. "Allow me, *ma'm'selle*." Snapping his fingers, he ordered, "Come here, you little pirate. Let's see what you've got."

To Melanie's amazement, the large black cat obediently came to the handsome stranger. Even more amazing, it dropped its prize into his palm. The infuriating beast then had the arrogance to preen and look smug about its actions.

Examining what he had retrieved, Viktor admired the workmanship of the jewelry. The pendant was an ornate filigree of gold, studded with garnets. Three large pearls were suspended from the lower edge, and the pendant was threaded onto a length of burgundy velvet ribbon.

"Thank you, *m'sieur*." She made a grab for the necklace. Viktor held it just out of reach, a challenging smile dancing in his eyes.

The mayor cleared his throat, scowling at her. "I apologize for my daughter's lack of manners."

"I said 'thank you' Papa." She pouted.

"So, you did, *ma'm'selle*." The vampire's eyes never left her. "Aren't you going to introduce us, Louie?"

"Of course, forgive me. *M'sieur* Brumble, this is my lovely, if ill-mannered, daughter, Melanie. My fault, of course. I fear I have spoiled her." He puffed with adoring pride. "Melanie, this is

Monsieur Thomas Brumble, of Boston. His family runs a profitable and prominent shipping company. He came here today to negotiate a trade agreement."

The girl knew her father's avarice well. It was a trait she shared with him. She smiled up at Viktor; not only handsome, but wealthy as well. "Thank you, again, for retrieving my pendant, *m'sieur*. Will you be staying in New Orleans long? It's such a long way from Boston. I imagine your wife misses you."

"Please, call me Thomas, and it was my pleasure." He smiled at her flirting. "I have other business to attend to in your lovely city, but I must sail as soon as I have finished. Unfortunately, I have no wife to miss me, as yet."

Both the mayor and his daughter perked up their ears at that. The father saw a means of cementing what promised to be a very profitable arrangement. Melanie saw that the man was both available and appreciative.

"Very well, Thomas. You must call me Melanie." She batted her lashes. "May I please have my pendant back now?"

"Of course." He moved to stand behind her. "If I may?"

She nodded and lifted her hair out of the way. Reaching around in front of her with the necklace, he made sure the pearl drops brushed against her cleavage. He drew it up slowly and brushed his fingertips against her nape, as he tied the ribbon.

"It is not too tight, I hope," he whispered close to her ear.

Melanie's pulse raced. She'd had suitors before, but none had ever been so bold, especially in front of her father. It made her blush and excited her, as well.

Louie saw it, too. He liked that the man was not intimidated by him. He also liked that "Brumble" was not the usual, money-grubbing young buck, looking to marry into wealth and a life of ease. He was wealthy in his own right and well-acquainted with work. He hadn't missed the sun-weathered complexion or the calloused hands and muscular build that were incongruous with the foppish attire.

"I'm sure *M'sieur* Brumble would like to stay for dinner, Melanie. Perhaps you could show him the gardens in the meantime."

Viktor made a show of turning the offer down. "Really, my Lord Mayor, I don't want to impose. I can join some of my officers at one of the common houses. I have to admit, I've acquired a taste for the cuisine here in such a short time. It's so much more flavorful than New English fare. Spicy."

"Nonsense, man. It's no imposition. Cook always prepares too much, and I'm positive Melanie will be glad of the company."

"Well, who am I to disappoint such a lovely lady?" He offered his arm. "Lead the way, *ma'm'selle*."

She actually giggled, as she took his arm and led him from the room.

Louie smiled smugly to himself, confident that he would soon be gaining a son-in-law as well as a business partner.

Viktor wandered through the gardens with Melanie, pretending to enjoy the vacuous small talk she barraged him with. He thought there were far more useful and entertaining things she could be doing with her tongue. Damn, but she was boring his balls off.

Finally, they reached a secluded spot. He stopped and looked around. "Good, they can't see us from here," he muttered to himself.

Melanie thought he was talking to her. "Are you sure?"

"Quite." The look he gave her was almost predatory. He was going to enjoy shutting her up.

Before he could act, however, she took the initiative. Standing on tiptoe, she wrapped her arms around his neck and pulled him down for a kiss. He returned the embrace and the kiss, retaking control of the situation. He did not release her when they broke from the kiss.

Rather than struggle, as he'd half expected, she gave him a sultry look. "You're not like the others," she said in a husky voice. "You are a masterful man, not a timid boy who is frightened of aggressive women."

"You've read me well, pet. Shall I tell you a secret?"

"Let me guess. You are really a pirate come to steal me away and ravish me." Her tone told him it was something she had probably fantasized about – often.

He chuckled wickedly. "Clever girl. How did you guess?"

Melanie laughed, but it had a nervous note to it. "You have a wicked sense of humor, Thomas."

He tightened his grip around her waist a bit. "Oh, but I'm not joking, pet. That is exactly what I am and why I am here. Oh," he added, "my name isn't Thomas Brumble, either. I killed the real Brumble weeks ago."

She started struggling, more angry than frightened. "This isn't funny. Let go! Who are you supposed to be, if you are not Thomas?"

"Captain Viktor Brandewyne. Perhaps you have heard of me?"

Her eyes grew large. She opened her mouth and took in a lungful of air, preparing to scream. He never gave her the chance. He covered her mouth with his own to muffle her cries. When she started struggling and flailing, he took them to the ground. Pinning her under his weight freed his hands to capture her arms.

After a few minutes, she stopped wriggling and began to respond to the kiss. Once he thought it was safe, he sat up, still straddling her. She gazed up at him, disheveled, with swollen lips and dilated pupils. He could smell that her body was ready for him.

He wouldn't take her here in the gardens, though. They had been out of sight long enough that her father would be sending someone to check on them soon.

"They'll be looking for you. It's time to leave."

"You'll never get past the gate or wall." She managed to muster some defiance.

"I've another secret for you, pet." He stood and lifted her in his arms so quickly it took her a moment to realize she was no longer on the ground. "I'm not human."

With ease, he launched them straight up about a hundred feet. Melanie squeaked in terror and clung to him with a death-grip.

"Don't drop me!"

"Wouldn't dream of it, pet. I need you alive and intact."

Chapter 24

Bainbridge made better time to Boston than he had hoped – or wished. He really wasn't looking forward to facing his employer. Tobias Brumble had a notoriously mercurial temper when it came to bad news. At least his report should remove himself and Zachary from suspicion.

Steeling himself, he knocked at the door of Brumble's house. He'd sent a short, coded message by homing pigeon when they'd made port in Bermuda. When he'd anchored in Boston, a message boy had been waiting at the docks. Tobias felt it better to discuss the matter in the privacy of his home, rather than his shipping offices.

A servant opened the door and took his coat and hat before ushering him to the study. For the moment it was empty. He didn't think that was a good sign.

Just as Tobias entered the room, his daughter passed by in the hallway. Before she could say so much as a hello to their guest, her father turned with a glower and shut the doors of the study.

Samantha recognized Mr. Bainbridge during the short glimpse. His presence here instead of her brother's did not bode well. Her father had been in an ill mood for several days now. Wondering if this had something to do with it, she eased the door open a crack to listen.

"What was all that balderdash about pirates, Bainbridge? What happened to the emeralds? Where is Zachary?"

"Unfortunately, it is not balderdash, sir. We fell prey to pirates, as did our contact, although the ship that attacked our contact was not the same one we encountered. The two survivors we rescued both claim that ship was led by a woman."

"A woman." Tobias sneered. "And you say there were only two survivors? That does not engender confidence in our partners in this venture. However, that still does not answer what happened to my son."

"We were deceived and drugged, sir. Zachary is held hostage by one of the most feared pirates to ever sail; Viktor Brandewyne. I believe he holds young Thomas, as well."

"You lie! Brandee is dead! He was removed from the lists months ago, when his ship was destroyed in a hurricane."

"The *Redfish* was destroyed, but the bastard has always had the devil's own luck at surviving. He's gotten his hands on a ship-o-the-line and was masquerading as such, complete with Royal Navy uniforms. And he knew the agreed upon signals. At first, I thought he'd gotten them from Thomas, but what I learned from the two survivors leads me to believe that he was in league with the female pirate. They both said she was asking for news of Brandee's whereabouts," Bainbridge knew he was grasping at hope that the theory would remove the younger Brumbles from suspicion.

Tobias still looked doubtful. "I am well aware of Bloody Vik Brandee's reputation, Mr. Bainbridge. If he really is alive, and that was who you encountered, why are you standing here unscathed?"

He'd know that question was coming. "He wanted me to deliver a message to you."

Brumble blinked, not sure what to make of that information. Although he knew the pirate's reputation, he had never met the man, nor had any of his ships fallen prey to him before the business with the emeralds.

"What possible message could he have for me, and why would he even know me? I've never encountered the man."

"He said he was taking your sons and your emeralds as partial payment for what he called your 'vile treatment in the past of one Jim Rigger.' He said this Rigger had been a friend of his. Perhaps he was a former crewman or cabin boy?"

Tobias mulled the information over. He could recall no former employee by the name of Rigger. It didn't surprise him that some man who had worked for him in the past might've turned to piracy. There were always a few ingrates in the crew that thought hard work was too much to demand for the pay they received.

Then it struck him. Brandee was believed to hail from Savannah. He seemed to remember some little street urchin that he'd taken on as cabin boy having jumped ship in that port. But that had been a few years before Brandee first made an appearance. Either the brat had teamed up with Brandee when he'd started out, or perhaps he was Brandee.

"Mr. Bainbridge, ready your ship to head out at high tide tomorrow. I'll have a message for you to deliver to Commodore Critchfield. He sails aboard the *HMS Quicksilver* and should be making for New Providence at this time of year. You say this pirate claiming to be Brandee had a warship and naval uniforms?"

"Aye, sir. The ship looks to be relatively new. She'd rate a first order and is copper clad. He calls her the *Incubus*."

Samantha had to be careful not to give away that she had listened to the conversation. Her father was very indulgent of her, but she did not trust him to restrain his temper with her.

She waited until after Bainbridge left to approach her father. "Papa, was there any news of my brothers?"

Tobias looked at his only remaining child. She looked so much like her mother. He wondered where the years had gone, and when had she become a young woman? Perhaps he should start scenting about for a husband for her. She would need a man to take care of her. He felt so old.

"Papa? Are you alright? You look quite pale." Sam worried, when he didn't answer right away. Truth be told, he looked like he'd aged several years in the relatively short time he'd been sequestered with Bainbridge.

He reached up and patted her hair, like he'd done when she'd been a little girl. "I'm afraid both of your brothers are lost, Sam. Now that I know which pirate is responsible, I no longer think Thomas was weak to just give himself over." He turned and went back into his study.

"I'll take my evening meal in here. Tell the cook to keep it light. I'm not very hungry."

"Yes, Papa. I'll bring it in myself."

"Thank you, Sam. You'll make some lucky man a fine wife." He gave her a weak smile. "Now if you'll excuse me, I've got to read over these reports Mr. Bainbridge brought. The more I know about this situation, the better I can arrange for protection of my ships."

She nodded and closed the doors behind her.

Once she was sure her father had turned in for the night, Samantha crept into his study. Using her spare key, she opened his desk and skimmed through the reports. She knew her father would never give her the full story. After all, she was female. He saw her as something to be protected and unable to understand business, politics or the ways of a man's world.

As she read, something deep within her hardened. It started out as white-hot rage until chilling fear tempered it into a resolute, razor-sharp, steel determination.

The draft of the letter to the Commodore let her know that her father had not so much given up hope of saving her brothers as suspected them of turning against him and joining up with this pirate, Viktor Brandewyne.

She sat for a few minutes, digesting all she had learned.

If her father was not going to make any attempt to find and rescue Thomas and Zachary, she would just have to arrange for it, herself. Making sure all the papers were placed where he'd left them, she returned to her chambers and set about gathering what she thought she would need.

As agreed, Bainbridge went to the Brumble & Sons Shipping office just before dawn. Tobias was waiting for him.

"Thank you for your punctuality, Captain Bainbridge. Is the *Shining Star* ready to sail?"

"The lads are loading the last of the provisions, as we speak, sir," he answered, placing a small, heavy locked box on the counting table. "You'll need a locksmith, I'm afraid. Captain Hermosa must have kept the key on his person. We'd already disposed of his body by the time we found the cash box. Even though it was well-hidden, I was surprised to find the pirates had not taken it."

"Indeed. It is fortunate for us they overlooked it. The Commodore expects to make a profit on this venture. Hopefully the contents of this box will allow us to recoup some of our losses." Tobias went over to a cabinet and removed a hammer and a small punch. "However, I don't think a locksmith will be necessary, Captain. I would prefer not to trust one with this in any case."

Bainbridge raised an eyebrow. "You can pick a lock?"

"Hardly," Tobias laughed harshly. "But I can remove the hinge pins."

The sea captain could slap himself for not having thought of that solution. Of course, it also made him wonder about Brumble's beginnings.

In short order, the trader had the box open. What he found inside made him smile. No wonder it had been so heavy. In addition to a great number of gold and silver coins, there were four small gold ingots. Bainbridge whistled appreciatively.

"Yes, that should do nicely." Brumble removed one of the ingots and counted out a fair amount of the coins. He then replaced the lid and tapped the hinge pins back into place. After locking the ingot in his safe, he bagged the coins and handed them over to Bainbridge. "That should be fair compensation for the hardships of this venture, George."

He took the sack of coins and hid it in his clothing. "Thank you, sir." Tobias was being uncharacteristically generous, and he was not about to question it or give his employer any cause to rethink the matter.

Brumble then handed him a sealed tube of stiffened oil cloth. "When you rendezvous with Commodore Critchfield give him the cash box and these papers."

"Aye, sir."

☠

When Samantha did not join him for the evening meal, Tobias demanded her whereabouts from the servant waiting on him.

"I do not know, sir," the nervous woman answered. "Perhaps her maid, Martha knows?"

"Send for the lass."

When she arrived, Martha almost had to be pushed into the room. Obviously, her mistress' father terrified the girl.

"Please do not beat me," she pled.

"Why would I beat you girl? I only want to know why my daughter did not come down for dinner."

The girl was still in a panic. "She said she was going to market this morning. She left with her basket but told me to stay home. I found this at her writing desk." She darted forward and placed a sealed note on the table then scurried back to the safety of the doorway.

He scowled at the folded paper with its drop of sealing wax bearing his personal seal. It bore no name or address on the outside. He understood the maid's fear. Samantha never went to market alone. Unless – could she have met some suitor that she knew would not meet his approval?

He opened the letter and read the contents.

Dear Papa,

You will not see me again. I love you, but I also love my brothers, and, unlike you, I believe them to be innocent of the crimes you accuse them of.

I have taken my dowry, Mother's jewels and your signet. I have disguised myself and am putting out to sea to search for the pirates that have taken my brothers. It is my hope to ransom them.

Sam

A quick search of her room and his study verified that the money, jewelry, and signet were missing. Also missing were some of Thomas' spare clothes.

Tucked in the top drawer of his desk, where he kept his signet, he found her hair, neatly braided and tied with her favorite ribbon.

Tamara A. Lowery

Chapter 25

Melanie cowered on the far side of the room from Viktor, pouting. Even as she glared at her captor, she remained curious about her surroundings. She was busy examining a rather erotic bit of statuary when Grimm entered.

"She's new. Is she one of Angelique's that survived the fire?"

"Hardly," Vik snorted. "Melanie is daughter of the Lord Mayor of New Orleans."

Grimm blinked at his captain. "It's not like you to stir up the local authorities unless they've done something to antagonize you, Vik."

"That's the beauty of it, Hezekiah." He grinned. "I didn't. As far as the mayor knows, she was kidnapped by one Thomas Brumble of Boston. He probably won't even start looking for her for a few days. He was ready enough to marry her off to 'Brumble' to seal a lucrative trade agreement. I imagine he thinks she's eloped and saved him the expense of a dower and wedding."

"My father would never!"

Viktor quieted her outburst with a look, then smirked. "If you truly believe that; you don't know him for the greedy bastard he is."

That got her ire up. Grimm leaned against the wall to watch the show. "How dare you belittle my father, you pirate! He is a great man! And you, what kind of pirate are you? You attack me in my father's garden; you fly away with me, if that really happened; you bring me here to this house of ill repute; and then you just sit over there fiddling with that stupid shell and some nasty, dirty old moss!"

Grimm chuckled, "Thought she looked a little too – clothed for you to have had her yet."

"Aye, and I think she's angrier that I haven't ravished her than that I kidnapped her or spoke my mind about her father." He laughed with his first mate.

"Stop talking about me as if I wasn't here!" she shrieked.

"Damn, she's almost as vocal as Belle." Grimm made a show of cleaning out his ear, causing Viktor to laugh harder.

The pirates' mirth at her expense proved more than Melanie could stand. She forgot her fear and rushed at Viktor, slapping and clawing. He restrained her easily enough, pinning her wrists behind her back. She was also pinned against him.

She deliberately pressed herself closer to him, looking up at him with lidded eyes and an angry pout. Even Grimm could read the lust in her body language.

"I do believe she wants you, Vik."

"That is her problem. I need some rope and a gag. I'm sure Celine has some lying about for her clients that enjoy that sort of thing."

Grimm left to check on it.

Melanie whined, "Why haven't you taken me? Is there something wrong with me? Is it because I'm a virgin?"

"Hardly, pet. Under other circumstances, I would have ruined you for any other man. But I did not take you away for my own pleasure. I have a buyer who requested you, specifically," he answered.

She once again grew indignant. "I am to be sold like a common slave?"

"You weren't listening. You've already been sold." Grimm returned with the requested items and Belladonna. The siren carried an armload of pouches stuffed with moss. "Thank you, Hezekiah. If you would gag her while I hold her? I think she's about to get vocal again."

The men made short work of binding the girl. Viktor then set her on one of the more comfortable couches. She squirmed and emitted muffled angry screams. Finally, he lightly slapped her, knocking her out. He had to be careful, due to his enhanced strength. He didn't want to mark her face or kill her.

His actions confused Belladonna, and she said so. "Why didn't you just bespell her? It would have been easier."

He looked at her then back at the girl. "Part of the agreement was that I not use my powers on her or her father. Jeorge wanted me to deliver her with both her mind and virtue intact."

"Hmph. I don't know why he'd want the brat. She's pretty enough for a human, I guess. But I could hear her tirade all the way downstairs. She seems to be an awful lot of trouble." The siren snorted. "For that matter, if he wants her so much, why didn't he get her himself?"

"A fair question, pet. I think she was a test. In all honesty, I don't think Jeorge expected me to be able to snatch her."

"Well, then he will be surprised when you deliver her tonight. I still don't like that you're going back there alone." She pouted.

"You don't trust him."

"No, I do not."

"Nor I. Don't worry, Belle. I have no intention of letting him catch me off guard."

Viktor waited until full dark to deliver his prisoner. It made it easier to get the girl out of Celine's and across the city to the house Jeorge was using, without being seen. He didn't think using flight to kidnap her technically broke his agreement, since he had not bespelled her at any time. But he didn't want to risk over-using the talent. It took a lot of energy, and he'd noticed that the ember seemed to go through more fuel when he did so.

He really needed the ember to last until he could get it back to Gloribeau. If it died before then, he was doomed to die from his curse. It went without saying that he wanted to avoid that fate.

He ended up having to knock the girl out again before leaving with her. He wrapped her in a sea bag and threw her over his shoulder. Since he was once again wearing his usual clothes, no one even gave him a second look, save for a few lustful glances in passing from some of the whores that worked the streets.

Melanie started to stir by the time he reached Jeorge's doorstep. He was debating tapping her again by the time the door opened. She had come awake enough to be panicked by the sea bag she was stuffed in. Muffled shrieks and wriggling were bound to draw attention, if he didn't get them inside soon.

The human who answered the door, did not speak. He merely bowed and motioned for Viktor to enter. Once inside, the man motioned for him to follow.

They were led to a room that was probably intended by the builders to be a formal dining room or ballroom. A large drapery partitioned the back of the room off from sight. The remainder of the room was furnished as a receiving area and resembled a throne room.

Jeorge sat in a sumptuously ornate yet comfortable chair. The two lesser chairs, both empty, flanked him. Memnette sat on a stool at his feet. Andre stood behind him. A few other vampires were scattered about the room.

"Welcome, Captain Brandewyne. Did you bring what I asked for?"

"I did." He set the sea bag down in a way that would put Melanie on her feet, then undid the tie at the top. He had to hold her to keep her from falling as he pulled the bag down off her.

She blinked, her eyes adjusting to the candlelight. Looking about, her panic abated, and she tried to mask her fear, nervousness and disorientation with anger. Seeing Viktor holding her arm, she growled and tried to pull free. He tightened his grip, causing her to try to shriek past the gag at him.

Jeorge smiled. "Good, you left her mind intact. But is her virtue intact? After all, my trackers tell me you kept her prisoner for quite some time at that brothel you seem so fond of."

"I am quite capable of controlling myself, Jeorge." Vik snorted. "She is still virgin."

"Ungag her, please."

Viktor raised an eyebrow. "Are you sure you want me to do that? She is much more pleasant to be around when she is silent."

Melanie made angry noises at that.

Mirth shining in his eyes, Jeorge nodded. "Yes. Untie her as well. There should be some sport to this, and it is only fair that she be able to defend herself."

He shrugged and did as asked. Apparently, he wasn't the only one who, liked to play with his food. It was quicker to use a knife to cut the ropes than try to untie the knots. Then he undid the gag.

She rounded on him, slapping. "You bastard! Let me go!"

"As you wish." He released his grip on her arm without ceremony. Not expecting it, she stumbled and fell with a squawk, her feet still tangled in the sea bag. "She's all yours."

In a blink, Jeorge stood before her, a hand extended to help her up. She looked at it warily before taking it.

"Who are you?"

"I am Jeorge. Don't worry, child; you will find I am a fair and generous master."

She tried to take her hand back but could not. Though gentle, she found the vampire's grip unbreakable. "I am not a child! You look to be about the same age as I am, and you are not my master! My father is the Lord Mayor! I am not someone to be sold as a common slave!"

He threw his head back with a delighted laugh, not bothering to hide his fangs. Melanie's eyes grew wide. She doubled her efforts to free herself. Every vampire in the room reacted to the scent of her fear. Only Viktor seemed unaffected.

Jeorge touched her face with his free hand. He maintained his hold on her hand without effort. She flinched and whimpered. "Please, let me go," she pled.

"You don't want me to do that, my dear. Right now, you are under my protection. You recognize what I am?"

She nodded, tears brightening her eyes. "You are the undead -- vampire," her voice was a shaky whisper.

He smiled and wiped away a tear with his thumb. "That is right. I was old when your grandparents were children, even though I appear to be a mere youth. If I were to release you right now, you would be fair game to any of the other vampires in this room, and they are all quite Hungry."

Melanie shook her head violently. "No, please, no."

"Then please, my dear, join me as my honored guest." He led her back to the dais and seated her in the chair to his left. He then motioned toward the chair to his right. "Captain, I would be honored if you would join us, as well."

Viktor decided not to insult his host by declining. He made himself comfortable. Melanie held onto the arms of her chair with a death grip. Jeorge's protection or not, he didn't think she would last much longer if she kept acting like prey. Not that he really cared. She was Jeorge's problem, not his.

Jeorge clapped his hands. A blank-faced human brought in a tray with a decanter, two tiny glasses, and a small, covered dish. He set the tray on a small side table and poured a dram of green liquor from the decanter into each glass. Then he un-lidded the dish and using tongs, removed a cube of sugar and placed it in a glass, repeating the process for the second glass. Replacing the cover on the sugar dish, he carried the two glasses to the dais and stood with his head bowed.

"Allow me to offer some refreshments," Jeorge took the glasses and offered one to Melanie then the other to Viktor.

"What is this?" she asked.

"Absinthe." Viktor raised an appreciative eyebrow. "I've heard of this, but never encountered it before. It is quite rare on this side of the world."

"Indeed," Jeorge confirmed. "I've a small stock of it that I brought with me when I came to this continent a century or so ago. I cannot enjoy it myself, although I was fond of it when I was still human. I like to use it for special occasions."

Melanie was curious in spite of her fear. "What is the occasion? Is it true that absinthe is an aphrodisiac?"

The vampire smiled at her. "It is one of the most powerful. That is why the serving is so small. I'm sure you've noticed that the sugar has absorbed all of what was in your glass. It is also quite bitter, hence the sugar. Please, try it. You have my word that I have not drugged it."

Viktor knew that last was directed at him, as well. He hadn't really been worried about it, though. Since his curse took effect, only blood or very strong magic could intoxicate him. He found the taste of the absinthe-soaked sugar mildly interesting. He preferred rum or brandy.

The effect on Melanie, however, was striking. She made a face at the underlying bitterness. She hadn't eaten since breakfast, so the alcohol hit hard and fast. She still gripped the arms of the chair, but it was to keep her seat rather than out of fear. Her eyes dilated, and her face flushed. Blood rushed to the surface of her skin all over her body.

Jeorge clapped his hands again, summoning three more humans, two women and a man. Viktor recognized him as one of the sleepers he'd found Angelique with in the crypts. The man who had served them raised his head and joined the others in the center of the room.

At a nod from their master, Andre and Memnette joined the other vampires, forming a ring around the humans. Jeorge stood, and all eyes went to him. "Rejoice, my children, for a new vampire shall join our kiss this night. Feed well."

The vampires needed no further prompting. Their descent on the humans reminded Viktor of a school of sharks after a shipwreck. Oddly, their victims never uttered a cry as they were slaughtered, drained bloodless in a matter of minutes.

When the vampires finished, Jeorge directed, "Andre, see to it that these four do not rise. They were not worthy to join us. The rest of you, leave us now."

The vampires filed out. Andre dragged the bodies out by their hair managing two in each hand and making it look easy. Memnette closed the doors, leaving Viktor and Melanie alone with Jeorge.

She still felt the effects of the absinthe, which made the feeding frenzy seem surreal. She also felt very aroused. "What a strange performance. Your actors were very convincing. I almost believe that they really were killed. I still do not know how this rogue deceived me into thinking he flew away with me."

"I thought you were instructed to leave her mind intact and free of your influence." The vampire's tone was dangerous.

Viktor's was just as cold. "I did. If I had not, she would not remember that detail of her abduction, and I could have led her here willingly instead of having to knock her unconscious and carry her like a bag of grain."

"Hmm, yes, there is that."

He stood and bowed to his host. "I thank you for your hospitality, sir. I have upheld my part of our bargain and delivered the girl to you. I trust you to keep your part and see to it that Celine and Angelique and their business remain unmolested. Now if you will excuse me, I must go hunt."

Jeorge waved in dismissal of the notion. "There is no need of that, *mon ami*. You brought your meal with you." The words were an eerie echo of Mother Celie's to him concerning Jim Rigger the night she had educated Viktor about what the curse had done and would do to him.

"Melanie is yours, sir. She was the price you named. Do with her what you will; I do not care. You said a new vampire was joining your kiss. It will not be me. I am not one to be tied to any one port, and I've business that may take me to the ends of the earth before I'm done."

Jeorge laughed, honestly delighted. "You misunderstand me, Captain. I would not want you in my kiss, no offense. I would always be watching my back, waiting for you to try to usurp me. No, the new vampire will be our sweet Melanie, here."

"What? No! I demand you take me back to my father at once!"

They both ignored her outburst. Jeorge continued, "It is my custom to make my children's last night of life as pleasurable as possible. It has occurred to me that since you enjoy the favor of the two most successful whores in New Orleans, you might be best suited to provide her that pleasure."

Viktor stroked his beard, considering. This vampire was a peculiar one. He asked for the girl to be delivered intact, then turned around and offered her up. Perhaps he was a voyeur. He'd encountered stranger quirks.

"I usually prefer privacy when I take a woman, especially one that's untried like she is, unless I'm making an example of them. Has she or her father wronged you in some way that you would want to humiliate her?"

Melanie blinked at her kidnapper. Hope sprang up that he might protect her from this creature. But the absinthe singing in her blood led her to feel hurt that he still wouldn't want her.

"I have no desire to humiliate her. Only I shall watch, to ensure that she receives the pleasure I believe she is due. Then at the height of that pleasure, I wish for you to have the honor of taking her life and giving her a new one."

She looked back and forth between them. "You mean I am to be raped then murdered?"

"No, child. You are not to be murdered. You will be freed from your mortality and reborn to a new life; one in which you will never get sick and never grow old."

"It wouldn't be rape, either." Viktor smirked. "You were willing enough earlier today, pet."

Jeorge gave him a questioning look.

"She was pouting because I wouldn't take her."

"I see." He smiled knowingly at his soon-to-be neophyte. She blushed furiously in response. "Of course, you will need a bed."

He walked over to the drapery and pulled a cord. The curtains parted to reveal a large, sumptuous bed that rivaled anything Viktor had encountered in the many, many brothels he'd visited.

Melanie froze at the sight. Viktor saw he was going to have to take charge of the situation. He moved to her and took her hands, pulling her to her feet. Her expression was of fearful shock. This really was going to happen.

"You should be careful what you wish for, pet." He raked her with a leer and made sure she saw him do it. "I intend to carry out my boast of ruining you for any other man."

Her blush renewed, and she giggled nervously, as he led her to the bed. It wasn't long before her fear was completely forgotten.

Tamara A. Lowery

Chapter 26

Celine glanced into the salon as she passed the room. What she saw irritated her enough to make her stop and go in.

"Hey, you. Stop that pacing! I just bought that rug last month. You are wearing a track in it!"

Belladonna snarled at her, needle-teeth showing. "To hell with your stupid rug, human."

"That rug cost me almost a month's work! It came from Persia. I will not have you ruining it!"

Grimm arrived just in time to catch the angry siren as she launched herself at the madam. It was all he could do to hold her. "Get out of here, Celine. I can't hold her for long," he grunted.

"She is ruining my new rug," she argued.

Belle renewed her attempt to get at her, forcing Grimm to lift her off the floor to reduce her leverage. "I'll pay for the bloody thing, let her ruin it! Now, run!"

"I will not flee in my own home!"

"Dammit woman! I don't have time to argue with you! She will kill you if she catches you. The damned carpet is not worth it. Now, scat!"

Celine finally realized the siren was a real danger without the pirate captain there to control her. She hastily made herself scarce.

Once he thought it safe, he set Belle back on her feet. He was grateful that she hadn't extended her claws. They could wreak havoc on human flesh. He had to shake her by the shoulders to get her attention.

"What the hell has gotten into you, lass?"

Belladonna had to focus for a few moments to make sense of who had her and what he'd asked. "Hezekiah?"

"No, the King of Spain," he replied irritably.

"Let go, Hezekiah."

"Not until you answer my question. What is wrong with you? You were about to slaughter someone who is very valuable to the Captain – over a piece of carpet!"

Her eyes flashed gold. "Viktor is risking a great deal, including the success of his quest just to secure her safety, and all she can do is bitch about me pacing on her stupid rug! Besides, she started it," she ended on a pout.

He felt like slapping her for her childishness, but he had to remind himself that she was not just a hysterical human female. If the siren was this upset, chances were that the concern was legitimate.

"Vik is more than capable of taking care of himself, lass," he tried to reassure her. "I think this is more about him not letting you go with him."

"It's not just that, although that is part of it." She desperately wanted him to understand the true danger to their captain. "It was Jeorge that dictated I not be with him tonight. How am I supposed to protect him, if I'm not with him?"

"What makes you so sure he's in any danger? All he had to do was deliver the girl."

Belle shot him a look that said he was a fool if he truly believed that was all. "Then why has he not returned yet? Do you really think anything to do with true vampires is ever that simple? They're crafty, and the old ones love playing mind games to fight the boredom. They are also very territorial. If Jeorge starts to think Viktor is a threat to his power or territory, things could get very ugly, very fast. The Captain is good, but he is badly outnumbered by beings that are just as powerful as he is."

Grimm started to get the idea, and he didn't like it one bit. "Do you think this vampire is more powerful?"

"No." She shook her head. "But he is more adept at wielding his power. He's had centuries to home his skills. Viktor is more powerful, but his power is fresh and raw. His control is amazing for being so new to this world, but he doesn't fully understand his abilities yet. They are still growing, and there are some he has yet to discover. Right now, with a creature like Jeorge, that makes him vulnerable."

"You know where they are meeting. He needs us to have his back." He started checking his weapons as he spoke.

Belladonna put a hand on his arm, stopping him. Her eyes were both sad and tortured. "We can't. If we were to show up now, Jeorge would take it as a breach of Viktor's word and possibly a threat. To explain we were there against orders would make him look weak. He would never forgive us for that, and you know it."

Grimm had to admit she was right, but he didn't like it. Sometimes the greatest threat to Viktor was Viktor.

"Damn. Well, now that I know that; I can't just sit here and wait. It would drive me mad. I'm going to go find a bottle and a wench. Why don't you go hunt? It might take your mind off things," he suggested.

"I can't!" She snarled in frustration. "The bastard bound me with a promise to stay here until he returns."

She looked so miserable that he flirted with the idea of bedding her to give them both a needed distraction. But he knew that if the experience didn't kill him, Vik most probably would. Belladonna belonged to Viktor.

He left to carry out his original plan.

Nearly an hour passed before Belle realized Grimm had been able to physically restrain her. That should not have been possible for a human. She remembered scenting a faint trace of familiar magic on him months ago, when they'd been searching for *Madre* Dorada. Why had she not pursued that hint?

Of course, Grimm seemed to be more loyal to Viktor than anyone else on the crew. Viktor certainly trusted him. She and Grimm were the only ones he didn't require to drink the special rum he used to ensure obedience among the crew. Belladonna knew the reason it was not required of her was because she had already bound herself to his will.

But he trusted Grimm. Of course, he trusted him. Why wouldn't he? Why was she even questioning it?

She shook her head and looked out the window at the sky. Morning was still a few hours away. There was nothing she could do except wait for her captain to return.

Heaven help him when he did. She was determined that he would never leave her in such a position of helplessness again.

Viktor took his time making his way back to Celine's. He constantly had to add moss to the ember in the shell. It had fared well all night long, not needing any kindling. It had actually grown quite warm when he had been draining Melanie. Now the damned thing had cooled and kept sputtering like it was going to die. He had to keep it alive and get it to Gloribeau today, if possible.

He picked up on the siren's ire and agitation as soon as he crossed Celine's wards. Odd, he should have been able to sense her before that. He got no indication that she had been shielding from him. He wondered if it was a side-effect of the wards or some meddling on Jeorge's part.

It was something he would have to figure out later. He didn't have time for that or for Belle's impending tantrum. Right at the moment, time was of the essence.

"You callous bastard!" She rounded on him as soon as he entered the room.

"Shut it." He silenced her with the most effective means available to him. It always took her a moment to recover from one of his kisses. He took advantage of that lag. "Where's Hezekiah?"

Damn, but she hated when he did that to her. She also loved it. Viktor always managed to confuse and frustrate her unlike any other male. The brief disorientation allowed her to pick up on his mood. Something was very wrong.

"He said he was going to find a bottle and a wench. What is wrong? What happened?"

"Find him. I'll send for Jon-Jon. Meet us at the skiff. I'd like to find Gloribeau today."

"Dammit woman! Don't you knock?" Grimm was halfway through a bottle. A partially naked woman straddled his lap, riding him.

"The Captain wants you," Belladonna replied tersely.

"Bugger." He'd always hated stopping in the middle. "Get off, lass. I've got to go."

Rather than comply, she started riding him harder. "Not yet, *mon ami*. I'm not finished yet."

He shoved her off roughly, stood up and began fastening his breeches. "Yes, you are."

Secretly, Belle enjoyed the brief glimpse she got. She knew nothing would ever take place between them, though. Viktor would never permit it.

The prostitute stood and snatched the bottle then took a swig. Swallowing angrily, she glared at the pirate. "Not so fast, *m'sieur*. There is still the matter of payment."

Retrieving the rest of his things on his way towards the door, he smirked over his shoulder. "Don't worry, lass. I won't charge you anything. You can keep the bottle."

The pirate and the siren left the woman sputtering in incoherent rage.

They arrived at the dock to find Jon-Jon loading several packages into the skiff. Viktor was tending the ember.

Belladonna looked questioningly at the amount of cargo. "I thought you intended to reach the Sister today. Why so many provisions?"

"René won't be in any shape to resume his duties for some time. Besides, he's terrified of the prospect of revisiting Glory. Celine asked us to deliver next month's shipment to her early, since we're going there anyway." Viktor shrugged. "I didn't see any harm in it. The witch seems to like me. I'd like to keep it that way."

She saw the logic in it. Staying in Gloribeau's favor could make things easier. Belle had a feeling she was the most powerful of all the Sisters. She hoped that they were able to reach her quickly. Just boarding the skiff, she felt her own powers starting to wane again.

"Shove off, Mr. Jon. The morning is almost past," Vik ordered. "Mr. Grimm, keep a check on our sounding. I don't want to waste time with unnecessary groundings."

"Aye," both men replied and set to their appointed tasks. Jon-Jon untied the mooring and began propelling the craft from the stern with a sturdy pole. Grimm took up his position at the bow with the sounding rod, checking the water's depth at regularly timed intervals.

About an hour into the swamps, Viktor spoke to Belle. "That sea bag to your right has more pouches of moss in it. Hand me one, pet. This damned thing keeps trying to die on me."

Silently, she did as he requested. A mild dizzy spell took her as she sat back down a bit awkwardly. She shook her head, trying to clear it.

Even though he was tending the ember, he noticed the change in the siren. "Pet?"

"She's growing stronger. Her power is interfering with mine."

"Like the last time?"

"Worse. Other than your presence, I'm already almost completely deaf and blind magically." She hugged herself, not looking at him. "I really don't feel like talking about it – or thinking about it."

If he didn't know better, he would've thought she was pouting. But he remembered how she had been the last time they'd entered these swamps. If her reaction to Gloribeau's magic was worse, she had to be miserable.

Very well, if she didn't want to think about it, he could give her a distraction.

"Why were you angry at me this morning?"

"Why do you care?" She threw it back at him irritably.

Viktor found himself actually stung by her words. He was not used to being questioned. He was the Captain. He was used to being obeyed. Yet once he thought about it, he found that he really did care. He tolerated more from the siren than he'd ever tolerated from anyone else, male or female. He did care, even though he wasn't sure why.

"Just satisfy my curiosity, pet," he finally replied.

She sighed and glared at him. Just curiosity. Why was she not surprised? She knew it was too much to hope that he really cared.

"All right, if you really want to know. You might as well have locked me in a cage, when you left to meet with Jeorge. By binding me to remain at Celine's, you denied me any means of distracting myself while you put yourself in extreme danger. I couldn't even go hunt!"

"You could have amused yourself with one of the clients."

She gave him a look. "As if that bitch would let me near any of her precious customers." She snorted. "She was pissy just because I was walking on her stupid carpet!"

He couldn't help but smile at her ire. Her color was up, her eyes were bright, and he thought it made her irresistibly cute. The thought of the effect telling her that would bring only heightened his amusement.

She noticed the smile. "It is not funny," she growled.

"I'm sorry, pet. I just can't picture the situation." He tried not to laugh.

"It definitely wasn't funny from my perspective," Grimm commented. "I had to hold her off and promise to pay for the damned thing to get Celine to get out of sight before she tore her up."

Viktor raised an eyebrow. "I'm impressed you escaped unscathed, Hezekiah. You know better than to get in the middle of a cat fight."

"Aye, but I'm not the one she was mad at. Besides, didn't see the sense in letting them go at it. Belle has a decided advantage, and I don't think it would've sat well with Gloribeau." He shrugged.

"Good man. I can always count on you to watch my back." He returned his attention to the siren. "I apologize for imprisoning you, pet. I didn't want you defying the agreement with Jeorge and shadowing me."

"Give me some credit, Captain." She managed to make the title sound like an insult.

Once again, Grimm spoke up. "She's a smart one, our Belle. After she told me why she was so upset and worried, she stopped me from going to you."

"And how did you manage that, pet? More importantly, why?"

"I know better than to give the appearance of weakness to a predator, especially one like Jeorge. If either of us had shown up behind you, against orders and your agreement, it would have made it look like you couldn't control your people."

He blinked at her. Once again, he had seriously underestimated her. He really needed to keep in mind that she was unlike any human female he had ever had dealings with.

"I am still angry with you."

Now she was pouting. "Out with it, then. What other offenses have I unknowingly committed?"

"Do not patronize me! You didn't come back until dawn! All you had to do was deliver the brat to him. That shouldn't have taken all night! What did he want with the silly little thing, anyway?"

"You are not my wife, woman."

That evasive reply spoke volumes to Belladonna. "You fucked her. You fool! Your agreement with Jeorge was to deliver her intact!"

Without warning, Viktor backhanded her sharply. "Do not speak to me in that tone ever again, Belladonna, not in front of my crew, strangers, nor in private." His tone was dangerously cold.

She wiped a shaking hand across her mouth and came away with blood. That blow had actually hurt. Her neck was sore because her reflexes were dull, and she had not seen the slap coming in time to at least roll with it. There was a wary fear in her eyes, when she met his angry gaze.

Viktor saw the fear. Rather than feeling vindicated, which was his usual reaction after delivering such a reprimand, he felt remorse. He really didn't want to break the siren's will. Although her temper and insubordination were irritating, they were also a refreshing change. He had enjoyed that she was not afraid of him.

Now it looked as if that had changed. The least he could do was answer her questions about why he had been at Jeorge's all night.

"He wanted the girl to be brought into his kiss. Apparently, he considers the event a night long process and celebration."

"So, you did not leave out of respect for your host? Was sex part of the celebration?" Belle's voice was wary, but still carried a note of defiance. He was relieved that she was not broken.

He nodded. "Yes. Jeorge prefers that his candidates die at the height of pleasure. Not only did he invite me to give her that pleasure, but to make her vampire as well."

"I wish you had never encountered any of the vampires here. Now you will never be entirely free from dealing with them." She sighed.

"What do you mean, pet? I fulfilled my part of the bargain. As long as he honors his part, there is no need for me to have any further dealings with him."

She shook her head. "I have to remind myself that you have not been vampire for very long. You are at a power level that it takes many at least a century to reach, but you don't have the experience or knowledge of vampire culture to go with that power. Jeorge has taken advantage of that fact, although I don't think he suspects your true power."

"How do you figure that, pet?"

"If he knew how strong you really are, he never would have allowed you to leave. As it is, he is curious about you. He had you followed yesterday. Now he has a direct means of keeping up with your movements, once the girl rises tonight. You made her; just as you can sense your cadre, any vampire you make can sense you."

He had never considered that, yet it made sense. After all, he used Lazarus to "see" things. It only made sense that the communication could go both ways. The question was what did he want to do with this information? He really didn't like that someone else could so easily track him. It was bad for business, so to speak.

"Can I block him?"

She thought about it for a moment before nodding. "Yes, but I would advise against blocking him entirely, at least initially. Let him see. Let him think you are unaware of his spying. He knows you will figure it out eventually. If he doesn't grow bored with his voyeurism, you can gradually start using the link to control what he sees."

Viktor mulled this over. "You're right. This will force me to continue dealings with Jeorge. It will be for the best to keep on a good footing with him. He will have information that could make things very uncomfortable for me if he were to give it to any of my enemies. I do not need that kind of distraction."

"You will have to be careful doing so, but you can use the link with the girl to find out what Jeorge knows about you and what he is doing while in her presence," she pointed out. "Since they are true vampires, and the girl is a new one, the link will only be open from sunset to sunrise. Only the very old, very powerful vampires can rise from their daytime death while the sun is still in the sky. Even then, they have to remain in places where the light cannot reach."

"That is good to know." He noticed that her color was off again. Some subliminal glow, the kind you don't really notice normally, was missing. Even her scent was almost human. That worried him. They needed to find Glory and get this over with as quickly as possible.

"You look tired, Belle. Why don't you rest?"

She flinched when he reached to caress her cheek. But then she relaxed. He wasn't going to hurt her. She must be tired; she had the irrational notion that he was worried about her.

She felt so sleepy. She only had a moment to wonder if he was willing her to sleep before she lost consciousness.

Chapter 27

Just as the last time, the swamp proved difficult to navigate. The more they tried to stay on course, the more of a maze it turned into. The canopy kept everything in a perpetual gloom. There was no way to tell the sun's position, which made telling directions nearly impossible.

Eventually, they found themselves reduced to just trying to keep to navigable channels through the trees. It didn't help that they seemed to be growing closer and closer together. If the waters were any shallower, Grimm would have sworn they had wandered over a storm-drowned hammock.

Jon-Jon was the first to complain, however. "I don't like this place, Cap'n. Feels like the trees are moving in to close around us."

"They are." Viktor's response surprised Grimm. He'd been thinking the same thing, but figured it was just a trick of the light. "Gloribeau is playing with us. The movement is almost too subtle to spot, but she is shuffling the trees. I don't know why she is prolonging our journey. It's taking more and more fuel to keep the ember alive. If it dies, she'll never regain her full power."

"She seems pretty powerful as she is," Grimm pointed out. "I'm starting to get the feeling she's not as worried about that ember as you are, Vik."

He growled. "I know the old man said the Sisters were not going to make things easy, but this is getting tedious."

A breeze played through the trees. There seemed to be the faint sound of a woman's laughter in the rustle and sigh.

Viktor narrowed his eyes. Low under his breath, so soft that Grimm was the only one on the skiff that heard him, he murmured, "Fine, I'll play it your way, old woman. I'll bide my time and keep the ember alive until you decide to show yourself."

The breeze whispered again. He could just pick out the word, "soon," echoing along it.

"Cap'n, she's not looking too good," Jon-Jon observed.

Viktor looked at the sleeping siren. She looked very pale, almost to the point of appearing gray. Dark circles marred the skin under her eyes. Her lips seemed colorless and cracked. Her breathing sounded labored, as well.

He reached out gently through their link. He did not want to wake her. She had told him in the past that it took a great deal of energy to maintain human form and that she had to either eat a great deal or sleep. She did not need sleep in her natural form. He had to concentrate to reach her. If he didn't know better, he would have thought she had actually become human. Her magic was almost non-existent, and her presence felt very weak.

"She's been away from the sea too long. This bayou is like poison to her. We need to finish with Gloribeau quickly and get her back to the ship."

Jeorge woke with a start. It had always been like that with him, ever since he had been made vampire. One second, he was dead to the world, and the next he was wide awake. Waking slowly was one of the few things he still missed about his humanity after all these centuries.

A glance at the clock told him the sun still rode the sky, but not for long this late afternoon. He would have to use the private access passage to reach the room his new acquisition lay in, waiting for the first night of her new life.

As expected, Melanie was still just a bloodless corpse. Under normal circumstances, she would not rise until sunset. It was that way for all new vampires.

That was another thing about Brandewyne that puzzled him. It was obvious that the pirate was still young as a vampire, but he was capable of things that only very old vampires were supposed to be able to do.

It was only in the last two decades that Jeorge had gained the ability to stay awake past sunrise, and then the most he could hope for was an hour. Viktor Brandewyne had not fallen asleep with the rising sun.

Jeorge desperately wanted to know how he managed that. The power and freedom that ability would grant him was tantalizing. It was time to employ an ability he did have which was unique to him, as far as he knew.

He discovered long ago by accident that he could cause a new-made vampire to arise to his call before sunset. He could do the same with vampires under a century old, but he did not think it wise to do so with any frequency. The older the vampire, the more likely they were to think it was their own power allowing them to rise early. That delusion tended to lead to rebellion.

Now he wanted to try out the new tool the pirate had given him. "Melanie, child, it is time to wake. I have a task for you."

As he called her, he took a small knife and slit his palm. He had not fed yet, so he was only able to squeeze out a few thick, nearly black drops of blood. He wiped them on her lips and sent his will into her. The wound did not bleed of itself, but neither did it heal. That would come later, after his first victim of the evening.

Melanie woke with a gasp. It was followed by a scream, as he had expected. She was being made violently aware of all the changes her body had undergone. Her senses were being assaulted by stimuli she never could have known as human, and of course, there was the Hunger.

All new vampires went through this on their first night. Jeorge likened it to birth-trauma.

"Welcome to your new life, child," he greeted her, once she calmed down.

"You called me, master? Why am I still naked? Where is my sire?" She spouted questions, then clutched her stomach and doubled over in pain. "*Mon Dieu*! I am so hungry!" she keened.

Patiently, he answered her questions. "Yes, I did. There was not time to dress you this morning, but I have clothes laid out for you. As for your sire's whereabouts, you are going to help me answer that."

"Food! Please! I am starving!"

"It is early yet, child. As soon as it is safe to go out, I will teach you to hunt. In the meantime, I need you to find Viktor Brandewyne."

"But I'm Hungry!"

Lightning quick, he slapped her; not hard, just enough to get her attention. "I need you to find your sire. You will do this, or you will stay Hungry."

Her eyes grew panicked. "But I don't know how! Please, master, don't starve me!"

Jeorge smiled. "I can teach you how. Do exactly as I tell you, and I give you my word that you will feast tonight. Now close your eyes and think of nothing but the one who made you."

Melanie obeyed, trying her best to ignore the gnawing pain in her belly. After a moment, the connection clicked into place. "I have him."

"Very good, child. Last night, there was a conch shell that he kept tied to his side, even while he made love to you. Does he still have it with him?"

"Yes. He is emptying ash from it and stuffing moss around a fire's ember he is carrying in it."

"Open your mind to his a little more, but not too much. He mustn't know we are watching him. You should be able to feel his thoughts. What are they right now?"

"The magic is growing weak. Time is running out. He has to find the witch soon. She is dying. He has to save her."

"The witch is dying?"

"No. Belladonna."

The siren. She was dying? How was that possible? Her kind was nearly immortal. They could be killed, but not easily, especially if they were close enough to the sea to get in it and repair any damage suffered.

"Where is he?"

"Deep in the bayous, looking for Granny Glory."

The swamp: that explained it. Jeorge was one of the very few who knew that black water was deadly to sea folk of any kind, especially if it was in a powerful witch's territory. The magicks clashed, with the native swamp magic always victorious. If the siren stayed in the swamp too long, her magic would die completely, and she would become a mortal human.

He had learned all he knew of sirens from his late sire. He had been connected to his mind the same way Melanie was to Viktor's at the moment, when his sire had killed Belle's sister. The knowledge had come with the very blood that had destroyed the bastard.

Viktor was instantly aware of Melanie the moment she rose. Her distraction with the change and her Hunger allowed him to listen to her without her knowledge. So, Jeorge could raise other vampires early. He wasn't sure what use that information was, but he made a note of it anyway.

Still, he was soon to dismiss the intrusion. He had other worries on his mind. The damned ember was going through the moss tinder at an alarming rate. The pouch he had was already empty. With Belle asleep, and Grimm and Jon-Jon busy navigating, he would have to get it himself.

Crouching rather than standing, to keep from upsetting the skiff, he leaned over the sleeping siren to get at the bag of moss-stuffed pouches. Her color seemed a little better, but he could barely detect her magic. Her scent had changed even more. She smelled completely like a human.

At that moment, she woke. For a moment, she didn't recognize Viktor; she only knew that a predator crouched over her. Her first instinct was to get away. She shoved him with all her might. If they had been on land, it would have been futile on her part. Her strength seemed to have fled along with her magic. But he wasn't expecting that reaction from her and was already a little off balance. The push managed to make him drop back into a sitting position.

Then Belle stood abruptly, rocking the boat. It threw her off balance, and she fell overboard with a startled yelp. She surfaced for a moment, thrashing wildly. Her eyes were filled with panic and remained human and gray. She reached for the boat and missed, then she slipped under the dark water.

"Dammit!" Viktor cursed and stripped off his coat.

"Captain! You can't go in after her. You know what she's like in the water," Grimm protested.

He looked at his first mate with a deadly glare. "She can't change in this swamp muck. Her magic has drained almost completely away since we came out here," he stated. "She'll drown!" He kicked off his boots.

Just as he was about to dive in, Grimm stopped him again. "The ember; it will go out in the water, and old Zeke warned that only you could carry it. I'll go in after her."

"No." Viktor's tone was adamant. "You'd never see her in this water. It has to be me. I can use the bond I have with her to locate her."

"You're going to abandon your quest?"

He smiled, "I never said that." Taking the shell, he shook the ember out into a wad of moss, which he wrapped around it. Then, he stuffed the wad into his mouth, like a plug of tobacco. A grimace was the only sign the heat caused him any pain.

The magic-laden ember secured, he dove over the side, plunging deep beneath the surface.

It felt like he was diving forever, before he finally reached the mucky bottom. Even with his keen eyesight, he could see nothing but his own limbs, and those only faintly. The water was too murky, and there simply wasn't enough light filtering through. If he wasn't careful, he would miss Belladonna, even if she was only inches away.

He called on their bond. At first, he felt nothing. Was he already too late? No, wait. There, to his left was just the faintest trace of her magic. Swimming toward it, he soon heard a frantic heartbeat. The closer he got, the weaker the rhythmic beating grew. She was running out of time.

He almost swam past her. His foot brushed something that didn't feel like muck or cypress knees. Feeling around, he discovered it was an arm. He pulled but ended up pulling himself to the siren rather than her to him.

Her eyes were open, but unseeing. Her heart still beat, but she was unconscious. Running his hands over her, he discovered she was tangled in submerged roots and vines. He used the dagger he kept at the nape of his neck to cut her free.

It was a fight for a while. Fresh tendrils seemed to snake out to re-snare her, even as he sliced and hacked at them. Her heartbeat grew slower. The ember in his mouth grew cooler.

On a hunch, he pulled the crystal out of his shirt. It glowed softly, allowing him to see what he was doing. It also had the effect of stilling the cursed vines that were giving him so much trouble.

Once he had her free, he pushed off for the surface with her.

Reaching the air, he found that the skiff was nowhere in sight. A quick scan of the area told him they weren't in the same part of the swamp they had gone into the water in. The island where Tulimanchulo had met its end was nearby. Viktor could see the scaffold and kettle.

He saw no one around when he pulled Belladonna ashore. Her nearly lifeless form flopped limply. No breath stirred her chest. Her pale face stared upwards with blue lips and sightless, glazed eyes. Lifting her, he draped her face-down over his shoulder then bounced her to put pressure on her stomach.

She vomited swamp water down his back. When he laid her down, she gasped and coughed, learning how to breathe again. Life returned to her eyes.

"Viktor?"

She passed out, even as he nodded. Listening, he heard her heartbeat strengthen, but it still sounded far too weak, even for a human.

Satisfied of her safety for the moment, he cast about for something to put the ember in. He'd left the shell on the skiff. It would have been too damp to use if he'd kept it with him, anyway. Unfortunately, nothing suitable seemed to be available.

Belle whimpered, drawing his attention back to her. Kneeling beside her, he brushed the wet hair from her face. He didn't like how clammy her skin felt. If she had been truly human, he would have set about building a fire to dry and warm her. But he wasn't sure of the best way to save the siren. Damn, but he hated to be made to feel helpless.

"I see you have returned to me, Viktor Brandewyne."

He was standing and facing Gloribeau in a split second, subconsciously placing himself between her and Belle.

"Did you bring what I sent you for?"

He nodded. Opening his mouth, he showed her the ember. She glided over to him, a seductive sway to her hips. Reaching up, she placed her hands on his shoulders, balancing herself.

"You have passed my test." She smiled then stretched up to kiss him.

He found himself grasping her waist and lifting her up for better access. He couldn't help but react to the friction of her voluptuous body sliding up his. She wrapped her arms around his neck, wriggling against him and making him moan in appreciation. As she deepened the kiss, she took the ember from his mouth into her own.

Breaking the kiss, but not the embrace, she leaned her head back and swallowed the ember whole. A slow wave of power spread out from the Sister.

Belladonna let out a strangled scream of pain, as the swamp magic rolled over her. Viktor looked over in her direction, wondering how he had gotten so far away. Even as he was thinking he should go to her, Gloribeau pulled his face back to hers, trying for another kiss.

With her full magic restored, she was the most powerful being he had ever encountered. The power, combined with her beauty and the scent of her readiness made for a potent aphrodisiac.

But he knew manipulation when he was the intended target of it. Gently but firmly, he set her back on the ground and deliberately walked back to Belle's side.

"I appreciate the offer, Gloribeau, believe me, I do. But she is dying. I need to get her out of here. She needs my help."

Glory vanished and rematerialized on the other side of the siren from him. "She is not dying physically. Only her magic is dying. If she does not return to the sea before the last ray of the setting sun vanishes, she will become human and mortal, but she will not die – right away."

He stooped and picked Belladonna up, still facing the Sister. "That is not acceptable. I am taking her back. I can't lose her."

"If you leave now, I cannot give you the magic you need."

"Then I will come back for it, once she is restored."

"You will not find me again, if you do that. Yes, the sea witch will return to normal, and will still be able to help you find my Sisters. But you will forever be lacking my part and will never be able to break the curse."

Viktor's face was set in stone, belying the tenderness with which he held the unconscious woman. "So be it. I will not condemn Belladonna to humanity."

He turned to leave.

Tamara A. Lowery

Chapter 28

Once again, Gloribeau transported to block his exit. She smiled solemnly and held out her hand. "Pass me the vial."

"Excuse me?"

"The vial that Celie gave you. You have passed my final test, Viktor Brandewyne. You chose helping another over the success of your quest as well as over the pleasure I offered you. Now at last, I can give you what you came for."

Irritated and relieved at the same time, he shifted Belle's body to drape over his shoulder, freeing one hand. He slipped the chain holding the silver vial over his head to hand it over then hesitated. "I have no null to make the exchange and keep our magicks from interacting."

Gloribeau laughed. "I am not Dorada. My magic will not suffer from contact with yours."

He handed her the vial, and she opened the cap and spit into it. Her spittle mingled with *Madre* Dorada's golden teardrop, emitting a soft glow, before she replaced the cap and handed the vial back to him. He returned it to its place about his neck.

As he shifted the siren back to a two-armed carrying position, Glory placed a hand gently on his arm. "I know you may never admit it to yourself or anyone else, but your actions show you love her. You will have to give up one of your crew for her in order to save her. She must feed to fully recover. But do not choose either of the trader's sons as her victim. They will prove valuable to you someday. Now fly, my friend. The sun is setting even as we speak.

He needed no further goading.

Grimm and Jon-Jon knew serious magic was afoot. The second after their captain jumped overboard, the trees shifted with a frightening speed, forcing away from that spot. They didn't have time to worry about helping the captain. They had to work fast to keep the boat from being crushed. It was apparent that someone or something wanted them to go in one direction only. Try as he might, Grimm could not spot any openings wide enough to allow them to change course.

After what seemed like forever, the trees finally opened up. It took a moment for them to realize where they had been directed.

"What is that witch up to?" Grimm muttered. They tied up at the same dock that René had brought them to the first time they had entered this swamp. As before, *flambeaux* illuminated the gloom, and no one was in evidence on the island.

"Reckon the Cap'n made it here, too?" Jon-Jon wondered aloud.

"Don't know. I don't see where it looks like anyone's here. All I can figure is that Gloribeau has a reason for steering us here."

"Of course, I do," a voice came from the catwalk. They turned to see the swamp witch gliding toward them. "You brought my supplies. Now how about you two boys unload them from your little boat?"

Grimm was amazed at the volume of magic pouring off her. He could only guess that Viktor had given her the ember. "Where is my Captain?"

Glory smiled warmly. "He chose well in picking you, Hezekiah Grimm. Your loyalty does you credit. He has received what he came for and taken the siren back to the sea to recover." She moved past them onto the small dock. Bending down, she retrieved the empty conch shell from the skiff. "Yes, this will come in handy. It is from Hell's Breath, isn't it?"

"Aye. The Captain used it to transport the ember."

"Good. Now, Hezekiah Grimm, Willoby Jon, I need you to bring the supplies Celine sent to my house. Then you will be free to rejoin your Captain and crew."

Both men were mesmerized by the sight of her as she walked back to the ladder to the catwalk, climbed it, and disappeared down the walk.

Melanie's inability to reconnect with her sire frustrated her. She could feel his life-force but was unable to "see" anything now. The vision had gone black shortly after seeing Belladonna fall into the swamp.

Jeorge wasn't very happy about it, either, but he couldn't punish the girl. She was new-born to her powers, and she had not had her first feed yet. He suspected that the lost connection had more to do with that than any possibility she had been detected.

The sun had just set. He decided to go ahead and take her out to teach her how to hunt.

Despite the risk to himself, Viktor plunged into the briny water with Belle the moment they reached the sea. She shifted immediately into her natural form, which made her awkward to hold. Her shark-like tail was just plain unwieldy.

He didn't like that she didn't regain consciousness. He had been prepared to exit the water quickly, to avoid an attack from her. The sun was about to disappear below the horizon. Hopefully, he wasn't too late.

Looking around, he saw he had emerged from the bayou country not far from the *Incubus*. Lashing out with his will, he snagged the first crewman his mind touched. Within minutes, the ill-fated sailor was swimming toward them, crewmates yelling at him to come back.

Viktor recognized the man as Bob Percher, one of the riggers. It was a shame he'd have to lose him. The man was a wizard at mending lines and sails.

"Pet, wake up." No response. Damn. How was he supposed to feed her if she remained unconscious? "Percher, come over here," he ordered.

The man obeyed, compelled by the vampire's will, but terror shone in his eyes. He knew exactly what was in store for him. "Have I done something to anger ye, Cap'n?"

"No, man. You've done nothing wrong in my eyes. You're just convenient and out of luck. Belle is dying and needs food – now." With blinding speed, he drew a blade and carved a hunk out of the man's arm.

Percher stared at the wound a full minute before realizing the pain. He let out a bloodcurdling scream at the same moment Viktor forced the gobbet of flesh into the siren's mouth.

The taste of fresh meat and the screams of prey were enough to revive her. The second he saw she was aware, Vik dropped her and flew up out of reach. She was a dangerous predator and just as likely to attack him as the chosen victim.

Percher continued to scream in panic. He stumbled in the shallow water, as he tried to blindly back away from the siren. His behavior only served to draw her attention. The smell of fear and blood sealed his fate.

Her weakened state erased any cognizant thought. She didn't even consider playing with her prey. She had to feed.

Percher's screams were abruptly cut short. Belladonna tore him in half. He was dead before he knew she'd made a move for him.

In her ravenous hunger, she completely consumed her victim in a matter of minutes. Looking around and seeing no one else in the water, she keened in hunger. Viktor was able to sense that she was about to start screeching at the frequency that could destroy a human's mind. He couldn't afford to lose his entire crew to her. He ordered another sailor to his death.

She went through five more pirates before her hunger was sated. Every man on deck or still aloft breathed an unsteady sigh of relief. The Captain's selection of victims had been haphazard at best, with no regard to position or skill.

With a thrust of her tail, she launched herself out of the water and caught one of the mooring lines. She pulled herself up, hand over hand. By the time she reached the deck, she had returned to human form. The pirates gave her a wide berth as she walked naked toward the Captain. Even Sniff made himself scarce. None wanted to take the chance she was still hungry.

Only Viktor stood fast. He knew she was not going to attack him now, for food, anyway. "Are you sure it is wise for you to play human so soon, pet? I would think you would want to recover your strength more."

She didn't answer. Instead, she stood on tiptoe, wrapped her arms around his neck and kissed him soundly. "Thank you for choosing me over Glory," she whispered. "You need to fetch your mates before she does to them what she did to René. Then we need to make ready to sail."

"You're in a hurry to get away from here?" He smiled, enjoying the feel of her in his arms. At the moment, he would rather take her below to his cabin than anything else.

"There is that. The further I am from her, the stronger I will grow. But we've another Sister of Power to track down."

"You had a vision."

She nodded. "Mexico."

Reluctantly, he released her. "Go below and get dressed. I'll go after Grimm and Jon-Jon."

Two sailors sat on coils of rope on the deck of their ship. They had the night watch, but they weren't really concerned about it. The captain and officers dined below. Their crewmates slept in one of the holds, resting up for the voyage ahead. The ship had finished taking on cargo about an hour before sunset but remained tied up in harbor. The harbor pilot wouldn't arrive until the morning to guide them back out to the Gulf.

So, they decided to play some dice. Viktor sat in the rigging above them, listening to their conversation and sizing them up to see if they would serve his purpose.

"Garn, Pierre. Who'd you get these dice from? They're heavy on one side. Keep rollin' threes."

"So I noticed, *mon ami*. I sort of borrowed them from Mr. Skrags."

"I knew that bastard was cheating! It won't go well for him if the rest of the crew finds out. Most of 'em already owe him half their pay for this trip."

"Perhaps he'd be willing to pay to keep that quiet, eh Larry?" Pierre smirked.

"That he might. That he might."

"I'll be glad when this run is over. Don't like playing packet. A working ship is no place for passengers, especially females. There'll be trouble among the crew, I'll wager."

"I don't think you lads will have to worry about that."

They looked up to see Viktor standing over them. The light behind him kept his face in shadow, and they mistook him for one of the passengers.

"Look here," Larry tried not to sound startled, "you shouldn't be up here after dark like this, sir. Deck's not a safe place to wander at night."

"No, it is not." Vik smiled.

Jon-Jon deposited the last bag of supplies in the corner of Gloribeau's shack. "That's all of it."

"If that's all you need, Gloribeau, we need to return to our ship. I'm sure the Captain is waiting on us," Grimm announced.

They turned to leave, only to find her blocking the door. Her skin looked so white against the silky black of her hair and gown that it seemed to glow. "Surely you don't have to leave so soon," she purred. "Your loyalty to your captain should be rewarded, after all."

Both men were struck by her unearthly beauty. Grimm could not remember encountering a more perfectly formed female. It was hard to believe that she had been a withered old crone when they'd first met her. Jon-Jon stood bewitched.

Glory reached up and undid the clasps of her dress. The garment slid to the floor in a silken puddle. "I know Viktor had to leave abruptly, but are you and Willoby really in such a hurry, Hezekiah?"

Grimm felt heat rise in his face and places lower. The swamp witch was truly magnificent. He actually took a few steps toward her, before he was aware he had.

"I am afraid they do, Gloribeau."

She turned to find the vampire outside behind her. She turned a smile of pure seduction on him. "You surprise me, Viktor Brandewyne. The siren was not enough to hold you?"

"I came to retrieve my mates, Sister. I need to set sail with all haste."

"I have need of these two," she said with a pout. "You are welcome to join us, but I cannot release them right away."

He inclined his head to her. "Your need is great. I can smell it from here. But my need of them is greater. So, I brought you substitutes for them. I remember the state you left René Thibideaux in and will not risk my mates to your sweet embrace."

She looked past him to the two frightened men he had kidnapped. They had not seen her yet. His body blocked their view.

"Bring them into the light, so I can inspect them."

"You lads heard her. In you go." He gave a tug on the rope he'd bound their wrists with, causing them to stumble.

"Gently, Captain Brandewyne," she chided. "They're no go to me damaged."

It was the second time she'd said his name, and it finally sank in to Pierre and Larry just exactly who had captured them. Viktor hadn't really bothered with introductions. Their terror was palpable. That he had flown them into the swamp hadn't helped.

Once they were inside, he handed the rope to the still naked witch. That drew their attention to her. To their credit, they quickly averted their eyes.

Larry pled hurriedly, "Run, lass, while you've got a chance! That's Bloody Vik Brandee!"

"*Oui, ma'm'selle*," Pierre chimed in. "He is *tres mal* pirate! Run! Don't let him catch and ravish you!"

They didn't understand why she started laughing. In fact, they almost forgot why they were afraid. Her laughter was extremely seductive. Even Viktor felt its pull. His single-mindedness kept him from going to her, and his will protected Jon-Jon. He wasn't sure how Grimm was able to resist. He could see by his first mate's face that it was a struggle for him.

"Oh, my dear boys." Glory laughed. "I am in no danger of that. Twice now, in fact, Captain Brandewyne has turned down the offer of my favors." She gave Vik a sultry smile. "I know his reasoning for it, but I still hold out hope he will return one day to take me up on it. The offer remains open."

"Perhaps." He carefully kept his tone neutral.

She circled the prisoners, looking them up and down. Once her assessment was complete, she gave a decisive nod. "They are young and appear to be healthy. They are even moderately attractive. You have a good eye for man-flesh, Captain."

"I've found it beneficial to know what pleases a woman."

"I accept your substitutes. You may take your men and be about your business." She dismissed him.

Just like that, the seductive power she wielded dropped away from the three pirates to concentrate solely on the two prisoners. Viktor wasn't about to question it. He quickly led his mates out of the shack.

Grimm started down the catwalk toward the dock. "Forget something, Hezekiah?"

"You didn't tie up at the dock?"

"I didn't bring a boat. The only boat at that dock is the one we brought the supplies in on. Although I doubt they'll survive to use it, leave it for those two to get out with."

Jon-Jon was confused. "How are we supposed to get back to the ship?"

In answer, Viktor put an arm around each man's waist. "Hold on tight."

Jon-Jon wouldn't have dared, but Grimm couldn't resist joking. "I like ye, Vik, but not like that."

"I could just drop you from a hundred feet up, Hezekiah."

"Fine. I'll hold you. But I want a big, fancy wedding."

"Heh," Jon-Jon barked, "you know you can't wear white."

Grimm made a kissy-face at the second mate. "Jealous."

Viktor had to chuckle at the banter. "Enough! If I start laughing too hard, I'm liable to drop both of you."

Looking down to see the treetops blur by underneath them, both pirates decided to leave the teasing off until they were safely on deck.

Chapter 29

Captain Bainbridge returned to his cabin to find a young man rifling his desk. "Ho! You, lad! What do you think you're about? I'll have you flogged for this!"

The youngster jumped, startled, but remained silent. Snatching the sealed message they were delivering, he tried to make a run for the door. Bainbridge moved more quickly than anticipated, however. He tripped the intruder, dropping him to the deck then pinning him there.

"No!" The interloper's voice was higher pitched than Bainbridge had expected, when he pried the papers away from him. The lad's face was smooth and free of fuzz. How young was he? There was also something very familiar about his features. If he didn't know better, he'd think his employer might have spawned the little bastard.

"I don't know what you want with these," he growled, "but you'll soon learn I do not tolerate thievery aboard my ship." He hoisted the lad to his feet to shake him, then noticed a tell-tale feature that stopped him cold. The "lad" had breasts.

The short hair and masculine clothes had fooled him at first, but he finally recognized the face he had seen on several occasions at his employer's home.

"Miss Samantha?"

Through the whole encounter, she had shown no fear. Even now, a quiet determination shone in her eyes. "You cannot deliver that message as it stands, Captain Bainbridge. To do so will condemn my brothers to the gallows and, for my safety, please address me as Sam aboard ship."

Bainbridge released her arm and bowed. "I am sorry for attacking you, Miss Brumble. I had no idea. Why are you here and dressed like that? Blast! Forgive my language, miss. I'll have to turn about so we can get you back to your father. He must be worried sick."

"No! You will not. I will not return to that man I once called father. I know what he put in that missive and who it is to. He has implicated my brothers, his own sons, in the acts of piracy that led to their disappearances and the loss of two shipments of emeralds."

He was stunned. "I don't know what you mean about that. My report to your father made no such implication, and I know nothing about any emeralds. Wherever did you get such a far-fetched idea?"

Sam scowled at him. "Do not think me simple or ignorant just because I am a woman, Captain. My father has already made that mistake. I have known about his smuggling operation almost since its inception."

"You place me in quite a predicament, miss."

She smiled. "Not as sticky a one as you may think. I can alter the message and seal the new version. Several times, I forged Father's handwriting and signature on notes for Thomas' tutors. My brother preferred to avoid getting a second beating for the same offense. Father was brutal enough," she explained, pulling the stolen seal from her pocket.

The captain had to admire her cleverness, but he still had a problem. His employer would not be pleased to learn she was aboard the *Shining Star*. He wasn't too happy himself having her aboard. Females on a ship tended to lead to trouble among the crew. Some runs lasted for months. That was a long time to go without a woman, and sailors in general were a rather uncivilized lot.

"Miss Brumble, a ship like this is not a safe place for a woman, especially one as comely as you, miss. Go ahead and alter the documents. I too believe in your brothers' innocence. But I have to either return you to your father or at least put you ashore in a safe port."

She shook her head, adamant. "You can't do that, Captain Bainbridge. I left a letter for Father. I've taken my mother's jewels and my dower. Hopefully it will be enough to ransom Thom and Zach."

"Are you mad, lass? Bloody Vik Brandee is the most feared pirate on these or any other waters!"

"No, sir. I am determined. I will win my brothers' freedom, if they are still alive, by whatever means I must." She refused to back down. "I have successfully been passing myself as a lad these past weeks. You even believed me to be male, when you caught me. Address me as Sam. The crew will never know the difference. Captain, you helped train my brothers. Teach me seamanship, too. I already know a few basics from listening to them, and Zach taught me knots to help him remember them, himself."

"You cannot be swayed from this perilous course?"

"No, I cannot."

"Very well, Sam," he hesitated over the name, "I will follow your tack, and we'll see where it takes us. Now go on and fix these." He handed her the sealed report. "Your father will find out, if I don't deliver them. Besides, the more eyes looking for Brandee, the better. Although, God have mercy if we find him; I doubt Brandee will."

"Cap'n, ye might want to take a look at this," the second mate said after knocking at the cabin door. Knowing the man was not prone to overreaction, he went up on deck to see what the problem was.

Floating around them in the water were several objects that were difficult to identify. "I've never seen a fish kill like this, Cap'n."

The captain peered more closely at the objects. "I don't think those are fish, Mr. Bartley. Have a few of the lads take the boats and gather those up. I want them on the deck before sunset. If it's what it looks like from here, she'll want to see it."

Bartley shuddered. Their passenger terrified him down to his bones. If this was something that might be of interest to her, he'd rather not deal with it. But the captain had given an order.

"Aye, Cap'n."

"What is so important that you ask me to postpone my breakfast, Captain Wormsloe?" she asked irritably.

"Mermaids, m'lady. About eight of them."

"Captain, I have seen mermaids before. We have merfolk in my native waters."

"These were found floating and bled out."

That got her attention. "Show me."

He led her to where the bodies were laid out. All eight had their throats torn out. Even as they watched, the horrendous wounds started to close.

"It is against our laws to turn any of the sea folk," she stated. "Some are toxic to us, but those that are not, are just as strong in magic. The resulting creature would be too much of a competitor for prey. This Brandewyne is foolish in his feeding habits. Have your men watch for similar groups. We may be able to follow them to him."

"What about these, m'lady? It looks like they will rise soon, at the rate they are healing."

"If you value your crew, behead them all now. Otherwise, they will wake with the Hunger. Couple that with their natural ability to lure sailors to them, and you will have a slaughter on your hands. Now I am going back to my cabin to feed."

Before the hour passed, the crew tossed the headless mermaids back into the sea. Wormsloe ordered the few that appeared to be pregnant skewered before disposing of their bodies. He didn't want to take the chance of the infection passing on to the unborn.

Zeke stared into his fire. The time approached rapidly. Soon, he would remind that wild girl of the commission he gave her months ago. She was the one who'd told that fool boy that mermaid blood wouldn't hurt him. She had to be the one to put down the monstrous predator Viktor had unknowingly created. Alyssa would give birth before long, then she would have to be destroyed.

THE END

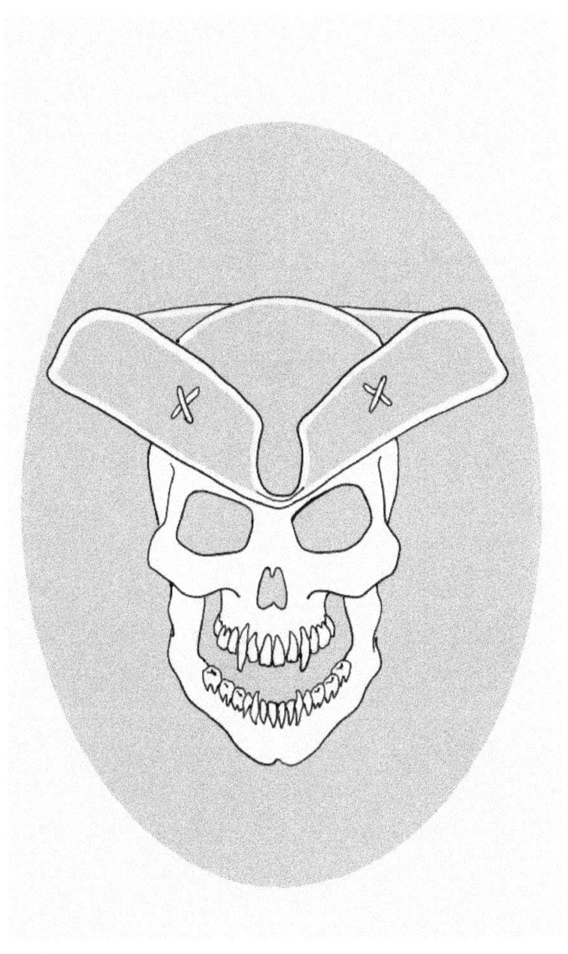

Tamara A. Lowery

About the Author

Tamara A. Lowery, who once considered herself close to becoming a Crazy Cat Lady is now down to three cats. She lives with them and her husband in Tennessee and builds cars to pay the bills when not writing. She's been writing since the early 1980s but only published since 2011.

In addition to the Waves of Darkness series, she is the author of a steampunk episodic serial, The Adventures of Pigg & Woolfe.

She hopes to release a short story collection sometime in the near future, as well.

Website: talowery.wordpress.com

Facebook: facebook.com/Waves.of.Darkness

Instagram: Instagram.com/talowery_author

Plurk: plurk.com/Viksbelle

Smashwords author Page: smashwords.com/profile/view/Viksbelle

YouTube: youtube.com/user/Viksbelle

Waves of Darkness

Tamara A. Lowery
Sisters of Power arc

Blood Curse

Demon Bayou

Silent Fathoms November 2022

Black Venom May 2023

Hell's Dodo November 2023

The Daedalus Enigma May 2024

Maelstrom of Fate November 2024

Daughters of the Dragon arc
Hunting the Dragon (still in draft)

The Adventures of Pigg & Woolfe

Season 1
The Girl Who Fell from the Sky (S.1 omnibus)

Episodes

A Chance Encounter

The Truce

In the Woolfe's Den

Chase the Lightning

Peril in the Philippines

Rendezvous in Hong Kong

Double Jeopardy

Chance and Fortune

Demon Bayou

The Italian Connection

Rescue at Sea

Ghost Riders in the Sky

Castle in the Clouds

Season 2

S.2 Omnibus (Title TBD) Coming January 2023

Episodes

Airborne Alliance January 2022

Under the Mountain February 2022

Reversal of Fortune March 2022

Frustrations April 2022

Going Underground May 2022

Evade and Elude June 2022

Escape July 2022

Sanctuary August 2022

Message in a Bottle September 2022

Strange Bedfellows October 2022

Family Reunion November 2022

Berthing Assignments December 2022

Season 3 2023

Season 4 2024

Tamara A. Lowery